"And now you should tell me what is on your list, princess."

"The list of things I wish to do?" she asked, her voice higher and softer than usual. He dipped his head down to whisper in her ear. Not that anybody was there, but he couldn't help himself.

"Yes. That list," he said, feeling the skin on her arms get goosebumps as he spoke.

"I want to go somewhere where it doesn't matter if I laugh loudly. I want to dance without worrying about how I look, or if I am executing a misstep."

She paused, and he felt his insides coil in anticipation of what she would say next. "But most of all, right now, I would like to kiss you," she said at last.

Which was both the best and the worst answer she could have given him.

By Megan Frampton

Dukes Behaving Badly
PUT UP YOUR DUKE
WHEN GOOD EARLS GO BAD (A Novella)
THE DUKE'S GUIDE TO CORRECT BEHAVIOR

PUT UP YOUR DUKE

MEGAN FRAMPTON

AVON
BOOKS

An Imprint of HarperCollinsPublishers

AVON BOOKS
An Imprint of HarperCollins*Publishers*
195 Broadway
New York, New York 10007

Copyright © 2015 by Megan Frampton
ISBN 978-0-06-235222-4
www.avonromance.com

First Avon Books mass market printing: July 2015

Printed in the U.S.A.

10 9 8 7 6 5 4 3 2 1

FROM THE UNEDITED VERSION OF A LADY OF MYSTERY'S SERIAL:

It was delightful outside, the sun shining directly overhead, the birds chirping loudly, while nannies walked their young charges in the park.

No one could have anticipated the ~~drama storm~~ horror that was to come, not on this perfect day in London.

Certainly not the young ~~girl~~ lady who sat waiting for her betrothed on a park bench.

But that is the nature of such tales, isn't it? Because if horror could be anticipated, perhaps it could be prevented.

—THE PRINCESS AND THE SCOUNDREL

Chapter 1

1842, London, the Gentleman's Pleasure House, Second Private Chamber on the Right

"And then what will you do to me?" Nicholas didn't care so much for the particulars of the response—he knew the woman currently sitting on his lap would do what he wanted her to, and he would be gentlemanly enough to ensure she found enjoyment as well.

He was a very egalitarian lover.

"What do you want me to do to you?" she countered.

Clearly, she did not know that when he asked a question, he wanted an answer, not another question. He suppressed the feeling of irritation and, yes, boredom, and concentrated instead on placing a strawberry between her breasts, then lowering his mouth to capture the succulent fruit. Of the strawberry, not her breast. That appetizing treat would be for later.

He put his mouth to her ear and spoke, so that neither of the two ladies, one on either side of him, could hear.

"I want to keep your mouth busy so you can't speak. And when you are able to speak, you'll be screaming my name."

She wriggled on his lap, her plush arse riding his cock, which had already jerked to attention. She leaned her head back on his shoulder. "I've heard about you, m'lord, and I am very eager to find out if what they say is true."

Nicholas wrapped his hands around her waist and slid his thumbs up so they were in the soft crease under her breasts.

This was his favorite part of being with a woman— the anticipation, wondering what her face would look like as she came apart, wondering how her body would feel under his hands, how she'd want him to take her. The actual doing of it, well, that was pleasurable as well, but none of the women he'd been with had lived up to his expectations.

But each time, with each new woman, he hoped this would be the one. This female would be able to send him to a new height of ecstasy, of wanting, of being able to lose himself, forget thinking just for a few moments of bliss; would be equal to him in bed, in conversation, in life.

Not that he thought he'd find that kind of woman here, in a house of ill repute, no matter how well it catered to men of his class. But he wasn't particularly interested in courting a young lady of his own class only to find, once he was married, that she was no true companion to him in bed or in conversation, but that he was now married to her—for life.

He'd considered it very seriously when he'd met a lady a year or so ago—but she'd entered into another engagement before he could figure out if he actually wanted to or not. So he remained single, and singly determined not to be wed, at least not unless he was absolutely certain about the wife in question.

But he wasn't going to eschew the pleasures of the bed just because he was pessimistic about his chances for long-term happiness. Short-term happiness, for now, would suit him just fine.

It seemed that other gentlemen in London felt the same way—the house was stocked with lovely women, rather like a well-tended fishpond, and it was as easy to catch one as baiting a hook. A hook made of money, and a few well-chosen words. He had both in abundance, which was why he currently had three women surrounding him.

He was in one of the more opulent chambers, not on the enormous bed that dominated the room, but instead seated on a long, low sofa upholstered in a dark purple hue. The furniture was also dark, and candles on several surfaces cast a warm, sensuous glow in the room. As though Nicholas and three willing ladies were not sensuous enough.

"M'lord?" The woman had turned in his lap so she faced him, while the other two women—women he'd had before, both of whom were quite skilled and enthusiastic—ruffled his hair and ran their fingers down his chest and murmured soft words, mostly involving him, and them, and what they were all going to do together later.

He was quite looking forward to it.

So he was not so happy when he heard his brother, Griffith, calling his name.

Griff wasn't bad, as brothers went; in fact Nicholas quite liked him. But Griff, unlike his older brother, did not habituate houses of ill repute, or even houses of good repute, instead usually staying in the library to spend more time reading.

"Excuse me, ladies," Nicholas said, removing the woman from his lap and placing her gently beside him on the sofa. He did up the buttons of his shirt and ran a hand through his hair, which he knew was entirely disheveled, thanks to the sensual stroking and playing that had been done to it.

"In here, Griff," he shouted, getting to his feet. He was just tucking his shirt back into his trousers when Griffith entered, his brother's eyes widening as he saw what must have appeared to be absolute and total debauchery in the room.

Or, as Nicholas liked to call it, Tuesday.

"What is it?" he asked, since Griff's mouth was opening and closing like a chiming cuckoo clock.

"Here." Griff thrust a piece of paper at him. "I don't think you'd believe me if I just told you."

Nicholas unfolded the paper, heavy parchment that already gave whatever was written on it more weight than he wanted. He scanned the lines, filled with legal jargon, and then raised his head to stare at his brother. "This says—this makes me—"

Griff nodded. "The Duke of Gage."

Nicholas looked back at the paper, as though it would explain it all. Well, it did, actually, but he couldn't comprehend all the *whereas*es, *in testimony*s, and *further review*s.

"This can't—but how?" He looked at his brother, as though Griff could explain it.

"It seems that there was a dispute of lineage in a different branch of our family, quite remote, but the end result is that the current Duke of Gage isn't really, because a few generations up there was some bigamy." His brother could explain it. Excellent.

Only now— "And the dukedom or whatever it is called goes to me? What about all the other relatives who were next in line?"

Griff shook his head. "That bigamous marriage affected many of the offspring. It's just like the War of the Roses, which began because John of Gaunt made his mistress his wife, and then that made their children not bastards, only—"

Nicholas punched his brother on the shoulder, not hard, just enough to make him stop talking. "I don't need a history lesson, and I sure as hell hope this doesn't result in a war."

"Right. Of course." Griff grinned and rubbed his shoulder. "Better you than me, I have to say."

Nicholas raised an eyebrow. "Well, if it were you, it would mean I was dead, so yes, I'm very glad it was me. So what do I do now?"

Griff shrugged. "The current duke is contesting the finding, of course, but it seems as though the legality of it is on your side. Or the illegality, rather."

Nicholas frowned. "And how is it that you know about this first, rather than me?"

Now his brother looked embarrassed. "Well, the solicitor came to the house, only you weren't there. And I thought you'd want to know right away."

Right. Because he was here, while his brother was at their shared abode, no doubt doing something worthy with his life rather than keeping company with no fewer than three loose women at a time. Unless that really was a worthy endeavor, and everyone in the world was wrong about suitable pursuits.

Not for the first time, Nicholas wondered just how it came to be that he and his brother were so different, yet so close—Griffith was happiest when his nose was buried in a book, while Nicholas was happiest when his nose was buried in a breast, preferably two.

His older sisters—both of whom were married— were entirely respectable as well, but they were only his half sisters, so they didn't count as much.

He turned to the women, who were busy with each

other. He had a pang as he saw just what one of them was doing to the other one, while the third watched, her eyes heavy with desire.

"It seems, my fair companions, that I have some urgent business that requires my attention."

All three of them paused to look at him, disappointment creeping over their expressions. The one in the middle, he thought her name was Sally, said in a pouting tone, "Are you sure? Your friend there could join us, just for a little while."

Nicholas glanced at Griff, whose face had turned an alarming shade of red. If it got any darker he would match the sofa, in fact. "I wish we could stay, ladies, but we have to go." He didn't want Griff to explode in some sort of embarrassed lust conflagration. That would be difficult to explain to their relatives.

He didn't wait for any response, just took Griff's arm and led him out the door, dropping a few coins into the hands of the woman who ran the establishment.

"So early?" she remarked, tucking the coins into her pocket. "We'll see you soon, my lord?"

Nicholas shook his head. "I regret to say I doubt I will be returning, at least not for some time. It appears I have a dukedom to inherit."

And with that, he pushed the door open and stepped out into the foggy night, his brother right behind.

"Miss Jane? You are waiting for ~~Mr.~~ Lord ArbuthnotShireSton?"

The lady glanced up from her ~~lap~~ book. "I am. And you are?"

She took a moment to look at him, noting his saturnine expression, his ink-black hair, his thin lips, his predatory air. She closed the book and met his gaze.

His eyes were like two dark wells, impossible to see to the bottom. She repressed a shudder.

The man didn't reply, just sat down on the bench beside her. He stretched his arm along the back of the bench so he nearly touched her. She flinched, then edged forward on the seat.

There were people all around them. She was safe. Wasn't she?

"And you are?" she repeated.

"I am the Prince of LaGordonza. And you are to be my bride."

—THE PRINCESS AND THE SCOUNDREL

Chapter 2

"Did you hear? About the Duke of Gage?"

Isabella's mother pursed her lips. "We have not heard anything. If you are about to spread idle gossip, Maria . . ."

Isabella's aunt bounced in her chair, setting her curled ringlets swinging around her head, her eyes wide with excitement. "No, not idle gossip, Jane! It appears that the Duke of Gage is not." Isabella's aunt was wearing an extravagantly wide skirt with several ruffles at the hem, and her motion made the ruffles lift up just slightly.

"Not what?" Isabella's mother's tone was aggravated, impatient, and imperious. Her usual tone.

"Not the Duke of Gage! Aren't you listening?"

Isabella pricked her finger on her embroidery. She didn't want to speak, barely wanted to breathe. Did this mean—?

"How can the Duke of Gage not be the Duke of

Gage?" her mother responded. "Honestly, it is hard to believe you and I are sisters; you are by far the silliest woman I have ever known."

Maria stiffened, her own lips tightening into a thin line. The curls stilled. "If you wish to hear the news from someone else, I beg you, continue to insult me. But don't be surprised when your precious plans for your precious daughter come to naught because her intended is a charlatan." She nodded in triumph. "And then where will you be?"

Not married to him, thank God, Isabella thought, even though the question was not addressed to her. She glanced at her mother, whose face had changed from its usual supercilious mien to something more hesitant.

That might be the most unexpected news today—that her mother was humbled, if only for a moment.

Isabella was wearing her most suitable gown for the occasion, of course; she was never less than perfectly gowned and coiffed and all those other things her mother deemed necessary for a future duchess. Which was also why she was doing embroidery when she'd much rather be with her sister out walking in the park, or being anyone but herself, actually.

"Tell me, then," her mother said in a clipped tone.

Her aunt, never one to hold a grudge—quite different from her sister in that regard as well—bounced again. "It seems that there was some sort of inquiry into the duke's lineage, for some legal dispute or another, and they've discovered some sort of impropriety in the duke's family, one that invalidates his right to be the duke."

Isabella wanted to shriek in joy, or hug her aunt, or run around the room waving her arms in triumph.

She did none of those things, only allowing herself to take a deep breath as she continued sewing. The duke might not be a duke any longer, but her mother was her mother in perpetuity, and would not appreciate it if her daughter were so uncircumspect.

Her mother rose, gesturing Isabella to stand as well. "We will have to find out precisely what is going on. Your father will wish to look into this."

Isabella felt herself shaking—in joy, or shock, she wasn't sure. The possibility of freedom, of not having to marry the duke, dangled before her like a beautiful jewel she just had to reach out and take. And her freedom was more precious than anything, since it was so rare, rarer than the rarest diamond. She'd never even had it, not for a moment of her life, whereas diamonds, for a lady in her position, were relatively easy to see, if not own.

Her mother glared at her, as though it were her fault the duke was no longer the duke. Isabella wished she could tell her mother that if she had the kind of power to unduke someone, she would have used that power to entirely extricate herself from any kind of marital agreement. Or maybe make herself look less beautiful so people would stop bothering her.

"Stop dawdling, Isabella. You can see yourself out, Maria?" It was not a question, but at least her mother gave her aunt the courtesy of pretending it was.

"Of course." Maria patted Isabella's hand. "I am certain you will be fine, Isabella. You will marry well, no matter who you marry."

Isabella merely nodded, even though she wished she could tell her aunt, tell somebody, how she felt about marrying well. About how marrying well meant a very different thing to her than it did to her family.

If she didn't have to marry the duke after all she could find someone, perhaps, who would care for her. That would be a good marriage, not one where her husband's title was more important than if he was a pleasant man. She didn't require love, but she wanted companionship, and friendliness, and perhaps a measure of fondness.

The duke—at least, the only Duke of Gage she currently knew—had never shown her any of those things, or any possibility of them, instead treating her as her mother did, as someone to be corrected and scolded into perfection.

Perfection Isabella had achieved, even though she wasn't proud of it. She had been molded into the perfect duchess, only now—only now it seemed as though there was no duke to fulfill her training. The thought made her want to laugh, if only because it so thoroughly ruined her mother's plans.

Freedom. Isabella had only occasionally allowed herself to think of what might be possible if her future weren't already determined; now that it was here, that it might well be her future, she was terrified.

What would she be if she wasn't the Duchess of Gage?

"You see, Your Grace, here are the papers that prove your right to the title." The solicitor, one of at least five who had been summoned to the room, pointed to a pile of documents that were not the type of reading material Nicholas usually entertained himself with—not that he would admit to reading novels, the more dramatic the better, to anyone.

First, none of the documents had anybody speaking to one another in terms of love. Second, the only mystery was whether Nicholas would fall asleep during their apparently unending explanations. And third, he couldn't wait for the end, not because then the happy couple would finally be happy together, with the villain vanquished, but because then it would be done.

But he didn't wander off, or interrupt the man who was speaking with a sly comment, or do anything he might have done if he were not the duke.

Only two hours into the title, and it had already changed him. The thought was an intriguing, if terrifying, one; he hadn't thought about how this might affect him, beyond the basic change of going from Not Being a Duke to Being a Duke.

How else would it change him?

Last night he'd been too bemused to even ponder what it meant; it had been too late to come to the solicitors' offices to learn the specifics, but this morning, he and Griff had gotten up at some ungodly hour—well, for Nicholas it was an ungodly hour, perhaps for Griff it was godly—and hastened over here to examine the documents themselves.

So far he'd nodded, and mm-hmed, and tried to look as though he understood everything they'd said to him. Griff, on the other hand, didn't have to try to look enthusiastic—he was clearly thrilled to be presented with reams of boring words on ancient pieces of paper.

Nicholas really did have to wonder if they actually had the same parents at all.

"And here, Your Grace"—the solicitor was pointing to yet another piece of paper—"you'll see that there are other, uh, obligations the duke—that is, the duke that was—had entered into." The man's finger shook, and Nicholas wondered if these documents were as exciting to the solicitor as a novel would be to him. And when the Lady of Mystery would begin her next serial. Those were words he'd like to read, unlike all the words currently in this room.

"What does it say?"

"It says, uh, it says, Your Grace, that there is a betrothal. To the Earl of Grosston's daughter. Lady Isabella Sawford, it seems her name is."

"And how does this affect me?"

The man cleared his throat. He didn't meet Nicholas's eyes. "It seems, Your Grace, that if the marriage does not occur between the earl's daughter and the Duke of Gage—no matter who holds the title—the dukedom will have difficulty maintaining its current income. That," he added, squinting down at the paper, "that the drought of two years ago forced the duke that was, the one who is no longer, into an agreement with the earl, and the earl has expended a not inconsiderable amount of money in propping up the duke's holdings."

"Let me see that," Griff said, taking it from the man's hand.

Nicholas uttered a snort. "Surely the earl can't expect that *this* Duke of Gage will have to fulfill *that* Duke of Gage's bargain. And what would the young lady wish? Expecting one husband, only to have another man as a substitute? It's not as easy as swapping out a horse in a team pulling a carriage."

"Of—of course not, Your Grace," the man replied. He spoke hesitantly, and for the first time since he'd gotten the news, Nicholas felt a twinge of uncertainty.

"He wouldn't, would he?" He addressed this to Griff, who was still staring at the paper in his hand.

Griff raised his head and looked at Nicholas. Suddenly he didn't seem quite so enthusiastic. "This is as legal a document as the papers proving that you are actually the duke. It appears, Nicholas, that in addition to inheriting a dukedom, you will also be inheriting a wife."

"You are mistaken, Your Highness." Jane kept her tone calm. Unruffled. Surely Anthony would be here soon?

"No, my pet." The man—the prince's oily tone washed over her like a perfect rainstorm, a deluge of pain and pride and princeliness instead of rain. "Your father has promised you to me, in exchange for ridding him of several pressing ~~debts~~ obligations. Your lord has agreed to step aside. He will not be coming for you now. Not ever," he added, reaching up one long finger to ~~tidy his hair~~ twirl his mustache.

—THE PRINCESS AND THE SCOUNDREL

Chapter 3

"And you won't have to be the duchess after all?" Margaret sat cross-legged on Isabella's bed, twirling a lock of hair around her finger. Both of them wore their nightgowns, only Isabella's—of course—was far nicer, festooned with ribbons and random pieces of lace. Margaret's was too short, and was made of plain white cotton.

Isabella plopped down on the bed next to her sister. "I hope not." Oh, how she hoped not. "The parents are spitting mad about it, but if the new duke says no, there's not much they can do. I wonder," she said, lying down and spreading her arms wide, "if there is any kind of market for Nearly Duchesses. They could probably get a good price for me, I have even perfected the nod that says, *I am grander than you, but I will not do you the discourtesy of saying it, even though we both know it is true.*" She made a mock disapproving noise. "All these lessons, only to find the duke that was to be my husband isn't a duke at all."

And thank goodness.

Margaret lay down next to her. "Do you think the earl will let the duke off the hook that easy?" Margaret had given up on calling their father Father when she'd overheard him dismissing her as "not being worth the cost of keeping her," since she lacked her older sister's beauty. Hence the lack of decoration on her nightgown.

Isabella felt a tightening in her chest, the same tightening that had been her constant companion since she'd been told of her fate three years ago. "I don't know. I hope the new Duke of Gage refuses to accede to the parents' wishes, I know nothing about him except that his name is Nicholas Smithfield, and he is unmarried. If only he were married already, there would be nothing they could do."

"Nicholas Smithfield?" Margaret sat up and looked at Isabella, her eyes round. "Nicholas Smithfield," she repeated, only the second time she spun the words out so each syllable had its own moment: *Nick-o-las Smith-fee-uld*.

Now the tightening became nearly a clenching. "Yes, that's the name, what do you know about him?"

Margaret smiled, and Isabella's chest eased just a fraction. Her sister wouldn't be nearly so jolly if there was something really horrible about the new duke.

Although knowing her sister, Margaret might be delighted if he were, say, renowned for being incredibly stupid or perhaps hating women whose names began with vowels.

"Only that he is supposed to be very popular with certain ladies, if you know what I mean," and then Margaret winked, of all things, and grinned wider.

Isabella swatted her sister on the arm. "How do you know about 'certain ladies' anyway? And how did you hear about the duke?"

Margaret's expression was smug. "Don't think girls who aren't out yet don't know anything."

"You always know more than I do," Isabella responded. It had been Margaret who'd told her about the deal with the duke in the first place, so that when Isabella's father informed her of it, she'd already gotten all her crying out, and had been able to maintain the icy reserve her parents seemed to require in their eldest daughter.

"That's right, I do," Margaret said in a satisfied tone of voice. "Well, my friend Harriet's sister had her debut last year, and she was wondering if Mr. Smithfield—your new duke—might ask permission to court her, since it seemed he did like her. Only then Lord Cavanaugh came up to scratch, and Harriet's sister took him instead, but in the meantime, she'd asked around, and heard all about him. I don't know where Harriet's sister heard, but their parents were not very enthusiastic about the possibility of your duke paying addresses to her, so there must have been some truth in it."

"He's not my duke," Isabella replied. *At least, I hope not*, she thought.

"Has the earl told you what to expect?" Margaret's

tone was much less happy; it made Isabella's heart ache to know that her sister knew full well what their parents thought of their youngest.

Not that they thought much of their oldest, either, but at least they paid attention to her, even if the attention they paid was usually in the form of admonishments.

And what Margaret didn't know, and couldn't ever know, was that the one time Isabella had tried to rebel, her mother had threatened to send Margaret away, not to let her have a debut or a chance to meet a gentleman who would appreciate Margaret's joyous sense of humor and sweet smile.

Isabella had never objected to anything her parents had asked of her since.

"No," she replied, her voice low. "No, he hasn't."

"The Duke of Gage, my lord," Lowton intoned before bowing and stepping aside to let the man enter.

Isabella kept her eyes down, not looking at him, hoping that if she didn't see him, he wouldn't exist.

That didn't work even in fairy tales, but for just a few moments she could pretend, couldn't she?

"Your Grace," her father said, stepping forward. Isabella felt her mother's elbow in her ribs and rose. "May I introduce my wife, the Countess of Grosston, and my daughter, Lady Isabella Sawford."

Isabella raised her head, her usual expression set on

her face, only to wish, when she saw him, that Margaret had also included the information that the new Duke of Gage was incredibly handsome.

Isabella was not small, but the duke appeared to be at least six inches taller than she. Probably even more; he towered over her father, who was himself larger than the average man. He had dark blond hair that swept back from a strong widow's peak, and piercing blue eyes—currently focused on her—above his autocratic nose. The intensity of his stare made it seem as though he might see inside to her very soul. His face was lean and sharply planed, his cheekbones strong, and he held himself with a command that he had to have been born with, not just assumed when he'd found himself suddenly a duke.

And his form; he was broad-shouldered and lean-hipped, and his long legs were encased in slim trousers that clung to his body in an almost indecent way. Or perhaps it just looked indecent because his whole self was so powerfully, handsomely male, and it was hard not to think of indecent things when one beheld him.

He was very plainly dressed, not wearing the fobs and signets and such that the last duke had worn. But he didn't need any ornamentation; the severity of his dress only highlighted the strong, sensuous beauty of his face.

No wonder certain ladies found him intriguing. It would be hard to imagine any lady—not just certain ones—wouldn't at least give him a second, if not a third, glance.

At this moment, in fact, she was staring back at him as thoroughly as he was looking at her.

"I am pleased to meet you," Isabella murmured. The duke inclined his head at her, his gaze still intent and focused.

"Isabella, could you excuse us? The duke and I have some business to discuss." Her father didn't even wait for her reply, just sat and gestured for the duke to sit as well.

"Isabella?" Now her father's tone was irritated; it usually took only one time for his command to be obeyed. But she couldn't take her eyes off him, it was as though she was thirsty and he was water.

Or not water—perhaps a rich, decadent liquor the likes of which were imbibed by ancient gods on their way to an orgy. Only now she was thinking of what he might taste like, and she could feel her face flushing as the improper thoughts chased through her mind.

"Of course. Excuse me," she said, finally breaking eye contact with him. She practically stumbled walking out the door—she, who had mastered the task of walking across a bushel of grapes in dancing slippers with a full water glass on her head, stumbled.

He put his hand out to steady her and she felt the contact like a burn on her skin. As though if she looked down at her arm she'd see his handprint there, even though he'd only touched her for a few seconds. And with a glove on, no less.

Oh dear. No matter what was going to happen—either she'd have to marry him, or she wouldn't—she was going to regret it, she was certain.

Nicholas wished he could shout, *Bravo!* and applaud at the earl's tactical move—showing just what he would be missing out on if he refused the bargain.

Because the earl's daughter was lovely, so beautiful it almost hurt the eyes to look at her. She had dark hair swept up in some sort of elegant style, revealing the graceful curve of her neck. Her eyes were dark as well, and huge, while her mouth—that mouth was the embodiment of sin. Lush, full, and dark red, it immediately presented images of what could be done with it.

Or perhaps that was only Nicholas's avid imagination.

Her body appeared to be spectacular as well, with round, full breasts, a small waist, and appealingly curved hips. He'd gotten good at gauging a woman's figure through her clothing, no matter what the fashion. But her gown, thankfully for his perusal, was made to highlight how she was made—the neckline was low, exposing the upper part of her bosom. The patterned fabric clung to her upper body, down to the tiny nipped-in waist that then spiraled out into a wide skirt that moved enticingly when she walked.

She was taller than most women he'd met, and of

course that set off some other imaginative thoughts, such as the possibilities that existed when partners had less than a foot of height separating them.

He could admire her all he wanted to, but the fact was that he still was here to negotiate a way out of this bargain without having to marry her. No matter how luscious she appeared. Because he'd had plenty of women—well, none as beautiful as she, but still—and he had yet to find the one he wished to be with for the rest of his life. And he didn't think a moment of admiration worth shackling himself to one woman forever.

"Shall we sit, Your Grace?" The earl gestured to a chair, easing himself into one opposite as he spoke.

Nicholas sat and inclined his head. "Well?"

It was a negotiating tactic he'd learned from his father, who'd had plenty of opportunity to question Nicholas about something or another. Stay quiet until the other person has spoken more than they probably wanted to, just to fill the silence.

"The thing is, Your Grace, that the Duke of Gage, the one who held the title until you—"

"I know who it was, there is no need to go over those details," Nicholas said. Another tactic? Make them lose their train of thought.

The earl crossed his arms over his chest. His expression was stern, as though Nicholas had done something wrong in being the actual duke. "Well, the thing is, is that I have spent a considerable amount of money. And the arrangement was that the duke would marry my daughter at the end of the Season. Her mother and I—" and at this he shot a worried look at the countess, and things clicked into place inside Nicholas's head. She was the one who was behind this, and judging by her expression, she was decided.

"We have invested a lot of time and capital with the promise that Isabella would one day be the Duchess of Gage." The countess spoke with a confident, arrogant tone that made Nicholas's skin crawl even as he admired it. She would not be distracted or deterred by anything he might do.

"You can see my predicament," Nicholas replied, spreading his hands out. "I have just found out that not only am I the duke, but that there is an impending duchess. That is a lot to digest within a mere twenty-four hours."

"Of course," the earl said.

"Of course," the countess said at the same time, "but the truth of the matter is that this agreement was done in good faith, and we expect the terms of it to be fulfilled, even if the representative has changed." He hoped to God that the countess's daughter wasn't nearly as terrifying.

Nicholas leaned forward, his elbows on his knees, his hands clasped loosely in front of him. "And what if I refuse the title? If I do not contest the previous duke's case?" It wasn't anything that had occurred to him until now, but right now, it felt as though a noose—a noose made of ducal strawberry leaves—was tightening about his neck, changing him forever.

And he rather liked who he'd been. Who he was.

Griff, of course, would have a fit at Nicholas refusing the title, but if taking it meant he had all this responsibility, not to mention a wife?

"You wouldn't." The earl spoke as though he could not believe Nicholas would even consider such a thing. And normally, Nicholas would agree with him—who would refuse a title just because it was accompanied by an unexpected marriage? Most men, perhaps all men, would just marry the woman and then maintain their previous habits. But Nicholas knew himself well enough to know that he would never dishonor his wife in that way, no matter who she was.

"I might," Nicholas replied. "Not that your daughter does not seem to be a lovely woman"—*perhaps the loveliest I've ever laid eyes on*—"but I do not like having my hand forced."

He let the words stop there and waited. He didn't have long.

The countess lifted her head and met his gaze, her eyes the same dark almond shape as her daughter's. The similarity made that noose feel tighter. "And you have considered what this would do to the dukedom? It seems as though you are entirely too rash, Your Grace," she said, emphasizing the honorific, "or selfish, because you are willing to risk not only your own reputation as an honorable man, but also a title that has been in existence for hundreds of years. How do you think our young Queen would respond if you did something so reprehensible? Would you even be accepted in respectable society?" She sniffed, as though she knew Nicholas's pre-duke society had generally been not so respectable. "Do you believe that we would have asked you here if we even thought for a moment the new documents were false?" She shook her head. "You are not what we intended for our daughter, but you do hold the title, whether you wish it or not. You will take the title and you will marry Isabella, or—" and she let the words just hang there, in an even better version than Nicholas's father had ever done, the implied threat nearly palpable in the salon.

But he could fill in the implications. If he carried through on his bluff, he would be ruining himself, Griff, and likely the future of all the industries and people who depended on the Duke of Gage's ownings to survive. Queen Victoria would be angry with him, anyone he might meet would have heard about him and his jilting of the dukedom, and he would be sentencing himself to a life of scandal and a bad reputation, a life that could never be redeemed.

And he could avoid all that if he just accepted a bride.

There was no decision to be made. He had to do it, even though it made his throat close over in anger.

"And your daughter?" Nicholas's words were uttered in a short clip.

"She will have no objection. She understands that an agreement is binding. And it is binding, Your Grace, we have no concerns about that."

That was the same conclusion Griff had reached after spending a few hours with the documents, only Griff hadn't talked about a binding agreement, but instead had looked grim and patted Nicholas's shoulder.

That was when Nicholas knew for certain there was nothing to be done. But he had to at least try, to see if his future in-laws could at all be swayed by any kind of reason or bluff or anything else he could throw at them.

It seemed he now knew the answer. And hoped his future wife did not take too much after her parents, particularly her mother.

Nicholas swallowed and nodded his head, just once. "Then it appears we have a wedding to discuss, my lord, my lady."

He wished he could return to the day before, when the only decision he'd had to make in terms of a woman was which of the three he'd have first.

From the unedited version of A Lady of Mystery's serial:

~~She could not believe her ears.~~ "I cannot believe my ears," she said, getting to her feet.

A nanny walking by gave her a strange look. Was she already tainted by the evil she felt rolling off him like a wave? Or maybe that was her imagination.

He reached into his pocket and drew out a heavy piece of parchment, dark ink—as dark as his hair, as his eyes—covering the creamy surface. "It is all here, pet. You are mine."

—The Princess and the Scoundrel

Chapter 4

Nicholas relished the impact when his opponent's fist caught him on the jaw. It hurt, hurt so goddamn much, and yet it felt satisfyingly real, and he knew he could, he would control the outcome.

Unlike the rest of his life.

He let the pain wash over him, then closed his eyes and breathed in, sharp, through his nose, feeling the curl of anger spread through him as swiftly and fiercely as the oxygen.

"Enough?" Flynn said, dancing on his heels. He'd been dancing and taunting during the whole match, and Nicholas had let him—he knew that the end would come, inevitably, as it always did, but he wanted to spool the match out as long as he could, because when it was over, it would be done. Finished.

Just like sex, he thought; the anticipation of it was so much better than seeing your opponent flat out on the floor (or the bed, depending on which activity it was).

He lived for the skirmish, the flirtation, whether it was between two well-paired fighters or two (or more) well-paired lovers.

"Never enough," he replied, then drew his arm back, stiffening it as it uncoiled from his body. He aimed for Flynn's stomach, right below where he held his hands to protect his heart.

And wasn't that another intriguing coincidence; Nicholas usually didn't protect his heart when fighting. Nor did he during sex.

Was that the problem?

He was overthinking when he should be boxing, he thought just before another punch hit him, this time in the gut. He crumpled over, his head dipping close to the floor, then rose up again and met Flynn's gaze.

His opponent was another one of the regulars at the boxing salon; Nicholas had fought him, and won, before. Flynn was shorter than Nicholas and wiry, a good fighter if he didn't get distracted by his own chatter.

"That was a good one, if I do say so myself," Flynn crowed.

Nicholas delivered a fierce, quick blow to his chin, Flynn's eyes widening as his head tipped back.

Flynn was definitely the victim of his own chatter. Or Nicholas's frustration about his own inability to control anything outside of the ring.

Nicholas refrained from asking Flynn if that punch

was good. It wouldn't do to fall victim to the same weakness his opponent had.

Instead, he concentrated on finishing the job, delivering blow after blow after blow to Flynn's midsection, until the man held his gloved hands up in surrender.

"Good match," Nicholas said as Flynn shook his head, as though to clear it.

"It was. Let's try it again when you're not so wound up about something," Flynn replied. He rubbed his hand along his jaw. "What do you have in your gloves, bricks? Hell, Smithfield."

Nicholas grimaced. "Sorry if it was too much."

Flynn shrugged. "Not too much, just that normally I can land more than a few on you before you finish me."

"Nicholas!" Nicholas turned at the sound of Griff's voice. His brother was fascinated by the ring, and the fighting, especially when Nicholas fought. Something about how humans took out their aggressions or some such nonsense.

"Griff, you want to step in here next?" Nicholas held up his fists in a boxing stance. "I'd be happy to pummel the stuffing out of you."

Griff rolled his eyes as he swung into the ring. "I know you would, and that's why I stay in the library, thanks very much. You all right?" he said, gesturing to Nicholas's nose.

Hm. He hadn't noticed, but he had started bleeding at some point. He just hoped it wasn't broken.

"Fine. Here, can you wipe my hands," he asked, holding his fists out. Griff drew a square of linen from his breast pocket and dabbed the blood away from Nicholas's knuckles.

"Did you go see them? The earl?" Griff added, as though Nicholas wouldn't know who "them" referred to.

"Yes."

Griff stopped what he was doing. "That bad?"

"Yes." Even though his intended was possibly the most gorgeous woman he'd ever seen. He hadn't chosen her. She might not be the one. No, he knew—she wasn't the one. How could she be, when he had tried so many?

But now he had no choice.

"How is the lady herself? Did you meet her?"

Nicholas uttered a soft snort. "She is lovely. But I do not want to marry anyone, especially not now when this is all so sudden anyway."

Griff shook his head and clucked his tongue. "I'm sorry. Could you just—just refuse to take the title? They wouldn't want you for their daughter then, would they?" Griff wrapped the linen around Nicholas's right hand.

Nicholas shook his head. "It's not that simple." He expelled a breath as Griff reached up to touch his nose. Not broken, thankfully, but definitely sore.

They'd had the same routine for over ten years now, since the first time Nicholas stepped into a ring, finding boxing the only way—well, one of the only two ways, and the other wasn't practical to do all the time—to relieve the constant anxiety and pressure in his head. Griff had followed him, as he always did, and Nicholas found his ministrations comforting, in an odd way, after he'd spent all his energy and anger in the ring.

Well. Perhaps not all his anger, he thought as he reviewed his meeting with Lady Isabella's parents.

"If I refuse the title—well, first I don't know if anyone is allowed to refuse a title, but even if I could, who would be the duke then? You? But the previous duke would then be able to make a better case for his keeping the title, I'd think, and it would go to the House of Lords, all of whom would dither about it for years, most likely, and meanwhile, the people who are under the duke's protection—the farmers, and workers, and towns—would suffer." He exhaled. "Not to mention what the Queen would have to say about it all. I can't even imagine. And I can't take the risk of doing that, just because I want to have my own say about my bride."

"Oh." Griff leaned past Nicholas to grab his shirt, then held it out for Nicholas to put on. He folded his arms across his chest and waited until the shirt was over Nicholas's head before he spoke. "Then I have to say," he began, looking Nicholas in the eye with his steady, firm, ever so direct gaze, "that I admire you for what you're doing."

Nicholas snorted. "Marrying a beautiful aristocrat?"

Griff shook his head slowly. "No. Not that. It's being

able to foresee the likely outcomes of your actions, and taking the course that is the best for the most people, even if it's not the best for you."

Nicholas felt a lump in his throat. "Thank you," he said in a gruff voice. "Now let's go see about that dukedom, shall we?"

And a bride, he thought to himself.

He and Griff were both quiet as Nicholas got himself rigged out again as a gentleman, not a brawler. What was there to say, anyway? They walked out of the club, Nicholas feeling the weight he'd escaped while in the ring with Flynn return with a vengeance. "Smithfield!" The voice was unfamiliar, but the tone was unfortunately not—dripping with scorn, like when someone made the mistake of thinking he was only a rake.

He usually got to correct them by letting them know he was a rake *and* a boxer. They did not speak to him that way again.

Nicholas paused on the sidewalk, Griff to his right. A gentleman strode up, right into Nicholas's face, his face red, his expression fearsome.

Lesser men would have stepped back. Perhaps wiser men would have as well.

Nicholas was neither lesser nor wiser, it seemed.

"You can't have it. You can't have her," the man said, poking Nicholas in the chest.

And, of course, Nicholas knew just who this was, and what "it" and "her" the man referred to.

"The former Duke of Gage, I presume," he said in his best rakish drawl. It was a tone designed to provoke, and apparently it worked quite well.

"Not former, you bastard," the man spat.

At this Nicholas allowed himself a chuckle. "It seems that you are the bastard, or at least that's what the documents say."

He didn't need Griff's inhalation to know a punch was forthcoming, and honestly, he'd had enough of those for the day. So he grabbed the man's wrist as it swung up, then twisted his arm around his back and leaned in close. "Listen, you may dispute it all you want, but stop thinking about yourself for just one minute. What would it do to drag this out? We both know that it's legal. Barristers have never been accused of being reckless, so the documents must be ironclad." How he wished they weren't, at least when it came to the papers this Duke of Gage had signed.

"I'll take this to the courts, you can be certain of that," the man said, his face flushing even brighter, his arm still painfully wrapped behind his back.

Nicholas leaned into his face and spoke in a whisper. "You do that. And I'll be waiting."

And with that, Nicholas released the man's arm so suddenly he staggered back, the malice on his face nearly tangible.

Nicholas and Griff watched as the former duke walked away, casting looks behind him and muttering darkly.

"He's not going to let it go that easily," Griff said in a matter-of-fact voice.

Or let her go. "Would you?" Nicholas replied, smoothing his jacket.

"And your people are pleased that I am to be your princess?" Jane stood ~~defiantly meekly~~ proudly in her parents' sitting room, the prince having just returned from planning the wedding.

It was raining outside, a fierce, driving wind banging against the windows, the shaking trees making long shadows on the rug. It was raining in her heart, too.

"They are indeed pleased," he replied in that unctuous tone, making a chill creep up her spine. If only she could do something to get out of her situation—but she was a woman, and had no resources, and nothing to counter his relentless pursuit.

If only there was someone out there who could help her.

And just then, she heard a knock at the door.

—THE PRINCESS AND THE SCOUNDREL

Chapter 5

Isabella sat as she'd been instructed, not allowing her back to touch the chair, her hands placed just so in her lap, her feet together, her spine straight. Her only tiny act of rebellion was to gaze out the window, not at her mother, who was speaking. "You and the duke will be married in two weeks. The ceremony will be held at St. Paul's, and your father and I will be hosting the breakfast after." Isabella's mother gave a sniff of disdain. "I presume you will wish your sister to stand up with you during the ceremony." She continued without waiting for an answer, which was a good thing; ever since that day, the New Duke Day, Isabella had been unable to carry on normal conversation, except for late at night with Margaret.

And even then it had taken most of Margaret's jokes and imitations to get her to speak in full sentences. Most of which began with "What am I going to do?" which wasn't precisely a sentence, and was usually accompanied with an enormous sob.

Because while she had been resigned to marrying that duke, undeniably unpleasant though he was, having experienced a few hours of freedom before it was snatched away made it nearly impossible for her to become resigned to marrying *this* duke.

Even though this duke was remarkably handsome. But that was the only thing she knew about him, and she knew well—her mother had been a beauty, in her day, and look how she had turned out—that external beauty was no predictor of what a person's internal beauty was.

"Are you listening, Isabella?" her mother's tone was sharp. She should be looking at her mother, that rebuke said. Like a dutiful child, she turned her head to meet her mother's eyes. They were in her mother's sitting room, her mother writing things down and consulting various notes, Isabella trying not to shout, while Margaret sat next to her, occasionally patting her hand.

Margaret's back touched the chair.

"Yes, Mother." Isabella hated whom she'd become through her parents' constant grooming. She was, she could say without false modesty, perfect. The perfect lady, perfectly able to do anything an aristocratic lady was supposed to be able to do—manage a household, do needlepoint, play the pianoforte, speak three languages, dress in the most impeccable gowns at all times—but inside, deep down where the true Isabella resided, it made her cringe every time she was called upon to perform.

The only person who understood that was Margaret, but Margaret wasn't able to do anything to help besides make the occasional sarcastic comment to divert their parents'— particularly her mother's—attention for a few moments.

"Will Isabella actually be dressed as a sacrificial lamb, or will that be implied with her wedding gown?"

Like now, for example.

"Margaret, don't be foolish," her mother replied, refusing to rise to the bait. She took one last look at the papers and made a face as though they, too, had disappointed her.

At least her mother was consistent—Isabella didn't think anything in the world would or could live up to her mother's expectations, and that included inanimate objects made of trees.

"But speaking of your wedding gown, I have to go out and consult with Madame LaFoy about it." Isabella made to stand, but her mother held her hand out. "There is no need for you to come as well, you would only get in the way."

And wasn't that the essence of how her mother thought about her? Someone who would get in the way if she actually expressed an opinion. Just once she'd like to tell her mother that no, she didn't actually like to take her tea the way her mother made it, nor was she particularly fond of the color pink, and sometimes she would like to choose what she would embroider—she was getting damn tired of roses.

And even saying "damn" in her head made her flinch. She wished she could not let it bother her, any of it, but she'd been trying to please her parents since she'd been born, it seemed, and she didn't know any other way to be.

Perhaps the question was not who would she be if she were not the Duchess of Gage, but who was she at all?

"Isabella!" From the tone of her sister's voice, it sounded as though Margaret had been calling her a few times.

"What?" Isabella dropped her needlepoint in her lap and looked at her sister. "What is it?"

"The countess will be gone for at least two hours— would you like to go for a walk in the park?"

Isabella repressed the feeling of *Oh, I shouldn't, I haven't checked with my parents.* "That would be lovely."

"Good," Margaret replied, jumping up immediately. "It's warm enough, we don't need shawls or anything, we can just go."

If only she could just go.

Isabella rose more slowly, nervous about doing something that wasn't precisely what she was supposed to do, but excited to do that type of thing as well.

"I wonder if we will see your intended." Margaret squinted at the watch pinned to the bodice of her gown. "It might be too early for him to be out yet."

"It's nearly two o'clock!" Isabella exclaimed. "Surely he is up by now? Not that I want to run into him, you understand."

Margaret shrugged. "From what I've heard, the new duke likes to stay up very late."

"Perhaps I shouldn't worry about getting to know him after we're married, since we won't be awake at the same time," Isabella replied.

Margaret's laughter accompanied them as they walked outside into the fresh air.

As they walked, half of Isabella's attention was on Margaret, while the other half was on her betrothed— she'd met him a few times in public, of course (and always in the evening), but he'd just scrutinized her with that intense gaze, and she'd felt herself start to heat up from the inside, wanting to fidget and squirm and do anything but be the focus of that stare—but knowing that her parents, especially her mother, would make her wish that unexpected body temperature was her biggest problem.

So she nodded, and murmured, "Yes, Your Grace," and "No, Your Grace" if he asked a question. Even if the question required more than a yes or a no.

At least she wasn't leading him into false expectations of what their marriage would be, she reasoned with herself. And if he thought she was an idiot, and he didn't want to marry her, no matter what agreements had been made? Well, that would be the ideal solution.

Except—except at certain moments, when the two of them were looking at each other, she could have sworn that there was something there, deep in his eyes. Some yearning that made her want to reach out and touch him, to smooth his hair, to tell him that he would find what he was looking for.

That was the only thing that was keeping her from falling apart entirely, and she wasn't certain if she was grateful or resentful of that fact.

And in two weeks she would be alone with him. Would be his wife for the rest of her life.

The ballroom was filled with most of Society, including many people who wished to meet the new Duke of Gage, but Nicholas had eyes for only one lady. A perfect lady, one who didn't seem to have any emotion. At all. "She seems to be made of ice," Nicholas muttered as he watched his intended walk out of the ballroom, her shoulders back, her hair perfectly coiffed, her gown lovely and fitting in all the right places.

"She might just be shy," Griff offered.

Nicholas turned to his brother, who stood at his elbow, and gave him a skeptical look, at which Griff shrugged as though it was the best rationalization he could come up with.

Which just meant that Griff, too, thought she was icy.

Both of them had spent the day embroiled in dukely

things, from deciding how best to allocate a loan that had been repaid, to agreeing to a new roof for one of the many barns on the property, to reviewing applicants for the estate manager position, the former manager having left when the former duke did.

Not to mention overseeing the installation of new furnishings for the duchess. His duchess.

He could have left everything up to the very capable upper staff who had come with the title, but somehow, despite everything, despite how cold she seemed, and how much he did not want this marriage, he wanted to choose everything himself. So he left Griff in the study to deal with some sort of field crop rotation, and he had tradesmen in to show him curtains, and bed linens, and coverlets, and all sorts of things he had had no idea were necessary for anyone to have.

And a bed, which was the only thing that was essential to him.

It irked him that he found her so cold and forbidding in her manner, and yet he wanted to possess her. He hadn't had a woman since he'd become the Duke of Gage. He hadn't had time, he didn't want to do anything to jeopardize his tenuous respectability, he was too tired.

He could give himself any number of reasons for not doing what he normally did, but the truth of it was that he didn't want any other woman. Not since seeing her.

He burned for her, counted the days—and nights—

until their wedding night. Chose just the right colors to complement her vivid coloring, so her bedroom was decorated in shades of rose, from the palest pink to the deepest fuchsia.

Griff had begun to mock him, but had stopped on seeing the look on his face.

And the wedding was in two weeks. In two weeks he could peel away her clothing, and work on melting the shards of ice that seemed to encase her heart.

Never mind that he might be the one in a puddle after their joining.

"It is so different from anything I've known before," she said. And it was true—there were strange, brightly colored birds flying overhead, people wearing clothing the likes of which she'd never seen, and him—her new husband.

The prince.

"Soon it will be as familiar to you as I am," he said, his voice a dark promise that sent a shudder up her spine.

—THE PRINCESS AND THE SCOUNDREL

Chapter 6

"Izzy?"

Isabella brushed the tears away from her cheeks as soon as she heard her sister's voice. She cleared her throat and concentrated on making her voice sound as normal as possible. As normal as it could sound, given that tomorrow was her wedding day. Two weeks had gone by, each day bringing her closer and closer to him. To being his wife, to leaving here, to practicing her perfection. Perfectly.

"Come in," she called, reaching up to smooth her hair, which had gotten mussed when she had flung herself, uncharacteristically and very unduchessly, onto the bed.

The door opened, and her sister entered, pausing as she surveyed the scene. "Did your stately demeanor explode or something?" she asked, walking to the bed. Isabella looked around guiltily, seeing the chaos she'd managed to create in just a few minutes—hairpins on the floor, pillows that were at the end of the bed, and perhaps the most damning, a hairbrush that had not just been pulled through her hair one hundred times.

So perhaps not all that chaotic after all.

Margaret bent down and began picking up the hairpins, making a chiding, clucking sound as she did so. "My lady must never try to do anything herself, what was she thinking?" she said, doing a credible imitation of their mother's lady's maid.

She dropped the pins into the bowl on Isabella's dressing table, then turned to look at her sister, her expression showing her worry as much as her teasing usually did.

"Are you all right?"

Isabella couldn't answer; the tears she'd been crying were choking her throat, and she could feel her eyes prickling as well. But this was Margaret, and Margaret, unlike everyone else in her world, would understand if she couldn't answer, couldn't be perfect every single second of every day.

"Oh, Izzy," her sister said in a sympathetic tone, noting her distress, then getting onto the bed and gathering her sister into her arms. Margaret was slight, and Isabella was substantially taller, so it was not the most comfortable position, physically at least, but to Isabella it felt wonderful.

"You could run away, you know." Margaret's tone

made it sound as though it were an entirely reasonable idea.

Isabella made a sound that in another woman, a woman who was not the most proper young lady ever who would eventually become a duchess, would have been deemed a grunt. "And just how can I run away?" She raised her head from where she'd buried it on Margaret's shoulder. "All I know is how to be elegant and beautiful and perfect. I have no skills, no money of my own, and no clue how to survive."

Margaret opened her mouth as if to protest, then snapped it shut again.

"Precisely," Isabella said, wishing her sister had been able to argue with her assessment at all. Then she wouldn't have felt so incredibly worthless. Because if her sister, who loved her most in the entire world, didn't even think she could do anything else, then she definitely could not do anything else.

"He is quite handsome," Margaret said, the tone of her voice revealing her skepticism. "At least you'll have something pleasant to look at across the breakfast table."

"For the rest of my life," Isabella said.

"Well, maybe he'll tire of you and leave you in the country with the children."

Isabella straightened on the bed and glared at her sister. "You are not helping."

"Well, what do you want me to do?"

Nothing. There was nothing that anyone could do, not even Isabella herself. Primarily not Isabella herself, in fact.

And that was the problem. She wished, just once, that she had fought back against what her parents had wanted for her, what they'd done to her, as soon as they realized that their eldest girl was going to be as beautiful as she was.

If only she had been allowed to not be perfect, just once, maybe the thought of not being perfect in this marriage—a marriage she didn't even want—wouldn't terrify her so much. She wished she wasn't so perfect—then she could just refuse.

But she was perfect, and her situation was not, and tomorrow she would be married to a brand-new duke about whom she knew two things: He was incredibly handsome, and he had very little experience with being a duke.

Whereas she was incredibly beautiful (she could admit it without false modesty) and she had a lot of training on how to be a duchess.

Which meant that going into this marriage they already had only one thing in common, and she didn't think being attractive was what made a marriage work.

"Izzy?" Her sister nudged her shoulder. "You know that if you're unhappy, if it's worse even than being here, you can tell me. We will find a way to fix it."

Isabella gave a dry chuckle. "The only way out of

marriage, as far as I know, is death. And I do not wish to die." She paused. "And I may not wish to be married to the duke, or to anyone, but I do not wish him to die. At least not until I get to know him."

"That sounds like an excellent plan," Margaret said. "And then, maybe—"

But whatever Margaret was about to say was lost as the door opened, revealing their mother, still wearing her evening gown, her face set in its normal disapproving expression. "Good, you are here," she said, shutting the door behind her, her disapproving look replaced by one of firm decision.

Oh dear. Isabella felt her stomach start to tighten, the way it normally did when her mother had that look on her face. To be honest, her stomach hurt most of the time she spoke to her mother, since she was bound to be found wanting in some way.

"Margaret, you need not stay." *Go, Margaret* was the real meaning.

"No, stay, Margaret." Isabella couldn't believe she had just contradicted her mother.

Judging by her mother's expression, she couldn't believe it, either.

"If you wish. Although what I have to say is not for an unmarried lady's ears," her mother said with a meaningful nod.

"Then I most definitely wish to stay," Margaret replied, bouncing on the bed in her enthusiasm.

The thought struck Isabella that this was to be the last night she and her sister would be together. Not that they wouldn't be together in the future, but this was the last night they would be together in their night rails, trading confidences and support.

Margaret must have sensed her distress—she usually did, after all—and reached to pat her hand while her mother settled herself in a chair adjacent to the bed.

"There are some things you should expect after marriage, Isabella," her mother began as Isabella's stomach tightened even more.

At this rate, perhaps she wouldn't need a corset, her waist would be so small from all the tightening.

The next morning arrived, despite Isabella wishing it wouldn't. She hadn't been able to eat anything except for a cup of tea (prepared the way her mother wanted) and had pushed a few eggs around on her plate. For once, her parents were too preoccupied to notice what she was doing. If only that inattention weren't because of Isabella's wedding day.

She'd been allowed to take breakfast in her wrapper, the one and only time Isabella had been allowed to be less than perfectly dressed for an occasion. But her wedding gown was pristine white, thanks to Queen Victoria, who'd apparently thought a bride wouldn't spill anything on her gown on her wedding day.

Of course Isabella's mother knew better, which was why Isabella wasn't wearing her gown at breakfast.

"Are you ready?" Margaret asked, giving Isabella's hair one last pat. Isabella's mother's lady's maid heaved a loud sigh and did something just where Margaret had touched.

"I suppose." Isabella ran her hands down her already well-smoothed gown, wishing there was just one more night she could have at home with Margaret, wishing that she hadn't had the ill fortune to be blessed with beauty and rank.

And then had to laugh at herself, as Margaret would if she could share her thoughts.

"The carriage is waiting, as is the duke." Their mother's voice arrived before she did, and Isabella felt herself straighten up automatically.

At least she didn't think the duke would be correcting her posture. That would be one of the benefits of marriage. Hopefully, slouching wouldn't be the only benefit.

"Coming, Mother," Isabella replied, gathering Margaret in her arms for one last hug.

"Just remember. We can figure it out, if you're miserable," Margaret whispered. Isabella felt the sting of tears in her eyelids, and gave a quick nod as she drew away. Even though there was nothing to be done, it at least felt as though someone cared about her.

"Come along, girls," their mother said.

Isabella drew a deep breath and stepped out into the hallway.

All too soon they arrived at the church, a crowd of carriages indicating that the best and finest of London Society had arrived to see the newly minted duke as well as, Isabella presumed, him marrying her.

She entered the church, her heart pounding, holding her breath and her spine as she walked down the aisle to the man who would have the care and keeping of her for the rest of her life.

"Come in!" Jane swiveled in her chair, hoping to see a white knight, a horse, or at least a messenger bearing the news that she wouldn't have to go through with it after all.

"Good evening, Jane."

He walked into the room like a stealthy predator, his black eyes gleaming as they rested on her. She felt as though she could see what he was thinking, what he was feeling, and it made her shiver.

"I wanted to give you this," he said, reaching into his breast pocket and withdrawing a slim case. He walked to stand in front of her, opening the case as he did so.

It was the most ~~gaudy hideous~~ beautiful thing she'd ever seen. He took it out of the box, then stepped around to stand in back of her.

"This was my mother's necklace," he said, sliding the

cool jewelry on her neck. She felt his fingers, also cool, hooking the chain fastening the clasp. "You will wear this at our first official event as husband and wife."

She swallowed, then touched the necklace. "Thank you," she said in a soft, nearly strangled voice.

The necklace felt like a collar, as though it tied her to him forever.

Could she ever take it off?

—THE PRINCESS AND THE SCOUNDREL

Chapter 7

Nicholas pushed the door open without waiting for her to reply to his knock.

"Oh!" she said, her voice high and unnatural. Not that he really knew what her actual voice sounded like; the most he'd heard her speak at one time were the vows she'd repeated that morning.

He wasn't sure whether to be grateful or not to have decided not to take the traditional honeymoon—on the one hand, there was the intended activity of a honeymoon, which he definitely wanted. But on the other hand, he was still so new to the title, and there were things that had to be done, and he also wanted to ensure that she was properly accepted, right away, as the Duchess of Gage, so they'd be attending parties and making calls rather than taking themselves off alone.

And now here he was in her room.

She sat at the dressing table, her lady's maid doing something to her hair.

"You won't be needed anymore this evening," Nicholas said to the woman. She glanced at Isabella, who inclined her head.

"Excuse me, Your Grace, Your Grace," the woman said, giving two quick curtseys as she walked to the door.

Nicholas waited until he heard the soft snick of the door shutting before moving to stand where the lady's maid had stood. He picked up a brush from the table and drew it toward her hair.

He saw her flinch. And felt his chest constrict.

"Go ahead," she said in a low tone. "You just— startled me." She lowered her head and he began to brush her hair. The long black strands rippled down her back like silk. It was astonishing that even her *hair* was beautiful—he'd never really thought much about a woman's hair, beyond if it was tickling his chest or getting in his mouth or anything, but her hair was glorious. He wanted to bury his face in it, wrap it around his throat, watch it hang over her naked body as she stood in front of him.

She made a little noise of satisfaction as he brushed, and the sound went straight to his cock. Dear God, if he could make her make a noise like that while in bed, this marriage might not be so terrible after all. Even if all he knew about her so far was that she was demure, and lovely, and quiet.

Like an elegant cat, one that knew just how it was

perceived, and just wanted occasional brushing and petting.

"The ceremony went well, I thought."

It was the first time she'd begun a conversation with him.

He cleared his throat and kept brushing, even though there were no snarls. "Yes, and the breakfast was good as well." He felt like punching himself for uttering such an inanity.

"I hadn't realized you knew the Duke of Rutherford," she continued. "His duchess is—quite unusual, isn't she?"

Nicholas's hands stilled. "The duke is one of my best friends, and his wife is a warm, generous woman." He didn't mean to speak brusquely, but it was clear he had, since her shoulders hunched as though he'd delivered a blow.

"I did not mean to offend you, Your Grace," she said, her voice hesitant.

"Nicholas. It seems ridiculous for you to call me Your Grace, since you are also Your Grace, and it could become confusing."

She met his gaze in the mirror. "Nicholas. And I am—"

"Isabella. I know." He laid the brush down on the dressing table and held his hand out, palm up. "Shall we to bed, Isabella?"

Her head dipped in a brief nod, and she stood, placing her fingers in his hand. He drew her toward the bed, his cock painfully hard as he smelled her scent, felt her warmth, glimpsed the shape of her through her nightgown, the fabric of which was somewhat sheer, but opaque enough for him to long for more details of what she looked like.

Her fingers were trembling.

"Are you all right?" he asked.

"Fine, Your— Nicholas, I am fine." Her voice trembled as well.

They reached the bed, and she looked at him. There was no mistaking the terror in her dark eyes.

He felt that fear hit low in his gut. "You are not all right, Isabella." He assisted her so she was sitting on the bed facing him. The bed was so high, her feet dangled off it, not reaching the ground.

She didn't look at him, but kept her gaze focused down. He doubted she was admiring the carpet, beautiful though it was.

He knelt down in front of her and took her hand in his. "You can tell me, you know."

At that, she did look at him, her eyes wide with— fear? Guilt? Worry? "Tell you what?"

"That you're nervous about this. About all this." He hesitated, hoping he could find the right words. He'd never had to before. This was new to him as well, only the new situation was one where a woman was reluctant to have sex with him. He decided not to share that with her. Instead, he tried his best to comfort her. "I've never—that is, I don't want to do anything you don't feel comfortable with."

She looked down again. Perhaps she really was admiring the carpet. He'd chosen it himself; it was pink and covered in roses.

"I am yours to do with what you will, Your— Nicholas."

He felt something harsh and mean unfurl in his chest. "I have never forced a woman, Isabella, and I am not going to start with my wife."

"This is my duty," she replied, her tone deadened.

So much for his erection; that had already diminished as soon as he'd realized she was most definitely not looking forward to any of this, and now it was nonexistent. It only remained to salvage something from his wedding night.

He released her hand and stood, glancing around the room. He knew full well everything that was in it, having overseen it himself. "Excuse me a moment, will you?" he said, leaving her still staring at the floor.

He stepped out into the hallway and into his room—he didn't want to remind her that their rooms connected, then she'd probably fall onto the carpet to inspect it more minutely.

"Your Grace," his valet said, jumping up from the chair he'd been dozing in.

"No need to get up, thank you, Miller," Nicholas replied, waving him back down. He'd acquired Miller along with the title, since his previous valet had decided to return to the country instead of staying with Nicholas and his new responsibilities. "I am just in here to get— Oh, here it is," he said, picking up the newspaper from the bedside table.

"I can iron that, if you like, Your Grace."

"There is no need, I'll just take this, if I might."

"Of course, Your Grace." Miller sounded shocked that Nicholas would even ask. Judging by what he knew about the former occupant of the title, he would have to guess that there were few requests, only commands.

His blood ran cold at the thought of that man having a wedding night with Isabella. Then hot with a savage fury as he thought about how the previous duke insisted that she was his.

"Over my dead body," he muttered, leaving the room. He paused for a moment outside her door, trying to put an expression on his face that was gentle, soothing, and friendly.

He had never worn such an expression in his entire life, so he hoped he didn't look like an idiot.

He entered the room and saw her, still sitting in that frozen position on the bed, still staring down.

"Isabella? I brought something for us tonight." Then winced as he realized that she might misunderstand his meaning. "That is, something for us to do together." Damn it, still not right. "Uh—just go sit in that chair, if you don't mind." He gestured to a chair, one of a pair, that was set in the corner of the room near one of the windows.

Isabella stood, as he'd asked, and walked to the chair he'd indicated. This was not going as her mother had suggested it might.

First of all, she was no longer on the bed, which was the only place she knew of for such activity to happen. Second, he didn't appear to be an animalistic beast who would then fall asleep shortly thereafter.

In fact, she'd have to admit that he was being altogether kind. Not at all what she'd thought he'd be, given how he'd been staring at her, and how he'd brushed her hair, as though intent on seduction.

And if she hadn't been so nervous about it all, about not knowing him, and worrying about how she'd behaved during the ceremony and the breakfast, and how her parents would treat Margaret now that she was out of the house—never mind that *she* was out of the house, when she'd never spent a night apart from her family— she would have been seduced.

Because honestly the way he'd touched her—not as though she were something to be worshipped, but as just another human, a human deserving of attention and care—made her want to learn more about him. His appearance just got better the closer one looked; the faint golden stubble on his strong jaw, the variations of blue in his eyes, changing with his mood; his bare throat, its strong Adam's apple reminding her, as though she needed reminding, that he was very definitely male.

And yet—and yet he wasn't demanding his male husbandly rights. He was, in fact, sitting down in the chair opposite her, unfolding a newspaper.

Should she have brought reading material to her wedding night?

"I haven't shared this with anyone," he said in what would have been a shy tone in any other man, "but I enjoy reading the serialized works in the paper, particularly the ones written by A Lady of Mystery. I was thinking that I could read one of the serials to you?"

Well. That was unexpected. "Of course, Your— Nicholas." Isabella placed her hands on her lap and kept her gaze on his face. He returned the look with a quick smile, and she felt—for just a moment—that she'd like to see what he was like as an animalistic beast.

"I don't have the first parts of the story, but basically, there's this lady who has been promised by her father to a prince, and she has no recourse but to agree to it." At that, he looked uncomfortable, as though realizing what he'd said.

And she had stiffened, too. It was altogether too close to her real situation, as he'd clearly noticed as well, and she had no idea what *he* thought about their marriage. It wasn't as though she could ask him, either; even if he said he hadn't wanted it, the fact remained that they were married. And would stay married until one of them died.

Wasn't that a cheery thought?

Not to mention she wouldn't even dare to ask such a thing of anybody. She couldn't even tell her mother her preference for one color or another, she wasn't about to question him as to his feelings about her, and how they came to be together, alone, in this room.

"Never mind that," he said, folding the newspaper up again. "I think there are cards in one of those drawers over there, perhaps we could play a game?"

He got up in a swift, elegant movement. She'd forgotten just how tall he was. His dressing gown was tied, but loosely, and underneath he only wore a nightshirt, one that came to mid-shin.

Goodness, even his lower legs were attractive.

"Here," he said, returning to sit in the chair and pulling a side table so it was between them. "I'll shuffle, and you can deal."

"What are we playing?" Besides the game of What Is the Strangest Way to Spend Your Wedding Night Ever?

He flipped through the cards until he found the one he wanted and withdrew it from the pack, showing it out to her. "The queen of clubs. That's our old maid." He handed her the rest of the pack, placing the queen underneath his chair. "Now deal."

"We're playing . . . Old Maid?" Her mother had not mentioned anything about there being card games during one's wedding night. The animalistic beast, the sleeping, the discomfort—all of that, but no card games.

Interesting. It seemed that her mother might have prepared her to be a duchess, but not to be the duchess to this particular duke.

Perhaps marriage would be more intriguing than she'd imagined. She dealt the cards, watching his elegant fingers as he arranged his hand, then allowed herself to look a bit farther down, to where the neck of his nightshirt was open. She saw a sprinkling of chest hair, and that sight made her breath catch, as though *she* might be the animalistic beast.

Her throat felt tight, and there was something else, too. Something that wanted . . . something, but she had no idea what it was.

But she was fairly certain it had everything to do with him.

She tried to push those thoughts away and concentrate on her wedding night. One that included card games.

"I can't be the old maid, I've just gotten married today," Isabella said with a smile as she held her last card. Nicholas had beaten her the previous five times they'd played, and she had gotten surprisingly engrossed in the game, which she hadn't played since she was probably six years old.

"It's not very sporting for me to constantly win, is it?" Nicholas said with a smirk that seemed to indicate he didn't care at all for not being sporting. "But I suppose that now that I am a duke, I should get accustomed to winning all the time, shouldn't I?" He spoke in a wry tone, but it pierced Isabella in a way he likely didn't intend.

"It is fine, Your— It is fine," Isabella said in a quiet voice. While they'd been playing she'd nearly forgotten who she was supposed to be, who he was, and what her future looked like now.

It had been a glorious moment of forgetting, but now she couldn't stop thinking about how odd all of this was, how her mother would be appalled.

Perhaps she wouldn't speak of it.

Nicholas frowned at her reply, then stood and held his hand out to her as he had when he first came into the room. Was now when they were going . . . ?

She kept her gaze focused just beyond his shoulder, not looking at him so that she wouldn't be able to see his intentions on his face. Because if she didn't see it, perhaps it wouldn't be so bad.

"Don't freeze up on me, princess," he said in a low tone.

Her eyes snapped to his face, and what she saw there was not lustful, or greedy, or wanting.

He had a gentle, almost kind, expression on his face, and that, more than anything, nearly made her weep.

"Let's get you into bed. You must be tired," he said.

He led her to the bed, where he drew down the cover and gestured for her to slip in, pulling the covers up to her chin. She lay blinking up at him, wondering just who this man was whom she'd married.

He got around to the other side and removed his dressing gown. Isabella saw one long leg slide under the covers, then he was beside her. He turned on his side and propped his head on his hand.

The candlelight made the planes of his face stand out even more sharply, and he was dangerously, seductively beautiful. She could see that, but she was, as he'd said, frozen inside, and couldn't feel anything. Except for the worry that she wouldn't be good enough at this.

"May I tell you a story?" he asked.

This wedding night was nothing like she'd expected, nothing at all.

"If you like," she replied. At least she knew she was very good at listening—her mother had trained her above all other things for that.

"Where are your parents?"

They had been cheered, and walked at the head of what seemed to be a never-ending parade, and Jane's arms had been filled three times over with flowers, the exotic flowers that were like nothing she had ever beheld before.

And now they were alone, and she might finally get to speak to him, to unravel the mystery of her new husband.

The prince's face froze, and Jane—Princess Jane now—held her breath as she waited for his reply.

At long last, he spoke. But he did not say anything, not anything that was at all close to answering the question. "They are . . . not here."

"Oh."

"You will not inquire about them again," he continued in an icy tone of voice.

"Oh," she repeated, this time in a much quieter tone.

That there was a mystery about her new husband and his family she had no doubt; she just hoped the mystery could be solved without causing pain.

She somehow doubted it would.

—THE PRINCESS AND THE SCOUNDREL

Chapter 8

"And then the whatchamacallit."

"The knight," she corrected in her soft voice.

He stifled a grin. "Of course, you're absolutely correct. The knight, well, he and his friends, including King Art, decided that they would go off and do all sorts of wonderful deeds and gather favors from well-born ladies in tournaments and jousts and that type of thing."

He cleared his throat. "The end."

She still lay on the bed next to him, her hands folded on her stomach. She hadn't moved.

Either to get closer to him or to leave entirely. So perhaps it was a draw?

"I do not think," she said after a moment, "that that is the actual story of King Arthur and the Knights of the Round Table." She made a little noise that might have been a chuckle, he wasn't certain. He definitely had not heard her laugh yet. "For one thing, their purpose was not to gather favors as though it were a contest. And King Arthur did not, as you said, just put a little bit of effort into pulling Excalibur—not named Swordie, as you said—out from the rock. It was magic, he was supposed to be the king."

He couldn't help but grin then. She sounded so affronted, but more importantly, she no longer sounded scared. He'd hoped to at least put her more at ease, and he surmised that if he couldn't charm or seduce her—and he knew very well that was out of the question, at least for this night—then he'd take her mind off what was supposed to be happening and instead put her mind onto something far less frightening.

For her, at least. His brain was entirely engrossed with the fact that he was in bed with his new wife and she was wearing just a thin night garment of some sort, and he hadn't had relations with any woman for over two weeks, and that might be a new record, and she was still so lovely, and she was his wife, goddamn it.

Or that last part might have been his more . . . male parts speaking, since his brain would never swear in frustration. Would it?

But he had reminded himself, only about every minute or so, that trying to lure her into something now would likely cause irreparable damage in the future. Their future together, since now they were man and wife. Nicholas and Isabella. Duke and duchess.

Storyteller and story corrector.

"Fine, then. Tomorrow you can tell the story." He held his breath waiting for her reply. Knowing, somehow, that it was crucial that they make it through this night, just a few scant hours, for their marriage to even have a possibility of success.

"You should continue. Perhaps you will improve with practice," she replied, and he felt his chest expand as he took a deep inhale.

"And I will bid you good night," he said, leaning over to kiss her on the forehead. "Rest well, Isabella."

"Th-Thank you, Nicholas."

He got up from the bed, allowed himself one last look at her—yes, still unbelievably beautiful, still lying in a bed, of all things, all soft, and warm, and as close to naked as a proper aristocratic virgin would be—and here he was taking himself off to his own bed, entirely alone, entirely sexually frustrated, and—

And entirely fine with that, if it meant he could still hold out hope for the future.

She didn't expect to feel lonely when he left.

She also hadn't expected to feel anything but used as the object of her new husband's animalistic passions.

But instead he'd played cards with her, told her a ridiculous story, and left her with only the type of goodnight kiss a parent might give a child.

She curled onto her side, the side where he'd been,

and touched her hand to the cover. It was warm from his body.

She swallowed, then leaned forward and sniffed the pillow. It had a distinct smell. His smell. Not that she knew what he smelled like, but this odor was not, as far as she could tell, on anything else in the room.

Although to prove that, she might have to go around sniffing every object, and that would be odd.

She would have to take it on faith that this was his smell. And she liked it; warm, and clean-smelling, but also somewhat spicy.

Like a plum pudding.

She heard a sound, and realized it was she. Laughing. She had hardly expected to be laughing on her wedding night—she had expected pain, and tears, and awkwardness.

She definitely hadn't expected to be on her own.

Marriage, thus far, was an entirely unexpected experience.

"Good morning, Your Grace."

Isabella blinked, staring up at the swirls of rose-colored satin on the ceiling. This was not home. This was— "Oh," she said, raising herself up on her elbows. "Good morning, um—" She tilted her head at the woman who stood at the foot of the bed, her hands loosely clasped in front of her, her expression entirely pleasant. Not as though Isabella had just forgotten her name.

"Robinson, Your Grace."

"Of course. Robinson. Good morning."

"Good morning."

At this rate, they'd be saying good morning until the afternoon.

It was lovely of someone—perhaps Nicholas?—to hire a lady's maid. Isabella had never liked the one she'd had at her parents' house since she suspected the woman reported on Isabella's activity to her mother.

"I brought you some tea and a few pastries the cook thought might tempt you."

Excellent. They'd gone beyond the greeting stage in only five minutes. And Isabella was famished—not eating for a few days prior to one's wedding would do that to a person. "Thank you, that would be lovely." Isabella struggled to sit up, only to have her lady's maid—Robinson—march swiftly over and begin to yank and plump pillows with a ferocity that did not seem, to Isabella, to be a first-thing-in-the-morning-type activity.

"What time is it?" she asked as the woman positioned Isabella's body just so.

"Nearly nine o'clock."

Hm. She would have thought she'd have slept longer. Although she hadn't done anything particularly strenuous the night before, and she had been exhausted by the day.

"And the duke? Does he expect me at breakfast?"

The woman's attitude went even more proper, if that was possible. "The duke is already out, Your Grace."

Out? Out already? Where out? Only she couldn't ask the lady's maid that question; that wasn't proper. A duchess, her mother had said, must behave as though she knows everything and is never surprised by anything.

But even her mother would have been surprised by the events of the night before.

Not that Isabella was going to share any of her wedding night experience with her mother. That was not only not proper, she didn't want to tell anyone what had—or hadn't—happened.

She didn't even know how she felt about it, except that she was more intrigued by her new husband than she had been when she only thought he was the handsomest, tallest gentleman she'd ever seen.

And she had thought herself rather intrigued, even then.

She picked up one of the pastries from the plate and took a bite. It was delicious, filled with apples and sugar and some sort of cream. An entirely duchesslike breakfast.

As she chewed, she glanced around the room. *Her* room. She hadn't taken that much of a look the night before, what with being terrified about the potential beastliness of her husband and all.

The room was spacious, of course, as befit her new

rank. It wasn't nearly as crowded with furniture and other items as her parents' rooms had been—on a few occasions Isabella's enormous skirts had whisked a few items of bric-a-brac off a table, making her mother frown even more than usual. It was—pleasant, Isabella thought in surprise. Had this been the earlier duke's mother's room? Or perhaps the earlier duke had gotten it done up for her? Because she didn't think the earlier duke—no matter how low she thought of him—was infatuated with the color pink, or any of its iterations.

She giggled at the thought. Robinson, who'd been folding her wrapper, glanced over at her and smiled. Isabella nearly smiled back before she recalled that one did not smile at the servants.

At least, that's what her mother had always said, adding that the duchess, specifically the Duchess of Gage, would be correct at all times, no matter if she was at court with the Queen or at home with the servants.

The Duchess of Gage. That's who she was now, not Lady Isabella Sawford, not even the Earl and Countess of Grosston's perfect daughter.

What would the future hold? Who would the Duchess of Gage be, when all was said and done?

"Just one more round, I promise." Nicholas sat in the corner of the boxing ring, Griff dabbing at his face with a towel.

"Do you want to get your nose broken? Or worse?" his brother said through his teeth, his eyes focused on his work.

"What's worse than having your nose broken?" Nicholas asked. Not that he cared about the answer, but he did care about distracting Griff enough so his brother wouldn't insist he stop.

He had to continue. He had to do something to release all this—whatever it was that burned inside him.

He had barely slept after leaving Isabella's room, his brain reexamining the images of the day—her, looking perfectly lovely in the church, speaking her vows in a soft, low voice. That evening, the look of poise replaced by a fearful look that seemed to pierce his chest somewhere in the vicinity of his heart. How she'd glanced at him when she'd thought he wasn't looking, a hesitant, worried expression on her face. How that expression had eased as they'd played cards, then returned when he led her to the bed.

How it had felt to have her lying next to him, so close. And yet so distant.

"Just one more," he said again to Griff.

His brother stepped back and looked at him with a disgusted expression on his face. "Fine. You're not going to mind whatever it is I want anyway, so you might as well get yourself pounded for a while longer. Maybe it'll shake some sense into your brain." He turned his head to yell into the main boxing area. "Anyone want to take on the new Duke of Gage? He seems to need a good pummeling."

Several heads turned, and then a few gentlemen, already dressed for fighting, stepped forward. Griff looked at each of them, then pointed to the largest. "You first. Make sure you don't think about the fact that your opponent is a duke. Or maybe you should, if it'll make the fight more intense."

The man laughed, spoke a few words to the other men who'd seemed interested, then stepped into the ring, his gaze fierce.

Nicholas felt the man's stare through his whole body, flowing out to his fists, which were itching to find their way to the man's face. He needed some sort of satisfaction, and if this was the only type he would get—well, he would take it.

Isabella wasn't precisely waiting for her husband, but she also hadn't done anything at all that morning except pick up embroidery and put it down.

Up, down. Up, down. At this rate the fabric would travel more than she had.

She was sitting on a surprisingly comfortable chair—again, nothing like her mother would own—in a small room that served as "the duchess's own private tea room," the butler had informed her. It had a large bank of windows on one side of the room, but the day was cloudy enough to require candles. Especially since she was supposedly embroidering. Even though she wasn't.

With the exception of the butler, who appeared at regular fifteen-minute intervals, she was alone. And she didn't know when she'd ever been left alone for so long before. It felt—odd. Which was probably why she couldn't concentrate on her embroidering.

She dropped it—again—when she heard the door swing open, heard the butler's voice speaking in a suitably obsequious tone.

And walked into the hallway, casually, as though she just happened to be walking by when he arrived. She did not bring the embroidery; it had traveled enough. "Oh, there you are," she said, keeping her voice neutral. No hint of *Where in heaven's name have you been/ were you so disappointed by last night?*, Thank goodness. Not that she'd even know how to speak as though she had any emotion at all—the only person to whom she'd allowed herself, her own self, to peek through was Margaret, and Margaret had gotten only a fraction of what Isabella was capable of.

Whatever that was.

He turned from handing his hat to the butler and she gasped at the sight. His face—his gorgeous, sharply planed face—looked as though someone had been doing embroidery on it.

"What happened to you? You," she said, gesturing to the butler, "go fetch some cloths, some hot water, and—and—"

"Some whiskey, too," he added, giving her a sly glance. "It looks worse than it is, I am fine."

The butler scurried off, leaving them alone in the hallway. She drew nearer, suppressing a gasp as she saw his face up close. "You are most definitely not fine. Come into the sitting room," she said, taking his arm and leading him back where she had been without waiting for a response.

He allowed himself to be led, his plum pudding scent tickling her nose, the heat and strength and all of him at her back, reminding her just what they had and hadn't done the night before.

"Sit there please, Your Grace," she said, putting her hands on his shoulders and pushing him down into one of the sturdier chairs. He glanced around the room, taking in the embroidery hoop, the tea things, and the footstool she'd been resting her feet on. "This is a pleasant room, isn't it?" he asked, as though he were merely on a social call and hadn't wandered in looking as though someone had mistaken his face for a door knocker against a particularly heavy door.

Or something.

He chuckled. "I haven't really explored much of the house yet. You know I've just moved in, probably two and a half weeks ago."

Of course. Two weeks since they'd first met, two weeks since she'd had her freedom, for a brief moment, only to have it snatched away in a sea of legalities and honor and funds and livelihoods.

What could one woman matter against all that?

So even though she hadn't the faintest idea of where she fit into this new life—her life—she couldn't chafe against it. At least, not too much.

And meanwhile, here he was, all bloody and bruised, but still with that roguish smile on his face, the one that, if she were that sort of woman, would render her weak in the knees.

As it was, she was only mildly shaky.

"Your Grace, Your Grace," the butler said, nodding first to her and then to Nicholas. They shared a conspiratorial glance, both recalling his words from the night before.

"You can put the things on that table, there," Isabella said. "And then you may go. I will attend His Grace."

The butler nodded and deposited an armful of white cloths and a bowl of steaming water on the table, then made his way to another table set against the wall, picking up a bottle of brown liquid and a glass.

"If there is nothing else, Your Grace, Your Grace," he said, bowing as he placed the bottle and glass onto the table.

Isabella drew nearer, taking one of the cloths and

dipping it into the water, then wrung it out. "Are you going to tell me what happened?"

He grinned and looked up at her. "Telling you someone hit my face isn't something you don't already know."

Isabella repressed a sigh, the kind usually only Margaret elicited, and instead concentrated on schooling her features into the neutral duchess expression she'd perfected after hours of practice.

Only then, when she did that, his grin receded. And he looked away from her face, to somewhere else in the room.

Had she somehow disappointed him? Was that why last night hadn't happened? And what was she going to do?

It didn't help. Having the largest man Griff could find for him to spar with hadn't reduced the impact of seeing her, still (as he well knew) a virgin, still impossibly beautiful.

Now also, it appeared, slightly bossy. Which surprised him, since the night before, the only substantive time they'd spent together had left him with the impression that she was meek. Soft-willed. Pleasant, but not compelling.

But this woman—she'd taken one look at him, and that gorgeous mouth had turned down in an expression of dismay, but she'd had the wherewithal to bark out orders to his butler—whose name Nicholas couldn't even remember, much less remember to order around—and insist he come sit so she could tend him.

"I know this will hurt, but it will hurt more if we don't do something," she said, seeming to have dropped her inquisition of just how he'd gotten himself so beaten.

You should see the other man, he wanted to say, but he doubted she'd appreciate the levity.

It did hurt, as she'd promised, and he inhaled sharply as the warm, wet cloth touched the corner of his eye, where his opponent had delivered one of his most lethal blows.

"Are you going to tell me?"

So she had not dropped her inquisition at all. Add "stubborn" to the list of what he knew about his bride.

He closed his eyes and leaned back in the chair. That forced her to move closer to him so she stood between his legs. Well. He couldn't have planned that better if he tried, could he?

"I like to consider myself a rather skilled pugilist," he said. "I've had worse results after a fight."

He felt her step back, and opened his eyes. Her expression was as near horrified as someone so perfectly appropriate could look. "You mean you chose to do this to yourself?" she asked in a hushed tone. As though she were too horrified to speak too audibly. "Deliberately?"

He wanted to laugh at just how appalled she seemed,

but he knew that would scare her off probably more than his cut-up and bloody face would.

"Yes, as it happens, I did." Nicholas reached up to rub his palm along his jaw. "Can you pour me some of that whiskey?" he asked.

She yanked his hand away, holding his fingers in hers. "Don't touch your face, not until I'm done," she said in that bossy tone. And not, he noticed, pouring him anything at all. "It's hard to believe anyone would want to do this to oneself, but then again, I am not a man."

Nicholas let his eyes drift over her, from her gorgeous face and its lush lips, currently pressed into a thin line, down over the fragile bones of her neck, over her breasts, her waist, her hips. Felt how warm and soft she was between his legs. "No, you are most definitely not a man," he said in a voice that had grown huskier over the past few minutes.

She blushed, but kept working on his face, dabbing the cloth into the water, then cleaning with a gentle touch. Nicholas winced a few times, but it really wasn't the worst he'd ever gotten. Never mind it hadn't had its intended result of making him want her less—if anything, he wanted to claim the spoils of his own particular brand of war and hoist her over his shoulder, take her to the bedroom, and ravish her until they were both speechless.

But that was not possible.

"What are your plans today?" he asked as she made a few last swipes at his face with the cloth.

She stilled. "I—I do not have any. I rather hoped, that is, I assumed we would spend the day together." Of course. Because most couples, ones that hadn't both been just thrust into entirely new situations, would be off on a honeymoon.

Nicholas felt her words like another punch. He'd already messed this marriage in myriad ways, and they had been married only twenty-four hours.

What might he accomplish in twenty-four days? Twenty-four years?

"Of course, that sounds like an excellent plan," he replied, as though he'd been thinking the same thing all along, and was just waiting for the opportunity to speak to her about it.

"You didn't even think about it, did you," she said in a flat voice, stepping back from his legs, looking at the carpet, again.

She didn't exhibit it, not at all, but he knew he'd hurt her.

"I hadn't, but that is because I wished to consult with you. Isn't that what a married couple should do? Consult with one another?" He had no idea, he hadn't seen what married couples did or didn't do with one another since he was small, before his father died, but it certainly sounded good.

She unbent a little, so perhaps it was the right tactic. "That is reasonable. So what would you like to do?"

Well, he hadn't thought she'd turn the question right back around at him so quickly. He reviewed what he'd done before he was a married man: visit boxing saloons, visit houses of ill repute, sit at home thinking about at least one of the two activities he'd done while he was out, ride horses, and read serial novels.

"Would you like to go for a ride in the park?"

Her face lit up, and he felt the pressure in his chest ease. "That would be lovely. I will just go change."

"Good," he replied. He would take her out for a ride in the carriage, they would talk about things not related to boxing or sex, and he would be able to get to know his bride better. If only he could stop thinking about the latter in regards to her, he would be fine.

He might never be fine.

Princess Jane soon grew accustomed to a life, so
different from her own, in the prince's castle. She
was awakened at dawn by the riotous singing of
those brightly plumed birds, she was served by no
fewer than ~~three~~ five maidservants at one time, she
ate delicious fruits she'd never seen before and spent
long hours escaping from the heat in a ~~bathtub~~ pool
reserved just for her.

But she might never become accustomed to her
husband. He didn't speak to her frequently, but when
he did, it was always to question her—not to allow
her to ask questions of him.

She knew, from their earlier conversation, that
there was something altogether ~~strange~~ mysterious
about him, but she didn't know if she wished to
unravel the mystery, or leave it alone.

What if her new husband was as dangerous as

he'd seemed when she first met him? What if she still managed to fall in love with him?

And how would she decide how she wished to proceed, when it came to him?

—THE PRINCESS AND THE SCOUNDREL

Chapter 9

Isabella hurried up the stairs, an odd excitement fluttering in her chest. There had been something so—so foreign about him, not in the foreign country sort of way, she could absolutely tell he was from England, as she was—but in an unknown territory sort of way.

He was entirely different from anyone she'd ever met. Even the men she'd met during her Seasons, even the previous—and unlamented duke—hadn't had the same force of personality this one had.

It was enticing and also frightening. At least, frightening to her. From what Margaret had intimated, he hadn't had any problems getting females to pay attention to him.

And why shouldn't they? He was handsome, seemed charming enough, and had a low, resonant voice that did interesting things to her insides when he spoke.

And he smelled like a plum pudding.

So yes, she was excited about going for a drive with

him. She would need to discover what type of man she had married, beyond the rudiments of looks, voice, and ability to punch and get punched, apparently.

That last item should not have also made her thrill in some sort of secret way, but it did. It absolutely did. What would it look like to see him in the midst of a boxing match? She knew enough to know that gentlemen—even dukes—did not wear their coats and waistcoats and cravats when they boxed. She didn't know what they did wear, but she knew it was less than what he would normally wear.

And again, for some reason, that intrigued her.

While she wouldn't say she herself was an animalistic beast, she did have to admit to wishing she could get a little . . . beastly with him.

The lowering thought occurred that perhaps he did not feel the same. Might not ever feel the same.

She wasn't vain, but she knew she was not only pretty, but beautiful—her parents had been telling her for years that her beauty was the only thing she had worth cultivating. So what could possibly be the problem? Was he in love with one of his former paramours? What if the lady wasn't a former paramour at all, but a current one?

And just what would Isabella do about it?

That was something she was going to have to think about.

"Your Grace!" Her lady's maid jumped up out of a

chair as Isabella opened the door. "I thought you were downstairs."

Isabella smiled. "Well, Robinson, I was, only now I am here. And I need your help—the duke, that is, my husband"—and was that the first time she'd said those two words?—"is taking me for a drive, and I need to change into a proper outfit."

"Of course, Your Grace," Robinson replied. She marched over to the wardrobe and flung the doors wide, revealing most of the clothing Isabella's mother had ordered as being appropriate for a duchess.

There was a lot of pink in there, Isabella noted with a sigh.

"Might I suggest this one?" Robinson said, withdrawing a garment that was, thankfully, not pink. It was a dark purple, and was tailored within an inch of its life, with clever darts ensuring that no one would mistake her for a man, but still, it was not pink.

"Should you wish it in the future, Your Grace, we can inquire of the tailor if we could commission one in pink." Robinson stepped back, holding the gown.

"No, that will not be necessary," Isabella said hastily. "The purple is fine."

It was only twenty minutes later that Isabella descended the staircase, holding the skirt of her gown up from the stairs, her hat placed just so on her hair.

He was waiting downstairs, pacing back and forth across the parquet, and it appeared he'd been running his hands through his hair, judging by its dishevelment.

And why was it that when a lady's hair was messy she looked . . . messy, whereas when a gentleman's hair was messy it merely made him look more attractive?

Or was that just he?

"I apologize that I kept you waiting, Nicholas," Isabella said.

He looked up at her as she descended the stairs, an odd, nearly predatory look on his face. It sent a shiver up her spine, and she automatically straightened in response. Her mother had told her often enough that showing a reaction was unseemly.

"No, of course not. You look lovely," he replied, taking her hand as she walked down the last few steps. He drew her fingers to his mouth, but kept his gaze on her. "Lovely," he repeated, kissing her fingers lightly. She felt the impact through her gloves, all the way through to her feet, it felt like.

"Thank you. Is the carriage ready?" she asked, hearing her voice a little shakier than it was before.

"Yes, I have some unexpected meetings later on today—things to do with accounts and such—so we cannot stay out long, but I did wish to show off my bride."

"If you are too busy, we can go another day." A lady must always give up her own pleasure in service of others.

He frowned, as though confused. "I've just said I wanted to go, and now you are asking if I don't want to? If you don't wish to, just say so."

Just say so. If only it were that easy. She hadn't been allowed to say anything of what she'd felt for nearly her whole life. The only person to whom she'd ever even admitted anything was her sister, and even then she felt constrained in her conversation.

"Of course I wish to go driving with you, Nicholas," she said in a bright tone. He gave her another quick, curious glance, then made a gesture for her to precede him to the door.

The butler opened the door with a bow. "Have a pleasant outing, Your Grace, Your Grace," he said in a very proper tone.

"Thank you, we shall," Nicholas said, putting his hand at Isabella's waist to guide her down the stairs.

No man had ever touched her like this, at least not when there was no music and dancing occurring. It felt so risqué, even though this was her husband, and had things gone as she'd been told they should have gone, he would have touched a lot more than her waist.

"Oh," Isabella exclaimed as she spotted the carriage. It wasn't the usual type her parents drove in—sturdy, large, with a coachman, four wheels, and four horses. This carriage looked nearly birdlike, with two wheels and just one single horse.

A groom waited for them, dressed in what Isabella

realized was the duke's livery. Thank goodness it wasn't pink.

"Thank you, um—" Nicholas began. "What is your name?"

The groom looked startled, as Isabella would have been in his place—she didn't know the names of half of the staff at her parents' house, it wasn't deemed necessary.

"Michael, Your Grace," the groom—barely a boy, as Isabella saw—replied with a visible swallow.

"Michael, can you hand me the whip? I will assist Her Ladyship into the carriage."

"Certainly," Michael said, walking to the back of the vehicle.

"Isabella, if I might?" Nicholas said, taking her hand.

"Of course." She felt the warmth, the strength of him with just the clasp of his hand. He put his other hand back on her waist, and she stepped up into the carriage, her heart racing more than it should be.

He sat beside her, and they were so close, they were nearly touching.

She had driven with gentlemen before, but always in a carriage, and always with someone else there.

Marriage was full of new experiences. Just not the ones she'd imagined before she was married.

"Michael," Nicholas called out, "is there anything I should know about this horse?"

"No, Your Grace. She's a right proper stepper, and her name's Lady."

"Lady," Nicholas repeated. "And so fitting she is going to be pulling a lady as well," he said, nodding toward Isabella.

Was he—flirting with her? Were husbands supposed to do that with their wives?

And why did she have no idea how to reply?

Nicholas felt like the stupidest kind of clod. Not that clods were, in general, noted for their intelligence, but he felt like the stupidest. He felt tongue-tied around this woman, this lady who was also his wife, and he seemed to be saying the things most likely to make her poker up and adopt that frigid mien that almost seemed ingrained in her.

And what if it was? What if he had married the world's iciest woman? To whom, he knew, he would be absolutely faithful, because he was not going to insult her. It was a potentially very depressing thought.

But he thought he'd caught a glimpse of something in her eyes, in her expression, that indicated that she was not entirely cold. She'd responded well enough the night before, to playing cards and being told stories. She'd seemed excited to go for a drive, but then he'd had to ruin it by telling her he had another obligation.

Was she so vain that she expected her husband to dance attendance on her at all times? Was that why she'd asked if he'd prefer not to go driving?

He didn't think he'd ever thought about a woman so much, at least not one with whom he was having sexual relations. Or thought so much about one woman in such a short time. Even if they were having relations.

"Where would you like to go? Anywhere in particular?" he asked, as much to get his own mind off her—not to mention sex—as to inquire as to her preference.

Which was, as it happened, no preference. "Wherever you would like," she said in that low, distant tone that managed to be both sensual and off-putting at the same time.

Just as she was.

She was sitting next to him, but it felt as though she were somewhere far off in the distance, a quiet, gorgeous star floating off in the night sky.

He decided to try again. Because if he didn't figure out who she was, and what she liked, he would never have a fulfilling, satisfactory marriage. Not to mention a fulfilling and satisfactory sex life. "I actually want to know, Isabella," he said firmly, "where you would like to go. I myself don't have any thoughts on it, I usually just go for a ride in the park, but if there is somewhere else—"

"The park is fine," she blurted out, then folded her hands carefully on her lap. "The park is fine," she repeated in a much calmer tone.

"The park, then," Nicholas said, turning the cabriolet in that direction. "But next time I ask you your opinion on something, I actually want your opinion, not what you think my opinion is, or that you don't have an opinion. Everyone has an opinion on something, even if it's disliking a particular food, or preferring one activity over another." And then he winced, since he knew what activity he would prefer, and he was guessing that was the last thing on her mind.

"Oh," she said in a quiet voice, and then stopped speaking altogether.

Well, that went well, he thought sourly as he drove them to the park. Now she was a silent lump, albeit a gorgeous, silent lump, sitting beside him on the seat.

And them with eternity to spend together. Wonderful.

But then—then she did speak. "The weather is nice today."

So it wasn't much, in terms of conversation, but it was more than she'd said in the past fifteen minutes, so he seized it like a drowning man grabs a rope from the shore.

"Yes, it is."

If a drowning man really didn't wish to grab that much rope. Perhaps hanging himself was a preferable idea. In which case he would need more rope.

"I was thinking—" he began, as she said, "Where did you—?"

"You first," he said, turning into the park.

"I was going to ask where you learned your story from last night. It was . . ."

Please don't say idiotic, he thought as she paused.

". . . creative."

He laughed, as much in relief as in humor. "Yes, creative is one word for it. My brother, Griffith—you met him at the wedding—he is the much more studious one in the family. He used to read all of those stories and then we would act them out, and he'd invariably get frustrated with me because I couldn't remember the details or names. Eventually, he just gave in and allowed me to tell them."

A greeting from nearby interrupted him just as he was about to ask her something about herself. "Your Grace!"

Nicholas cursed inwardly as some titled gentlefolk or another greeted them. This was nearly the longest conversation they'd had to date.

To be fair, he had brought her out in public in an open carriage, so it was highly unlikely they wouldn't be interrupted.

He slowed Lady to a stop and squinted to see who was speaking. "Oh, hello, my lord." He had no idea who the well-dressed couple were, but they looked vaguely familiar.

"Good afternoon, Lady Truscott, Lord Truscott." It seemed his wife knew them, at least.

The pair were older, with generous laugh lines in their faces, and both were smiling at his wife, as though delighted to see her.

Well, he was delighted to see her as well, but he doubted it was for the same reason.

"I would have thought you two would be off on a

honeymoon!" Lord Truscott exclaimed. "If the lady were my wife, I would have made sure to be alone with her. You've broken a lot of hearts, Your Grace," the man chided, wagging his finger at Isabella.

The man didn't mean it to be an accusation, but Nicholas still felt guilty, for not taking her away, for not knowing more about her past. What if she had left someone behind? Someone who wasn't a duke, whom her father hadn't bought for her?

What if she was cold because she'd given all her warmth to someone else?

He dared to glance over at her, as though it would be written on her face, but all he saw was her usual polite Society smile.

"The duke is only newly succeeded to his title, as you know, so we thought it best to remain in town for the time being," Isabella said.

It sounded reasonable, and yet—they hadn't discussed anything of the sort. At least not together. He and Griff had thought a honeymoon should wait, given that the dukedom and then the wedding had come so quickly, one after the other.

She hadn't even been given a chance to acquiesce to his decision. He'd just decided.

"Your Grace," another voice called, and both he and Isabella turned their heads.

It was his wife's father, riding up on a gorgeous horse

that did not suit the earl's disapproving expression.

It was so early in the day, and yet he'd already managed to annoy his new father-in-law. He tried not to feel triumphant at that.

But that was disrespectful to his wife, although, if he wasn't mistaken, she'd stiffened up even more beside him, returning to the posture she'd had when they started driving.

"Good morning, Isabella," the earl said before turning his attention to Nicholas. "I stopped by your town house this morning, but you had already gone out."

Yes, I had to pummel somebody so I could relieve my frustration at not bedding my wife.

"Yes" was all Nicholas allowed himself to say.

"Well, and you were out, and—" The earl was clearly uncomfortable at not saying whatever he wished he could say, and neither Nicholas nor Isabella was helping him.

But Lord Truscott did. "Spit it out, man! What do you need to talk about?"

Nicholas bit back a laugh as he concentrated on smoothing his features.

"I—well, there are things to discuss." What those things could possibly be Nicholas couldn't guess—he couldn't very well marry another one of the earl's daughters.

Isabella took his fingers in hers. He felt them trembling.

"Of course. You can make an appointment with my secretary"—even though he didn't have one yet—"and I will be happy to see you then."

It was a dismissal, and as he spoke, he felt Isabella's hand tighten on his.

Interesting.

"Your mother will be sending an invitation for you to dine with us soon," the earl said to Isabella. "She was just saying she is looking forward to hearing what improvements you might be making to the duke's town house."

"The duke and I have not yet discussed that. There has been no time, as of yet," his wife replied in her iciest tone.

Even more interesting.

The earl's expression tightened. As though he wished he could shout, but was preventing himself from doing so.

And if he did dare, Nicholas thought it was likely bad form for him to punch his father-in-law in the jaw.

Instead, he decided to punch him metaphorically. "The duchess and I will be pleased to invite you and the countess to our town house in one of the upcoming weeks. For now," he said, lifting Isabella's not quite as trembling hand to his lips, "we are currently too busy to commit to any engagements." He folded her hand in his and tucked it into his side. "Do give the countess our best wishes, would you?"

Well, it wasn't as though he could actually say, *Get out of here now.*

The earl's face flushed red, and his gaze darted between Nicholas and Isabella. "Fine, excuse me," he said, turning his horse around abruptly, then galloping off.

He felt her exhale.

Lord Truscott was not so discreet, letting out a bark of laughter that he quickly smothered as his wife elbowed him.

"If you will excuse us," Nicholas said, nodding to the Truscotts, "I wish to show my wife the pond at the other end of the park."

Lord Truscott grinned. "Of course! With a lovely bride like that, I'm surprised you're not home right now 'showing her the pond.'" The last bit was offered with a wink, which Nicholas returned.

Because there was no reason for anyone to suspect theirs was not a usual marriage, at least not usual yet—and now he knew he would have to patiently woo his wife to get her to trust him enough to make it a true, usual marriage.

Or spend the rest of his life getting punches thrown at him.

"Why can't I ask you any questions?" Jane wished she was less intrigued by her husband. He scared her, but he hadn't hurt her—yet.

She saw how his jaw tightened, and it felt as though something was squeezing the air out of her lungs.

"You just did." His tone was as harsh as it had been the first time they'd met—but now she wasn't frightened. At least, not that much.

"I mean a real question."

He turned his head and stared into her eyes, a piercing stare that made her swallow. "Go ahead, pet. Ask me anything. If you dare."

—THE PRINCESS AND THE SCOUNDREL

Chapter 10

Nicholas urged the horse forward, and Isabella grasped the side of the carriage to keep her perfect balance on the seat. She didn't think he would notice that her hands were not correctly placed in her lap. Now that she was no longer holding on to his hands for dear life, that is.

But all that brought up a more difficult thought—what *did* he think of her? She hadn't spoken except for a few words for the entire day. She felt as though she'd barely breathed.

"Are you all right?" His tone didn't sound as though he thought the worst of her; if anything, it was solicitous.

Oh, lovely, he must think she was an idiot. An idiot who happened to be married to him.

"I—I am fine," she managed to say in a nearly normal tone of voice. Which was to say, without expressing any emotion whatsoever. If Margaret were here, perhaps Isabella could have released some of the feelings racing around her, like a strong gust of wind playing havoc with a handful of ribbons.

And that was an idiotic image, too. Maybe she was an idiot. After all, the only thing that had ever been cultivated was her and her ability to pour tea without pouring it on herself.

She and Margaret had had governesses, but Isabella's schooling had always come second to her duchess training.

"If you wish to visit your parents, of course we can," Nicholas continued. She wished he were still holding her hand. She wished she could just crawl right inside him so he could hold her forever.

And was she so little of a person herself she needed another person to make her strong?

The very thought made her straighten in her seat and take a few deep breaths.

"I'm relieved to hear you breathing. I was worried you might expire, and that would be awkward to explain."

She smothered a laugh, glancing around to make sure nobody had heard him. Or her, for that matter.

"We're alone, princess. You can laugh if you want to." His voice was deep, its lowest tones seeming as though it were sending something down her spine, all the way to her toes.

"I am fine," she said stiffly, wishing she could just express herself. Just once.

She felt him sigh next to her, and felt more of an idiot than before. What was wrong with her? Oh—nothing. And everything. She was perfect, the perfect daughter, the perfect debutante, the perfect duchess.

The perfect dunce.

"I do not wish to visit my parents," she blurted out, so fast and so quick it sounded like *Idonotwishtovisit-myparents.*

He made an amused noise and shook his head, sending a few blond strands tumbling forward. Not that she noticed. Not that she itched to sweep them back and let her fingers linger there.

Not any of those things. The ribbons twirled and spun inside her head, and she wished she could just shake herself free of all this fancy.

"We agree on at least one thing, wife," he replied, a dry, amused tone in his voice.

And then she did laugh. Granted, it was more of a chuckle, but it indicated humor, at least.

"I wonder," she began, pushing herself to speak, "what else we might have in common."

He did look at her then, a hint of curiosity—and flirtation?—in his steady gaze. "Perhaps you could tell me what you like."

"Well," she said slowly, "I liked your story last night. I liked playing cards." *I did not necessarily like sleeping on my own, but then again, I don't know that I'd like doing whatever it is married couples do.*

"That is an excellent start," he said. "How do you feel about rainy days?" He spoke as though the question was of the utmost importance.

She answered just as solemnly. "I find them to be quite wet. But not entirely unpleasant."

"As do I." He took her hand again, threading his fingers through hers. "I believe that the basis of a good marriage—at least so I have observed—is that the husband and wife have things in common, or things on which they can politely disagree."

His hand was so warm. She felt anchored there with him, as though it were just the two of them in the world, as though she would follow wherever he led her, as long as he still held her hand.

It was a dangerous feeling, and not one she'd ever experienced before.

Even he didn't know what he was saying. But at least she'd lost that frozen look from before, and her fingers in his felt right. Even though as soon as he touched her, his thoughts immediately turned to touching her elsewhere.

Although to be honest, his thoughts were pretty much there even if she was standing at the other end of Buckingham Palace encased in ice.

"What do you like?" she asked. He could tell, now, the difference between her very polite Society voice and her somewhat polite conversational voice. And was grateful that he merited the latter.

Which then of course made him wonder what her voice would sound like in the throes of passion—if she begged for him to touch her, or if she told him what she liked in bed.

And so much for not getting an erection in public. He shifted on the carriage seat, hoping she wouldn't notice and get frightened again.

"I don't think anyone has asked me that before," she said. "Except for my sister."

Ah, now that was a very different tone indeed—when she mentioned her sister, her voice got softer, more filled with emotion.

"So you like your sister, I presume?" He would give her the easy answers, to start with, and then hopefully proceed to more difficult—not to say harder—ones: *Do you like it when I touch you here? What position is best for you?*

Can we do it again?

"I do." She sounded more confident. "Her name is Margaret, I believe you met her during our wedding."

Nicholas searched his mind for images of women at his wedding who weren't his wife, and found a few bobbing up in his memory. "Is she dark-haired? And was sitting with your parents?"

"Yes, that's she. She's my best friend as well as my sister."

"Perhaps we should invite her to a dinner party, even though we won't be asking your parents."

She let out a shocked gasp and held her hand up to her mouth to smother it. "Oh, my goodness, and wouldn't that make my parents furious." She paused, then shook her head. "But we can't, Margaret is still there at home with them, I wouldn't want to cause her any problems."

From the way she spoke, it sounded as though there were already problems. Not that he'd had a high opinion of his in-laws, based on their manipulation of him; but it now appeared he and his wife had that in common as well.

"But you still haven't answered my question," she said, her tone returning to the more polite conversational tone. "What do you like?"

Up to now, I couldn't answer that question in polite company, he thought. He wasn't sure if he should be proud or chagrined to admit that. "I like good wine, and carriage rides, and you already know—since I've confessed it—I like reading serials in the paper. My brother doesn't even know that about me." Because Griff would never miss an opportunity to tease him about it, and he got enough jabs from Griff about his lack of seriousness as it was.

But when there were women, and punching, and wine to be enjoyed, who had time for seriousness?

Of course, that was before one had inexplicably inherited a title that required one suddenly become responsible. As well as become married.

And suddenly they were having a conversation, a real conversation as people did who were thrown together for—well, for eternity.

"I like carriage rides, thank goodness, because wouldn't that be awkward if I said I didn't, and here we are?" she asked, uncurling her fingers from his and gesturing to the horses.

His wife might have, if he was not mistaken, almost made a joke!

"And wine?"

She shrugged. "I haven't had much, my mother doesn't think it looks proper for a young lady to imbibe too much."

While Isabella's mother had a point—some of Nicholas's wildest adventures were after having a few glasses of wine—he didn't like how that sounded. As though her mother had constrained her.

He began speaking in a deliberately pompous tone. "Now that you are a respectable married woman, I expect you to have no fewer than two glasses with dinner. And maybe—if you are feeling daring—a glass of sherry after."

She shook her head, as though it were an automatic response, then paused and met his eyes, her gaze direct and intense. "I think I should do just that, husband. And other things that were not allowed when I was a young unmarried lady." Only just as she said that, she must have realized what it sounded like, and her whole face turned a bright shade of pink, and her eyes widened.

She looked adorable, and he absolutely, positively could not laugh at her.

"We will make a list, then," he said in as neutral a tone as possible, given that he, too, was thinking of all the things that were now allowed for a young lady who was married—to him. "Of everything you weren't allowed to do before, and we will tick them off as we do them."

She smiled, and the color in her face lessened just a bit. Thank goodness. "That sounds like a lovely way to begin a marriage, Nicholas. Thank you," she said, taking his hand in hers and turning his palm up so she could place her fingers in it. "Let's begin this evening."

"Why don't you speak of them?" She trembled as she spoke, hoping he wouldn't hit her. Or banish her. Or take her off to some dark dungeon.

Only that kind of thing only happened in stories, didn't it?

Well—didn't it?

"Of whom?"

She exhaled, as irked by his deliberate obtuseness as relieved he hadn't done any of those other things. Except the dungeon; that might be fun to visit.

"Your parents. Your family. Who are you?"

He leaped up from his chair at that, striding over to kneel in front of her. He put his palms on either side of her ~~head~~ face and leaned in so closely she could see ~~the pores on his nose~~ his individual eyelashes.

"I am yours."

—THE PRINCESS AND THE SCOUNDREL

Chapter 11

"Thank you, Robinson, that will be all." Isabella took the brush from her maid and gestured to the door. She wouldn't expect him for at least another twenty minutes or so, but what if he arrived early? And what if he thought she wasn't welcoming enough, because her maid was here? Not that Robinson hadn't been there the previous evening, but that was before she'd known what to expect. What he would expect.

Although everything about marriage so far was entirely unexpected, at least to her. Presumably—and hopefully—to him, as well, since she didn't think he'd been married before.

Robinson curtseyed, a knowing look on her face. Isabella wished she could tell the woman it wasn't that, even though she barely knew what *that* was—which of course was the problem in the first place.

"Sleep well, Your Grace," Robinson said as she opened the door and left, closing it softly behind her.

What if he *had* been married before? What if his wife had died, and he had loved her desperately, and that was why he couldn't bring himself to do anything with her?

But then if that were so, how could he have the reputation he did?

And now she was back to thinking it was just she. From what Margaret said, he seemed to have no trouble doing that (again, whatever *that* was) with a multitude of women, with the exception of his wife.

"Good evening, Isabella."

She jumped in her chair, flinging the brush into the air. He snagged it, mid-flight, then bowed as he presented it back to her.

"Thank you. I—I didn't hear you come in."

He grinned, and a few strands of that errant hair fell over his eyes. How could messy hair make someone look more attractive? And yet, she had the proof right here. "I would hope not, or I would have to say you had a remarkable interpretation of an appropriate greeting." His grin faded. "And I would imagine you are nothing if not appropriate, at all times."

Was she imagining it, or did he sound disappointed? That she wasn't appropriate all the time? What kind of man had she married?

Oh yes. The kind that liked telling quirky stories, and snuck up on people, and who looked even more attractive if his hair was disheveled.

So she seemed to have married a stealthy storyteller who did just fine not owning a brush.

"I could be inappropriate, if that is what you wish," Isabella said, deliberately not looking at the bed. Not looking at him, either, in case her thoughts showed on her face.

She heard a quick intake of breath, then a gusty exhale, and then he did what he'd done the night before—knelt in front of her, only now he rested his forearms on her thighs as he took her hands in his. The weight felt right, and she wished she could feel all of him on her. All of his weight, making her feel every single inch of his body imprinted on hers.

She swallowed, in her thoughts as well as in reality, as she felt the weight of his gaze settle on her face. She had to look at him then.

And what she saw in his eyes—well, she wasn't sure any man had ever looked at her like that. She didn't know what it was. She didn't even know if she liked it or not. Just that it was . . . different.

"Listen to me, and know this, Isabella." He paused. "Wife." He glanced down at their entwined fingers. "I want you to be who you are. Not who you think you should be, or who you think I want you to be."

She felt the sting of tears in her eyes.

"It might end up that we—well, that we find we don't have that much in common after all. But one thing we should have in common is that both of us should be free to be whoever we truly are."

She barely restrained herself from asking him, *Who am I?* She'd asked herself the same question, and if she didn't know, how would it be possible for him to have an answer?

"Isabella?" His voice was soft, but his grip tightened on her fingers, as though he was concerned about her.

Not only did he not want to do that with her, he thought she was some sort of fragile flower who required kneeling in front of, and soft voices and reassurances of being true to oneself.

Whatever that was.

She drew her hands away and straightened in the chair, looking off into the corner as though it was far more fascinating than her husband.

It was not. Not at all.

In fact, the more she thought about it, the more she was fascinated by him. But fascinated or not, she was sitting here, not speaking, while he knelt in front of her, his fragile flower, and she couldn't have that any longer. "I am fine. I am me," she added, feeling incredibly ridiculous for saying that.

He uttered a soft snort and rose, then held his hand out to her. "Come, I believe I have a story to tell."

She stood and let him lead her to the bed. Where, apparently, there were stories to be told. Even if nothing else would happen there.

Nicholas didn't think he was making much sense. The first problem was that she was just so damn gorgeous, and more than half of his mind was transfixed with just looking at her. The entirety of his penis was definitely focused on her, and his fingers—well, probably at least eight of them itched to touch her, to find out if the skin all over her body was as soft as her hands. The other two just wanted to watch. Not that fingers watched, but he couldn't parse all that out right now, not when his mind—and all the rest of him—was in such a muddle.

The second problem was that he'd never had to talk much to women to get them into bed, and he hadn't really wanted them anywhere else.

But her? She was his wife, and even if she weren't, she was *different*. He wanted to know her, to find out what she thought about things, things as banal as the weather, and what kind of wine she might end up liking, if she liked it at all, and what she actually thought of her parents, and if she thought less of him for liking melodramatic stories, or what kinds of stories she might like. If she liked them at all.

But meanwhile, she was on the bed, and he got himself up there, too, sitting close but not too close to her, but close enough that her scent wafted into his nose and somehow, of course it did, that made him even harder.

It was a good thing he was a gentleman, or he'd be taking her hard and fast right now.

He'd never chafed so much at being a gentleman. But

more than taking her, he wanted her to give herself to him, and that would only happen if he wooed her.

If he stayed gentlemanly, even though many parts of him were objecting to that.

"What kind of story would you like to hear?" he asked, shifting so as to try to hide the obvious interest his penis had in her.

She looked down, lacing her fingers together in her lap. At least she wasn't looking at *his* lap. "Whatever story you wish to tell."

A silence, with Nicholas about to speak when she finally, finally spoke again. "That is, I think I would like to hear a story. About you." And then she turned her head to look at him, her dark eyes revealing a warmth he had glimpsed only in a few fleeting seconds.

"And what about me?" He reviewed his stories and came to the speedy conclusion that perhaps two and a half of them were appropriate.

She offered a shy half smile. "Tell me something you and your brother—Gruff?—did together when you were little."

Nicholas laughed as he leaned over to nudge her shoulder with his. "Griff. Although Gruff might be a better descriptor, especially if I happen to interrupt his studies."

"Griff. That's right. Please don't tell him I called him that," she said, her tone taking on a hesitancy that made him angry. Not at her, but at whomever had so chided her that she couldn't even joke.

Drink wine and be able to laugh at something. Two goals that, if he were able to accomplish those, might find him closer to getting to know, truly know, his wife.

And then—but he couldn't think about that, he had to think about childhood and something amusing he could tell her.

As opposed to, say, telling her just how much he wanted her, how he was desperate to see the shape of her underneath her delicate nightclothes.

Or how much he wanted her to see what was underneath his not-as-delicate nightclothes.

None of that.

Nicholas shoved all that away and began speaking. "Griff, as you may have surmised, is the more studious brother, and he needed to be lured away from his books. So I would learn just enough details of some history event and then suggest we go act it out, and see what would happen."

"How old were you?" Now she didn't sound hesitant. She sounded interested, and it was odd to discover that he was interested in telling her as well.

"I was twelve and Griff was nine or ten when we first started." He tilted his head back against the headboard, looking up at the ceiling as he recalled. "Griff was fascinated by early British history, and so we did the invasion of England and the Magna Carta and Robin Hood quite a lot. I always got to play William the Conqueror, but I didn't always win."

"I find that hard to believe." She spoke in a low, warm tone.

Damn it. Here he was trying to be gentlemanly, only she was complimenting him in just the kind of way that would make his masculine pride preen and wish to show her what else he was capable of: making her forget how appropriate she thought she should be, what it was like to come from a man's mouth.

How it felt to lie together after vigorous fucking, utterly sated and content.

Not that he'd ever felt the need to do that with any of his previous women before. But now he longed for it, he even—God help him—wanted to murmur something sweet in her ear that wasn't necessarily a ploy for more sex.

"Griff is far more clever than I. I had speed and daring, but Griff . . ." He paused to chuckle. "Griff can talk the bark off a tree."

"Whatever that means," she said.

He did laugh harder then. "Precisely. My brother is the one with the skilled tongue," damn it, had he actually said that? "I have just had to rely on my— Well, I'm not sure what."

"And now," she said, leaning over to bump his shoulder as he'd done to hers, "it sounds as though you are fishing for compliments."

He reached out and took one of her hands in his. "Naturally. Because every man wants to know his lady appreciates him."

She seemed to freeze for just a moment, then let out a soft sigh that did shuddery things to his insides. "You said earlier that we had to be true to ourselves. That there was the chance that we might not like each other."

"That we might not have that much in common," he corrected. "That's a very different thing. Of course, if you do end up disliking me, well, that is a problem."

And then he did something that made his heart pound, knowing that this might be the action that scared her away, but he couldn't not. She needed this and he most certainly wanted it.

He dropped her hand, raising his arm up over his head and sliding it over her shoulders, nudging her body forward so his arm could go around her waist.

She was warm and soft and felt absolutely right there, and he held his breath, hoping she wouldn't freeze again, or permit what he was doing just because he wanted it.

And then exhaled as he felt her body relax, just a fraction, into the circle of his arms, and she let out another soft sigh, this one nearly one of contentment.

"I don't think I dislike you, Nicholas," she said, speaking in a quiet tone somewhere in the vicinity of his chest.

And at that moment, Nicholas felt as proud as though he had single-handedly conquered not just England, but the entire world.

"What will you do with me, Princess?" her husband asked.

She wrinkled her brow. "What do you mean?"

He spread his arms wide. "I told you. I am yours. What will you do with me?"

"I don't understand." This man, this confusing prince of a man, her husband, had insisted she marry him, had taken her off to his country, had refused to answer her questions, even the most general ones, and now he dared to say he was hers?

But she didn't say any of that. Not aloud, at least.

"I have loved you since the first moment I beheld you," he said, his voice deep with emotion. "I chose you as my bride because I am yours."

"That doesn't make sense," she blurted out before she could think. "But if that's so, perhaps you could do something for me."

"What, Princess? What can I do for you?"

A feeling came over her, the likes of which she'd never experienced before, and she smiled.

—THE PRINCESS AND THE SCOUNDREL

Chapter 12

Isabella woke at some ludicrously early time in the morning to discover she was alone, pillowless, and cold.

She heard herself make another one of those if-she-weren't-a-duchess-it'd-be-a-grunt noises, then whacked the bed in search of her pillow. It was halfway down the bed, which was also where the coverlet had gotten to. She scooped both of them up in her arms and dragged them up the bed.

There was something to be said for efficiency.

The last thing she recalled before she must have fallen asleep was something about his sisters, both of whom were older than he, were married, and had children.

Given how their marriage had gone thus far, she doubted she would ever have a child. Because while she was ignorant about the specifics of what happened between a husband and his wife, she knew well enough to know that talking did not spontaneously generate children.

Because if they did, imagine how many more would have been born to all the gossips of the *ton*?

That thought set off a snort, a sound even she was surprised to hear coming from her.

At least she was laughing. She didn't laugh. Not unless Margaret was there, and was telling her something funny. She'd never found something amusing herself, so this was a revelation.

What else might she discover, now that she was a married woman living—albeit oddly—away from her parents?

For the first time, it seemed as though what she might become could be preferable to who she was. Perhaps she'd be a woman who could grunt, and snort, and giggle. Perhaps she could even work herself up into telling a joke herself. The closest she'd come to that was—well, nothing.

She couldn't tell a joke. Jokes and amusement were not things that were required, or even wanted, in a duchess. At least she presumed her mother would say that if she'd dared to ask.

But even in the short time she'd been married, she felt as though her husband, a duke himself, would want her to be amused and amusing and possibly even tell a joke.

She hadn't lied when she'd told him she didn't dislike him. She did like him, even if she was still prone to startle when she thought about how she was married. To him.

It had felt lovely last night, his arm wrapped around her, his low, rumbly voice speaking to her alone. And last night, he'd shared some of who he was with her, which felt even more special.

She liked that he felt about his brother, Griff, as she did about Margaret. He couldn't be a horrible person, could he, if he loved his relative so much? And she should, she was, past the point where she was concerned he was a horrible person—a horrible person wouldn't have played cards with her, and encouraged her to say what she felt.

It wouldn't have felt so right to be sitting on the bed with him, his arm wrapped around his shoulders.

Although she hadn't had much contact with men, much less men who looked like him—beautiful men, men who could look as they did, but who had black hearts. So perhaps he would become something horrible, the Horrible Husband from one of the stories he'd admitted to reading.

She didn't think so, but she'd trusted people not to hurt her before, and they had gone ahead and done so—such as her parents, who had told her she had freedom when really they were scheming to marry her off to whoever would boost their own social success the most. Margaret was the only one who hadn't.

She had to be on her guard, of course, but meanwhile she could just enjoy being with him, looking at him, and, yes, being held by him.

"Your Grace?" Someone shook her shoulder. She turned her head and met her lady's maid's gaze.

"Your Grace, I am sorry to wake you, but it is eleven o'clock, and your sister has just arrived. Should I ask her to come back later?"

Isabella flung the covers off her body as she shook her head. "No, just ask her to come up here and I'll get dressed."

"Yes, Your Grace," Robinson replied, dipping a quick curtsey as she left the room. Isabella swung her legs over the side of the bed and stood on the carpet, its thick plushness nearly swallowing her bare feet.

What would it be like to just lie down on that carpet? Would she get swallowed up inside its softness?

She shook her head at her own whimsy. And when had she ever been whimsical before? Next thing she'd be telling stories about King Art and the Swordie.

A smile was still on her face as the door opened again, Margaret coming in with a look of concern on her face. A look that eased as she saw her sister.

Only to have it get all concerned again when Isabella burst into tears.

"I'm fine, I'm fine," Isabella said, her nose buried in her sister's shoulder. She lifted her head and looked into her sister's eyes, her very best feature. Right now, however, they were narrowed as she returned Isabella's gaze.

"You don't seem fine," Margaret said in a matter-of-fact voice. Isabella glanced at Robinson, who was carefully not looking at them. Hopefully she wasn't shocked that her employer had just been as unduchess-like as possible, displaying emotion before breakfast. Not that expressing emotion was preferable at any time, but first thing in the morning (at least, first thing at eleven o'clock), even without the benefit of tea, made it seem even more shocking.

"Robinson, could you ask someone to get tea for us? And something to eat."

"I'm not hun—" Margaret began, only to clamp her mouth shut at Isabella's glare. "That is, I am famished," she said as she rolled her eyes at her sister.

"Please ask for a full breakfast, and we will wait for our tea until it is all ready." That should give them at least twenty minutes alone.

"Of course, Your Grace," Robinson said, her gaze darting between the two sisters as though she knew exactly what was going on.

But Isabella wasn't about to confide in her lady's maid about anything, not if she wasn't entirely sure she could even trust her husband. So she nodded in reply, then put her hand on Margaret's arm and drew her over to the bed, then frowned as she saw how rumpled it all was. It looked as though things had been going on there that most definitely hadn't, and she wasn't sure she wanted to have to explain all of that, at least not now, to her sister.

"Let's sit here," she said, moving to one of the rose-colored couches in her room. They sat, Isabella taking Margaret's hand.

"You are all right?" Margaret sounded suspicious. And Isabella couldn't blame her; the first thing she'd done was cry. Not to mention she thought perhaps the last time she'd seen Margaret she'd been crying.

There were a lot of tears to be shed, apparently.

"I am, actually." She gestured to her eyes. "Even though it might seem as though I am not."

Margaret seemed to visibly sag in relief. "Thank goodness, I wasn't sure what I would do if you weren't. Except I would do something." She said the last part in a very decided tone of voice, and Isabella was glad she had at least—and only—one person she could rely on. Even if that person didn't know what she'd do in case of emergency. But at least she'd probably pass her a handkerchief, or pat her back, or try to make her laugh.

"How is he?" Margaret got a coy, curious expression on her face. "And how is that?"

The last thing Isabella wanted to do was discuss what she and her husband were and were not doing. Even with her sister.

So she just sat there, wondering what to say as Margaret continued to regard her with that knowing look.

And more silence.

Until—"You're not going to tell me, are you?" Isabella wanted to laugh at Margaret's outraged tone of voice, only she didn't think her sister would appreciate it.

"Is it that bad?" her sister asked in a whisper, as though there was anyone else there.

"It's . . ." Isabella wanted just to tell her, *It's not, and we're not, and I have no idea*, only she didn't want to admit, even to her sister, that she hadn't become a wife in the true technical way.

"Is it that good?" her sister said, this time in an even more hushed tone, as though she couldn't believe it.

Well, if she were going to lie by omission, better to do it this way. She didn't answer, just smiled as though she had a secret.

Margaret leaned against the sofa back, crossing her arms over her chest. It didn't appear as though Isabella's knowing look was going to satisfy her. "You're not going to tell me!" she said in an outraged tone.

Isabella shook her head slowly. She hadn't ever done this before, actually teased her sister (much less lied to her), but it felt fun.

Instead of continuing to be annoyed, however, Margaret did the very Margaret-like thing of laughing and then hugging her sister, so tightly it felt as though she was squashing Isabella's lungs.

"Let me breathe!" Isabella gasped, poking her sister on the shoulder.

The door opened just as Isabella was simultaneously laughing and wheezing, and Nicholas strode in, stopping as he saw the two of them on the sofa.

"Good morning," he said in an amused tone, as

though he were privy to the joke. Which wasn't true, since even Margaret didn't know, but Isabella couldn't think about all of that when she got a good look at his face.

She was up and had her fingers on the worst cut, the one just on his cheekbone, before she could even think.

"Again? You did this again?"

Nicholas shrugged and looked over her shoulder at Margaret. "You're Margaret, aren't you?"

"Don't speak," Isabella said through clenched teeth. How could he continue to have this violence inflicted on him—willingly?

What else would he allow to be done to him?

That thought brought up images she didn't even know she had anywhere in her brain, and she felt her cheeks get hot.

Isabella shook her head and might have made some sort of disgruntled unduchesslike noise before walking to her dressing table, where a handkerchief and a basin of water were laid out for her morning ablutions. She dipped the cotton fabric into the water and wrung it out.

"I am, Your Grace," Margaret replied, in as amused a tone as before.

Could she not see her new brother-in-law looked like he'd fallen face-first into a mountain? Or she did see it, and she wasn't worried about it?

Either her sister had vision problems, or she was totally blasé about her new brother-in-law meeting one of those things she'd seen washerwomen using for clothing. With his face.

She put the damp cloth up to his face and began to wipe the blood off.

"How are you? Your sister has told me some about you, I am looking forward to getting to know you."

She paused in her ministrations to glare at him. And then turned her head and glared at her sister. And back at him. "Did nobody but me notice that you happen to be in my bedroom bleeding? That perhaps we could save the social niceties until there isn't blood gushing everywhere?"

"It's hardly gushing," Margaret said. Isabella heard the movement of her sister getting up from the couch, and soon enough, she felt Margaret at her back. "It's the worst there," she said, pointing over Isabella's shoulder at the cut on the cheekbone, which had begun to puff out around the wound.

"I've had worse done to me," Nicholas said, crossing his arms over his chest.

"I can imagine," Isabella muttered as she dabbed at the cuts.

"What happened?" Margaret asked over Isabella's shoulder. Isabella didn't have to see her to know her sister was on tiptoe looking, since Isabella was so much taller.

"I got hit." Nicholas replied with a smirk that showed he knew just how much he was—and wasn't—saying.

"I can see that. The question is, who hit you?" As usual, her sister forged ahead, her curiosity always winning out over her discretion. Whereas Isabella didn't allow herself to be curious, and she was always discreet.

And look where it had gotten her. An untouched wife whose new husband seemed to have a penchant for getting himself hurt.

Nicholas shrugged. "There were a few, actually. The first one only managed a few hits before I knocked him out. Then there was a really large man, but I don't think he was used to fighting someone with skill. After he tried to squeeze me, I knocked him off balance and he went down. He did land this, though," he said, pointing to his cheekbone. "And the last one—well, that was my brother." He grinned. "Seems Griff was irritated at me because now that I'm a duke, I shouldn't be brawling, or something like that."

"And your brother is not wrong," Isabella said in a low voice.

He narrowed his eyes at her, but he didn't get a chance to say anything when the door opened, a phalanx of servants bearing trays pouring into Isabella's bedroom. Too late, she realized she was wearing just her nightdress, and it wouldn't be appropriate for the servants to see her.

But it seemed that he had realized that sooner, since

he turned around and faced them, maneuvering her so she was behind him.

He was so tall. She often felt beautiful, because she simply was, but she never felt as though she were delicate. But now, with her nose practically in between his shoulder blades, she did. One of his hands was behind him, his fingers resting on her arm, and she felt the contact as though it were a bolt of lightning streaking through her body.

She inhaled, and her whole self was flooded with him—he smelled more than he had when she'd been curled up with him in bed, but it wasn't an unpleasant odor. Or maybe she only thought it wasn't unpleasant because it was he.

It smelled like earth and exertion and power. And, to be honest, sweat.

It smelled good. She wished she could lean forward and just bury her nose into him, breathe in all that odor, have it surround her, envelop her, until it was her scent, too.

"Your Grace, Your Grace, my lady." The butler gestured to a low table in front of the sofa. "There, please." The footmen—at least three of them—carried silver trays, which they put down. A fragrant aroma, albeit not as fragrant as Nicholas, wafted from the serving platters. She smelled bacon, bread, coffee, and chocolate, and suddenly she was very hungry.

"Is there anything else?" the butler asked, glancing from Nicholas back to her.

"That should be fine," Margaret replied. Isabella saw Nicholas's shoulders shake, as though he were squelching a laugh.

Meanwhile, she was squelching the urge to kick her sister.

"Yes, thank you, uh." Nicholas tilted his head. "I don't recall your name."

"Renning, Your Grace," the butler said, bowing again.

"Renning. Of course. That will be all, Renning."

The servants exited as quietly as they had entered. He dropped his hand from her arm, and she missed the contact already.

Margaret had already uncovered two of the servers, and gestured to Isabella with a crisp strip of bacon in her hand. "Thanks for this, only I've got to get back. I told the countess I was just going to return a book to the lending library, and I know I won't be missed, but I wouldn't want her to notice how long I've been."

"It was a pleasure to see you again, Lady Margaret," Nicholas said, sounding both sincere and amused. "Please come visit us whenever you like."

That warmed the parts of Isabella that hadn't already been warmed by all the breathing of his scent she'd engaged in.

"Oh, and the earl and the countess said they'd be

coming by for your at-home later today. I thought I'd let you know," Margaret said in a voice laden with meaning so it was obvious it really meant *I thought I'd warn you.*

"Thank you," Isabella replied in a neutral tone. Wonderful. She would have to face them, a not quite really officially married wife with her handsome, earthy-smelling husband (well, presumably he would take a bath, so never mind), and their faint praise that usually masked disapproval of some sort.

Imagine if her mother found out what had really— She couldn't breathe for a moment.

She couldn't let that happen. She'd have to figure out some way to make it appear as though she were a normal wife, a normal duchess, so her mother would never know the reality.

If she did know, she had no doubt her parents would find a way to leverage the already difficult situation to their advantage, and she already liked the duke far more than she did them.

She was already a consummate actress, pretending to be interested in things she wasn't, pretending she wasn't nervous each and every time she entered a ballroom. She would just have to fool her parents.

"So I will see you later. A pleasure to meet you, Your Grace." Margaret gave Isabella a quick kiss on the cheek, curtseyed to Nicholas, grabbed another piece of bacon, and was out the door within seconds.

Isabella swallowed. She was alone with him—well,

except for the company of all the food—he smelled wonderful, he had gone and gotten himself hit a lot for some reason, and he also still didn't seem to want to make this marriage a real one. A fact that she was beginning to resent.

"Nicholas, we should talk."

From the unedited version of A Lady of Mystery's serial:

"I want you to do something for me." Jane turned and faced him, his normally saturnine expression having changed into something softer.

Had she done that?

"What is it, Princess?" he asked.

"I want you to trust me. Trust me entirely."

He regarded her for what seemed like ~~an eternity~~ a moment, then nodded. "I do."

"I want to be able to leave." She held her head up as she spoke and then spun on her heel, leaving the room as quickly as she could.

Leaving him behind.

—The Princess and the Scoundrel

Chapter 13

"We should talk." Were there three words more likely to strike terror into a man's heart when spoken by a lady?

Well, there were those *other* three words, but Nicholas didn't think she was likely to tell him those anytime soon.

It wasn't working. His going off to fight to stave off the wanting of her.

He'd slipped out of her bedroom just after she'd fallen asleep. His arm had already gone to sleep, and it was difficult to disengage himself from her without waking her. But if she woke, she'd likely be all relaxed and comfortable, and he would look down at her gorgeous face, and full, soft mouth and he didn't know if he could resist leaning down and taking a kiss.

And then, since he was Nicholas Smithfield, after all, renowned for his skill with ladies, he wouldn't stop there. That is, not unless she wanted him to stop. He'd slide his fingers down her arm, to her waist, hold her as he kissed her slowly, languorously, then more intensely as she reacted—as she would. He knew he was good in bed, he'd been told enough, and not just by women he'd paid for the privilege.

He'd even had a few of the paid women asking him to return, no charge, just for the pleasure he brought them.

He was not necessarily proud that lovemaking and boxing appeared to be his only skills. But he wasn't necessarily unproud, either. Not that he could tell his wife about his prowess in those areas—she'd already made it clear she didn't understand at all why he liked to box, and he wasn't going to share any details of the other sport with her.

So he'd gotten himself pummeled this morning, and then walked into her bedroom only to find her in her nightdress and then insisting on fussing over him. Not scared of him anymore, at least, but that only made his desire for her come roaring back, even more strongly than before, when all he'd seen was her face.

Now he'd heard her voice, and spoken with her, and knew she wasn't the ice princess he'd thought. She was a warm, gorgeous, kind woman, and he wanted to get into bed with her and not let her out until she told him what she really wanted. Or screamed his name, whichever came first. So to speak.

But that would definitely take time. Because it was

a long way between dabbing a cloth on cuts caused by fighting, and allowing him—no, *joining* him—in a bout, preferably more, in sweaty, intense, passionate lovemaking.

"What is there to talk about?" He went and sat on the couch, patting the seat next to her.

He tried to keep his tone light, not to startle her. Although she had brought the topic up in the first place, hadn't she? So maybe she should be trying to keep her tone light.

He was already muddled, and she had spoken only those three words. He didn't think a female had ever unsettled him this much before. Scratch that. He knew. He took a piece of bacon from the server and chewed as he thought about that.

She sat down next to him, drawing into the corner of the sofa so there was no possibility of their touching. "I know that my parents forced you to marry me," she said, biting her lip as she gazed off into the corner. "I don't blame you for being angry."

And he had been. Still was, when he thought about her parents, and what they'd threatened to do if he didn't go along with the previous duke's agreement. But it wouldn't be fair to take it out on her. Was that what she thought he was doing?

"I'm not angry at you," he replied. Hopefully that would clarify it.

"So then . . ." and she paused, still gnawing at her lip.

Ah. His terrified bride wasn't too terrified to ask him why they hadn't had sex yet. Although he had no idea what she was feeling about that fact—she was a master at hiding her emotions. Perhaps if the whole duke thing didn't work out she could rebuild their fortune by gambling.

"So then why have we not—?" and he made a vague gesture in the air, but one that she apparently understood, since she turned the color of a bright sunset. She complemented the color of the sofa quite well, in fact.

"Yes, that." She took a deep breath, one that did interesting things to her nightdress. "Was there—is there—someone you—you cared for? Someone you love?"

Nicholas thought back to a few weeks ago, when Griff had arrived with the news. There had been three women present, and while he'd been fond of them, of course, theirs was a working relationship.

The only person he'd ever loved in his life was his brother. He cared for his sisters, of course, but they were older, and married, and they'd never really been a part of his life. Just Griff.

"No."

"Then—?"

How would he explain it, when all he wanted to do was have sexual relations with her? And yet was not? But some part of him, a part that he barely knew, recognized that rushing things with her would take their marriage on an irrevocable course, and he wanted a true marriage. A real marriage, one where there might, at least, be trust and friendship.

Plus passionate interludes of fucking, but that was understood. By him, at least.

"Instead of asking me if I was angry about our sudden marriage, I should be asking you." He reached out and took her hand, which had been plucking at the fabric of her nightdress since she sat. "Are you angry? Is there someone you were interested in?"

She froze, and for a moment, he thought she might say yes. *Yes, Nicholas, I was in love with a pleasant man who could tell me a story without mucking it up and who would have come to our marriage as pure as I am.*

In other words, exactly the opposite of him.

But she didn't. Eventually, slowly, she turned her head to look at him. That terrified look hadn't returned, precisely, but she looked wary. "No, there is no one."

And thank goodness, because he knew he couldn't have given her up, not now, not even with them not having consummated their union. He was that much of a selfish bastard, he was ashamed to admit, that he didn't want anyone else to have her. Plus it would have taken an extreme amount of effort for him to woo her away from another gentleman she thought she was in love with.

Not that he couldn't have done it; he'd done it before. But it would be far easier to woo her if there was just her own self in the way of their eventual, and very real, marriage.

Not to mention the fucking. He couldn't seem to stop thinking about it, actually, which would make wooing her with delicacy and care even harder. So to speak.

But meanwhile, it seemed she had more to add. *Focus, Nicholas*, he reminded himself. And not on how lovely she looked, or how he wished it were he biting her lip.

"Until you asked, I hadn't really thought about it," she said in a low, trembling tone. Not as though she was scared, thank goodness, but as though some huge emotion had overwhelmed her. "My parents told me what they'd done, the first time, with the duke, and then there was the change, with you, and they said they'd arranged it for me to marry you instead." She raised wide, wondering eyes to his face. "Why hasn't anyone asked? Why didn't I ask?"

She was so lovely, and so hurting. And here he was, having just gone to a boxing ring to get his face smashed so he could stop wanting her, at least for a little while, only it wasn't working. It absolutely was not working.

But he would have to hold out for longer, that was clear.

"*I'm* asking," he replied. "I want to know."

She just looked at him, shaking her head. "No, you don't." She withdrew her hand from his. "People say they do, but then all they really want is something from you. Of course," she continued, giving a rueful laugh, "the thing most men want from me is yours for the taking. Only you haven't. Taken, that is."

Not from lack of wanting, that was certain. But Nicholas wasn't about to take. He wanted to receive what she gave.

No matter how long that might take.

Jane knew she wanted to leave, but she wasn't sure where she wanted to go. And that was the difficulty, especially because she had nowhere to go to.

She'd left her home when she'd married him—did she really want to return there? They'd let her go, after all.

And with him, she had everything she could possibly want—only she still didn't know who he was, or why he'd taken her. Why he'd wanted her in the first place.

There was something so mysterious about him, so untrustworthy it seemed ridiculous to ask him to trust her. When she didn't trust him.

But if she didn't walk away, she wouldn't know if she really wanted to come back.

And so she walked out of the castle, crossed the moat, nodded at a few of the villagers who greeted her, and set off down the road. To somewhere.

—THE PRINCESS AND THE SCOUNDREL

Chapter 14

Isabella glanced at him, noticing how his lips had thinned, how the grip he had on her hand had tightened. His eyes looked . . . *fierce*, as though he were on his way to challenging someone.

Perhaps that was a constant state for him, which was why he kept arriving home with cuts and bruised knuckles and smelling of him, only more so.

In which case she would very much have to wonder about the man she'd married. But she knew he wouldn't hurt her. Physically, at least.

"I won't hurt you," he said. Almost as though he was reading her mind. "I want to get to know you, Isabella," he said, squeezing her hand. His expression eased. "I have an idea. Since I am so wonderful at telling stories," he said, waggling his eyebrows at her, "how about we trade. For every story I tell, you tell me something about you."

"What could you possibly want to know?" The question burst from her before she could even think. Most people just wanted to know what she thought about them. But she didn't think that was what he was asking for. What he was asking for was something far odder, at least in her experience. Unique, in fact.

"Whatever you wish to tell me. I believe we agreed to tick off a list of things you hadn't done before, but wished to? Isn't telling someone something about you one of the items on that list?"

She felt her eyes widen as she considered it. He might not be able to tell a story well, but he was certainly observant. That he understood what she was trying to say, when even she wasn't certain what she was trying to say—well, it was enough to render her speechless. Although that was the opposite of what he wanted, wasn't it? The whole point of this conversation was that it be a conversation.

In which case, she would have to converse.

"Isabella?"

Right. She hadn't been conversing. Except with herself, and she didn't want to be a part of that conversation now.

"Yes, I suppose it is," she said, looking down at their clasped hands. His hands were large, much larger than hers. Which made perfect sense, given that he was so much larger than she, but she'd never really thought about the size of a person's hands before, and now here she was, looking at the back of his hand, his long, thick fingers, and thinking all sorts of things that she couldn't even say to herself.

So much for conversing with anyone at all.

"I should go take a bath, I am sure I am smelly," he said, loosening his grip. "Your parents, and likely every other interested person in the world, will be coming by for our first at-home. Unless you'd prefer that we take some more time before meeting with anyone. Since . . ." and he made that vague gesture again, as though she were supposed to not be a virgin when she met people as his duchess.

"No, today is fine." She wished she could ask him to sit with her for just a few more minutes, and perhaps even ask him if she could bury her nose in his shirt, just to inhale his essence some more, but that would be something about her that she wasn't altogether certain she wanted him to know. For goodness' sake, it was something she almost didn't want to know about herself, and hadn't known until she'd married him, and now suddenly it seemed her nose was her most engaged body part.

"Then, if you'll excuse me," he said, rising from the sofa and grabbing another piece of bacon.

"Of course." She spoke in her usual tone, distant, correct, but it sounded entirely off with him.

"Of course," he echoed, then walked out of the room, closing the door sharply behind him.

She wished she was able to let go, just let go of who

she was, and who she had become, and speak as naturally as he and Margaret did.

Perhaps she would find plenty of time to practice, since it seemed she would not be engaging in any other activities, at least not until she could speak with him about it—highly doubtful—or he did something about it himself.

Was that an advantage to the situation, or something that would make her hurt more in the long run? Would she ever be wise enough to recognize the difference?

Nicholas walked down the hallway to his room, counting the steps as he went. He'd counted this morning, and found it was just twenty-three steps between his bedroom and that of his wife's.

Fourteen, fifteen, sixteen—if he just turned around and went back, he could be with her again in under a minute. He could remove her nightshift within five, and have her on her back and under him in another five. Seven, if he was taking his time.

But that wouldn't be the right thing to do, no matter how much he wanted it. She might be asking him why now, but she hadn't asked him why not yet.

Until she did, until she wanted him herself, not just out of duty or obligation or because people had told her that was what married people do together, and she was now a married person, he would stay away from her.

Until she asked. And then, oh Lord, and then he would make up for lost time in the best way he knew how. Until then, however, it was twenty-three steps of agony between here and there, between heaven and— not heaven.

"Your Grace." Miller sprang up from the chair and rushed to hold the door open. "Your Grace?" he repeated, his expression showing confusion and not a small amount of concern.

"I am fine, Miller. I want a bath."

Nicholas sat on the bed and began to undo his cravat, toeing his shoes off as he did.

"Let me assist, Your Grace," Miller said, getting down on the carpet.

Nicholas waved his foot at him. "No, please, just get me a bath. I can take care of my clothing." Of course he felt immediately bad when he saw how Miller's face fell. Given that all the man had to do was take care of Nicholas's clothing and getting dressed and such, and that Nicholas had effectively told him not to do his job—well, no wonder he looked disappointed.

"But now that I think of it, perhaps you could help me." Miller's face brightened, and he went to work, divesting Nicholas of his clothing faster than Nicholas could, even with an incentive such as a willing, naked woman in his bed.

He couldn't think of that. Shouldn't think of that, especially with his valet in the room. He didn't even want to think of what Miller would think if he—well, he couldn't think of that, either.

"Here, Your Grace," Miller said, holding up a dressing gown so Nicholas just had to slide his arms in. "I'll ask about a bath right now."

"Thank you."

Miller left and Nicholas allowed himself to spread out flat on the bed, his arms splayed wide, looking up at the ceiling.

How had he gotten into this situation?

Oh, right. He'd been the next in line for a dukedom, somehow, and had gotten it, and a wife, in the space of two weeks.

It could have happened to anybody.

At that thought, Nicholas chuckled ruefully. But also grateful it had been he who had become the duke, and married her, and not some awful man who would have taken advantage of her.

He had to keep that in mind, so that he didn't end up being the awful man.

It seemed only a few minutes later that Nicholas was lowering his naked and sore body into the tub in his sitting room. The steam gathered in a cloud above the water, and he braced himself for the heat.

"Thank you, Miller, that will be all." He did not want his valet to watch him bathe, of all things.

"Certainly, Your Grace." From Miller's tone, it sounded as though his valet had no desire to watch him bathe, either. And who said the aristocracy and their servants were constantly at odds? He and Miller were in total agreement.

"The towel is just over here," Miller gestured to a long, low bureau upon which rested, expectedly enough, a towel. Nicholas had a moment's thought that perhaps dukes were supposed to be blindly oblivious to things, which was why their servants pointed them out so often, but then realized his servants were just ensuring their master had everything he needed so he wouldn't bother them overly much.

He didn't blame them. He hated to be bothered himself.

"Thank you."

Miller nodded and left.

Nicholas had his arms draped over the sides of the tub, which was actually large enough for his frame. He'd never been able to take a bath without having his legs bent at an awkward angle so his body could be wet.

There were some advantages to being a duke, then.

He grabbed the soap and began to lather it in his hands, his thoughts wandering beyond her and their situation to other things he had to take care of. He'd had a reprieve of a few weeks as he got ready for his wedding and sorted out some of the paperwork—or rather, Griff had—but he knew that there were things he would have to deal with, as the duke, very soon.

That would be far less interesting than dealing with his wife, but far less fraught with potential danger. His business dealings might falter if he made the wrong decision, but they wouldn't be irrevocably damaged.

But meanwhile, he and his still untouched bride were to have their first at-home, and her parents were coming, as was—likely—all of Society intent on seeing what the new duke looked like.

In which case he should stop thinking and get to washing.

"Isabella," he said in that low tone that seemed to send a shiver down her spine. That or the room was cold.

She glanced over at the fire currently burning merrily in the fireplace. No, the room was not cold. It was he.

"When do you expect them to arrive?"

She didn't need to ask who "them" was. She'd been fretting about it since Margaret told her, which was silly since she'd seen them every day of her entire life until three days ago.

She glanced up at the large clock in the corner. "Not too long now. Mother prides herself on being punctual."

"Would you like some time alone with your mother?" He spoke in a neutral tone of voice, but she felt as though she could tell what he was thinking—*Please don't say yes, that woman is a bad influence on you, I don't wish to be married to anybody remotely like her.*

Or perhaps that was just she.

"No, thank you." She couldn't repress an involuntary shudder. Something she thought he saw as well, judging by how his eyes narrowed.

She wished she didn't feel so helpless—maybe if she were more confident and self-assured he wouldn't have rejected her. Was it possible he didn't find her attractive because she was so needy and trembling?

She straightened her spine and met his gaze. She could be the woman he must want, someone capable and strong and self-possessed. The duchess she'd trained for years to be. "Thank you for your concern, Nicholas, but I am fine." Perhaps if she said it enough they would both believe it.

He opened his mouth as though to reply, then shook his head and turned his back to her, going to stand by the fire.

And then it didn't matter that the room was warm, she felt suddenly chilled. As though someone had dropped an ice cube down her back, and she was required not to react.

"Your Grace, Your Grace?" Renning's voice made Isabella jump.

"Yes, Renning?" Nicholas sounded nearly as cool as Isabella felt.

"Your Grace's parents are here. The Earl and Countess of Grosston," he clarified.

Nicholas glanced quickly at Isabella, then nodded at Renning. "Please send them in. And bring tea."

In just a few moments, it seemed, Isabella's parents and Margaret were seated in the receiving room, Isabella's breathing had increased, and she had a tense ache in her belly.

In other words, it felt precisely as it had before she was married, only now there was a gorgeous six-foot-tall duke who was part of the scene as well.

Her parents walked in, her mother with that superior look of disdain she'd perfected likely long before Isabella had even been born. Did she have to practice in the mirror first? Or did it just come naturally?

Her mother's expression eased as she glanced around the room, which was as sumptuous as any newly minted duke could expect. The carpet, while not as thick as the one in Isabella's room, was opulently colored, lavishly overflowing with flowers and vines and other designs. The sofas—there were three of them—were all suitably fragile and precious-looking, as though only the most deserving person could sit down without breaking the furniture.

Naturally, her mother chose the most fragile-looking sofa to sit on, while her father sat in a chair adjacent. Isabella held their breath until it appeared the furniture would hold.

"Isabella, you and the duke will be holding a ball."

It was not even close to a question. Perhaps closer to a proclamation.

Isabella glanced at her mother, then at Nicholas, who'd placed himself—and his large frame—next to the fireplace, his arm resting casually on the mantel.

But Isabella thought she saw his mouth tighten, and his fist curl, and she had a brief, panicked thought that he would punch her mother. Well, the first thought was panicked; the second thought that crossed her mind might have been wishful.

"We will consider it." He spoke in a firm voice as though the topic was finished.

Isabella felt a sharp pride that he, at least, was not cowed by her mother.

"Particularly since the former duke—the duke that was—is going about London telling anyone who will listen that he is the rightful owner of the title. If you wish to keep your name out of the papers, and yourself out of the courts, you will work on making friends in powerful places," her father added. Apparently not realizing the topic had been concluded.

"And what if he does?" Now Nicholas sounded nearly as pompous and full of himself as the duke that was had.

"It might not matter to you now," Isabella's mother said with a sniff, "although it should. Because this would be your first official appearance as husband and wife, and as duke and duchess. These things cannot be overestimated." She sniffed again, as though she couldn't believe she had to continue laying out just how important this was. "And what about your children? If there is any breath of scandal when they are born, they might suffer." A pause as Isabella steadfastly concentrated on not meeting Nicholas's gaze. "And if there is scandal attached to your family, it will attach to ours. And Margaret will suffer."

Everyone turned to look at Margaret, whose eyes widened. "I promise you, I will not be suffering. No matter what that other duke does." She caught Isabella's eye and winked, so quickly Isabella thought she might have imagined it. What was her sister up to?

"I would like to present Isabella as my bride, and so perhaps a ball is the way to do it." He paused. "If that would not be too much work for you?" His comment was directed at Isabella, but her mother responded.

"Of course it is not. Isabella knows everything there is to know about running a great house, and that includes the proper way to have a party."

She did. That was one area she absolutely knew— how best to entertain so it was clear that the entertaining person was by far the most magnificent person, but also to ensure none of the guests felt slighted. It was a very delicate matter, and she knew she was even better at it than her mother was.

Not that being better than her mother at something was admirable; her mother was pitiful in the areas of empathy, simple kindness, and a desire to help her fellow man. Unless it benefited her or her family (and even then it depended which members of the family), she didn't bother.

"Then I shall leave everything to my very capable bride." Nicholas's tone was warmer than before, and Isabella felt an answering warmth.

Although by this time her temperature had gone up and down so much she felt feverish.

"I will assist Isabella, naturally." Again, not a question, or even anything other than a proclamation.

But it seemed Nicholas did not entirely understand her mother's tone. "I don't think Isabella requires any help. In fact," he said, pushing away from the mantelpiece and coming to stand next to her, "I think it is best if she does it all on her own. We don't want anyone saying my duchess is anything less than entirely capable, do we? That would definitely cause a scandal."

Isabella felt her eyes widen as Margaret smothered a giggle.

"If that is what you wish, Your Grace." Her mother's tone was clipped.

But it didn't appear that that bothered Nicholas at all. "Excellent! And I am wondering where Renning went with that tea." Nicholas placed his hand on Isabella's shoulder for just a moment, then went and yanked on the pull to summon a servant. The door opened immediately, revealing the butler in question holding a large silver tray.

"Your Grace, I apologize for the delay, but Cook had just made biscuits, and she wanted to send them here directly from the oven."

And, yes, there were the most delicious aromas coming from the tray, which Renning brought into the room and set down on the table in front of the biggest sofa. Isabella and her mother both moved instinctively to the teapot, but Isabella's mother halted as she saw her daughter's movement.

"That is right, I had forgotten. Now you are the mistress of your own household, you will be pouring tea." If only that pronouncement and the subsequent scrutiny didn't make her so nervous.

Not so nervous she wouldn't perform impeccably, she never made a misstep, but nervous enough that her insides fluttered and she wasn't certain she would be able to enjoy any of the biscuits Cook had sent up.

And she didn't know how he took his tea. That might seem minor, but if her mother saw she didn't even know how her new husband took his tea, what else might her mother suspect she didn't know?

All of a sudden, she felt frozen. More chilled than before, as though she had been thrust into an ice house and left on her own. She concentrated on taking a deep breath, but it felt as though she could only draw quick, hurried breaths.

"Isabella, today I will take my tea differently than usual," Nicholas spoke in an entirely casual tone, but she knew he had somehow realized what was going through her mind and was taking pity on her.

"Yes?" she asked, poised to pour out the tea.

His mouth quirked up in a smile, so quick she would have missed it if she hadn't been staring at his mouth. A habit she did not wish to break. "Yes, I would like milk and just one teaspoon of sugar."

He leaned toward her and kissed her, gently, on the cheek. "You are sweet enough for me," he said in a tone that was audible to everyone, yet still managed to sound intimate.

Isabella felt herself start to blush.

And wished that he really felt that way.

FROM THE UNEDITED VERSION OF A LADY OF MYSTERY'S SERIAL:

"Thank goodness you've gotten away!" Those were the first words Jane heard as she entered her parents' house. Uttered by her family's housekeeper, who had been with the family so long she was family herself.

"I didn't get away, Mary," Jane said, feeling suddenly irritated. "I left. The two things are quite different."

"Never mind, dearie, just let me take your cloak and bring you to see your mother. She hasn't been the same since you married that gentleman." Mary said "gentleman" the way other people might say "snake."

If her mother felt that way about her marrying him—why had she let it happen?

Jane took in the house, with all its familiar trappings. The worn cupboard, where her favorite cup was. The stone floor in the kitchen, leading to the dark wood of the hallway and the more presentable rooms. The cloaks hanging suspended on hooks in the entryway.

And yet even though she'd thought of how all she wanted was to return home, she couldn't suppress a sigh as she thought about him, and what he'd looked like as she left.

And she wished she hadn't left after all.

—THE PRINCESS AND THE SCOUNDREL

Chapter 15

"It was such a surprise when we heard the news, Your Grace."

Nicholas had no idea what the name of the woman addressing him was, just that she was dressed in something that made her look like an upside-down pudding, and that she kept fluttering her eyelashes at him.

He wanted to offer her a handkerchief to fish out whatever it was in her eye, perhaps that would make her stop. Because he was a married man, even though he was celibate for the first time since that first time, back when he was seventeen years old or so.

It was ironic, but if he had to wait for Isabella to want him, he would. Even if it meant he went without sex for a month. He just hoped it wouldn't be for a year.

The lady—because she was a lady, even if her eyelashes were untoward—sat on one of the couches, a tiny plate holding a cookie in one hand and a fan in the other. She was just one of the many members of the highest society who had come to call today, and there was a low buzz of conversation in the room and many covert glances cast at him, and at Isabella.

"The news that I was the duke, or that I had gotten married? Or both?" He didn't really care about the answer, but he knew he had to make conversation, and he couldn't say what was on his mind—how he'd felt watching as Isabella and her parents conversed, how he'd noticed her whole body stiffening and her demeanor growing more and more rigid with every passing moment.

So he might as well make banal comments until they were alone, and he could try to draw her out, discover what would melt his ice princess's heart.

"Your Grace, you are so clever!" the lady exclaimed, tapping him on the arm with her fan.

Nicholas had been accused of many things, especially by ladies, but never of being clever. He would have to tell Griff what she'd said.

"My lady," he replied, bowing. He looked over the lady's head and found Isabella, who was seated at the other end of the room. "My wife requires my attention, if you will excuse me?" he said, even though Isabella hadn't even looked at him. She was conversing with another unidentified lady, the expression on her face faultlessly polite.

"Certainly, Your Grace," the lady replied, but Nicholas barely registered her words.

"Nicholas." A hand gripped his arm, and he had a momentary response of wanting to punch the hand's owner, only then he recalled he was in the drawing room, not the boxing ring.

Plus it was Griff. Well, not that he wouldn't—and hadn't—punched his brother in the past, but this wasn't the place.

"What is it?" he said, still keeping his eyes on Isabella. She'd met his gaze and her lips curved up in her most polite smile.

He hated that smile. At least when it was directed to him. He wanted to see her smile only at him, not give him the look she bestowed on any idiot who crossed her path.

He wanted her to want him.

"I have some business matters to discuss with you." Griff sounded more serious than usual, so it must have been important. Of course, with Griff "important" could mean nearly anything—like when one of the maids had accidentally scorched his lucky cravat while ironing, the one that he'd worn taking all his exams. Or when he'd gotten only the second highest mark in his class.

But Griff's cravat looked fine, and he wasn't in school at the moment, so likely it was something actually important.

"Come to my study," Nicholas said, nodding to Isabella to let her know he was leaving the room. She nodded in reply, her expression entirely serene.

The two of them walked out, Nicholas dodging more ladies who had come to gawk at the new duke and his bride. Or at least it felt that way.

A footman stood at attention in the hallway, but Nicholas waved him off. "In here." Nicholas flung the door to his study open, allowing Griff to enter before going in and shutting the door behind them.

He turned to look at his brother. "Well, what is it? Are you here to tell me I'm now the king of some tiny island somewhere?"

Griff snorted. At least Nicholas was usually able to make his brother laugh.

"No, although it does have to do with your inheritance. It seemed so clear before, I went over the paperwork myself. And we knew he would cause a fuss, that was to be expected, but—"

"There is always a 'but,' isn't there?" Nicholas walked over to his desk and sat down behind it, pushing the chair away so he could spread his legs out. "Sit down, we might as well be comfortable while you tell me the bad news."

Griff sat down on the closest chair. "It's not bad news, precisely, it's just inconvenient."

Nicholas rolled his eyes. "Bad, inconvenient, whatever. Just tell me."

Griff nodded and took a deep breath. The kind he always took when he was about to lecture Nicholas for at least an hour.

"Succinctly," Nicholas added. He glanced over to the sideboard where there were, thankfully, a few bottles of some brown-colored liquor. He thought he might have need of something if Griff went on in his usual way.

"The paperwork is correct, you are the duke, there is no question, but the previous duke has managed to convince some members of Parliament to at least review the evidence."

"So there is a question." He leaned forward and tapped his finger on the desk. "What does that mean to me? I can't do anything besides standing behind the paperwork that got me here in the first place."

Griff sighed, crossing his arms over his chest. "No, you can't, but if it starts to feel as though he will win, in the court of public opinion, at least, you will find your life much more difficult."

Nicholas snorted as he rose and headed for the sideboard. "It is not as though being a duke is that difficult. All I have to do is stand around and look haughty."

"And manage your estates, and appear in the House of Lords, and ensure your workers and the people who rent from you are satisfied, and any number of things I have no clue what you're supposed to be doing." Griff narrowed his gaze. "You haven't been doing any of those things, have you?" he said in an accusing tone.

Well, no, he hadn't, but Griff should have known that. Because the only things he had done had been with his brother.

But looking at Griff's expression, Nicholas felt wrong about saying just that. He had been doing dukely things, namely getting to know his wife, getting punched each morning, and wandering about his new town house. Wasn't that enough?

Judging by the look on Griff's face, it was not.

"I haven't. And if you want me to, you're going to have to come help me."

Griff's eyes widened. "Help you how?"

Nicholas felt a broad grin creep across his face. "You can be my new secretary. It makes perfect sense. You've already helped me deal with some of the most urgent business, and of course there is always more. I won't trust anyone half as much as I trust you." He spread his arms out. "Why didn't we think of it before?"

"Probably because 'we,'" Griff said, emphasizing the pronoun, "hadn't given thought to anything."

"Well," Nicholas replied, tilting his now half-full glass to his brother, "*we* will fix that. Won't we?"

Griff sighed again. Something his brother did frequently in his presence, Nicholas realized. "Fine. I will help you deal with all the requirements of being a duke, if you will . . ."

He paused, and Nicholas felt a tightening in his stomach. What would his brother ask for?

"Teach me what you know about ladies."

Of all the things Nicholas had expected his brother to say, it certainly was not that. But if there was a list of things that Nicholas could possibly instruct his brother on, that would be the only item.

"We have an agreement." He held his hand out and Griff grasped it, and shook.

He had a new secretary, one whom he trusted implicitly, and he also had another duty added on to all the other duties that he'd apparently been neglecting.

Meanwhile, the top item on his list—his wife—was swiftly becoming the only thing he cared about.

Finally the day was over. It had been exhausting; she'd had to make polite conversation for most of the day with people she'd known forever, but who didn't know her at all. And now they were to give a ball, when those same people would come to her house and expect something living up to the title, the house, the odd situation of her being here, married, with him, and yet none of them would know anything. Not about her, not about them, not about anything.

She was so intent on her thoughts that she didn't realize he was in her bedroom until she heard his voice. "Robinson, correct?"

For such a large man, Nicholas was very light on his feet. Perhaps it had to do with all that boxing he did. Or he was just graceful. It didn't matter, but it did surprise her.

"Yes, Your Grace." Robinson stopped brushing Isabella's hair and stood at attention, waiting for whatever he was about to say.

That was one of the benefits of being a duke—even her mother had had to listen to him, to pay attention to him, when she usually just ignored whatever anybody said if she didn't feel like listening.

But he'd stood up to her mother, stood up for her, and she was grateful to him. And then he'd kissed her on the cheek, and made that nonsensical comment about her being sweet, and she felt as though she were melting.

"The duchess will not need you any longer tonight." He plucked the brush from her maid's hand and made a shooing gesture. "Enjoy the rest of your evening."

"Certainly, Your Grace," Robinson replied, bobbing a quick curtsey and then leaving the room, pausing only to straighten one ribbon on the dressing table that had dared to be askew.

Nicholas didn't ask, just drew the brush through her hair, meeting her gaze in the mirror. "You have lovely hair," he said in a low voice. That same one, damn him, that made her all trembly inside and made her wish he would just do something instead of making her wait.

Although what she was waiting for—well, she had no clue. Beyond the animalistic passion her mother had mentioned, and she just couldn't picture Nicholas being an animal at all.

But she wanted . . . something. Only she didn't know

what it was. Even if it was some sort of calling up an animalistic beast, or whatever her mother had warned her about, it might be preferable to all this anticipation, this worry she wasn't good enough, that she would never find out what it was all about.

"Thank you," she said at last, her voice sounding much breathier than she'd like it to. His hand paused mid-stroke, and she saw his eyelids lower, as though he were thinking of something. "Thank you for earlier, with my parents, and thank you for this afternoon. My mother is the one to have said it," she said in a rueful tone of voice, "but it is important that we appear absolutely . . . correct." She felt her chest tighten.

"We passed the first test, I believe," he said. "There was no doubt but that you would, given how perfect you are, but my manners are in question."

Perfect? He thought she was perfect? And why wasn't she flattered by that? Instead, she felt as though she wished to assure him she had foibles, and concerns, and every so often she pretended to cough when she actually had to burp.

But he didn't know any of that. She had to accept the compliment for what it was, and not as a judgment. "As long as none of our guests challenged you to a boxing match, I presume you would be presentable as well." She spoke in a light tone that belied her inner thoughts.

He chuckled, shaking his head. "Not that I wouldn't like to punch some of those people—a few of them implied I had bought my way into the title, as though I could manufacture hundreds-year-old documents. They should ask Griff about how capable I'd be at that kind of deception."

She put her hand on his, the one brushing her hair. "I think my hair is well taken care of. Would you—?" She couldn't believe she was asking this, much less that it didn't mean what it was supposed to mean. "Would you like to go sit on the bed?"

That look again. The eyelids lowered, a quick glance down her face, down further, then a visible swallow. "Of course. I believe you have some talking to do."

"Only after I hear your story," she said, taking the hand he held out to assist her in rising. Not that she needed it, but she did need to touch him. To feel as though there was at least some human contact in her life.

She'd gone far too long without it, it seemed—she craved it, craved leaning against him, as she had the night before, feeling the strength of his chest under her head, the long length of his body resting alongside hers.

And he didn't have to know how much she wanted, did he? For all he knew, she could just be enjoying the moment of sharing conversation. Of him telling her some ridiculous story, and then her telling him something she'd always wanted to do.

"What story shall I tell you?" he asked, getting onto the bed and stretching out his long legs. It was a good thing she had a bed fit for a duchess—or a small village—because she doubted a regular bed would fit him.

And then they'd be squashed together, and their bodies would be touching even more, and—enough of that, she told herself sternly. He couldn't know just where her thoughts were going.

"Perhaps about St. George and the Dragon?" She got onto the bed after him and slid under his arm, as though it were understood that that was the position they'd be in. Thankfully, he didn't jump or push her away or say anything.

"Too many dragons," he said, his voice a low rumble she felt under her cheek.

"Oliver Cromwell's rebellion?" she offered, knowing he would likely reject that as well. Somehow, though, that didn't make her feel like a failure for not getting it right. She felt, rather, as though they were teasing each other.

Except for Margaret, she had neither teased nor been teased. She thought she might almost like it.

"Too puritanical," he said, a hint of laughter in his tone.

She slapped his chest lightly, then let her hand rest there. On him. "Then you decide."

He covered her hand with his. "How about a fairy tale? Sleeping Beauty, perhaps?"

She snuggled further into his chest, taking surreptitious sniffs of his delicious Nicholas scent. It was definitely more plum pudding-y today, but either scent he had, she loved it.

"That would be fine," she replied. "As long as the princess gets a chance to have some adventures before she marries the prince." Then went still as she realized just what she'd said.

"Adventure it is," he replied smoothly, and she hoped he wasn't thinking about the implications of what she'd said, because, oh goodness, what if he thought she was talking about herself and what if he decided he didn't want her, and didn't want her to have any adventures and would send her off to the country with only one gown and an ancient maidservant who was scared of fire, and—

"Breathe, princess," he said, patting her on the arm. "I promise, I won't make you breathless until later."

She hiccupped a breath, wishing she could tell him how she'd taken what he'd said, only she couldn't, not with that big thing hanging between them.

That is, the fact that they hadn't had marital relations.

She was even mortified at where her own thoughts went. It was simpler when she didn't want and feel so much.

"Once upon a time," he began, his fingers idly stroking the bare skin of her arm, just below the sleeve of her nightdress.

She laughed in all the places he'd wanted her to, even though she insisted on correcting the ending to the story—instead of the princess heading off to fairyland to enact revenge on the mean fairy, as he'd recounted, she said that the princess would not be so petty, and would just let the mean fairy come to her own bad ends.

Nicholas would have to tell her the story of how the mean fairy got her comeuppance another night. And how revealing was it that he was picturing the mean fairy as his new mother-in-law?

"And now you should tell me what is on your list, princess." He felt her stiffen in his arms, but she didn't run away. Not yet, at least.

Was this how it felt to try to tame a deer or some other fragile, woodland creature? This constant worrying and tentativeness?

Because if so he had a lot more sympathy with zoo-keepers.

"The list of things I wish to do?" she asked, her voice higher and softer than usual. He dipped his head down to whisper in her ear. Not that anybody was there, but he couldn't help himself.

"Yes. That list," he said, feeling the skin on her arms get goose bumps as he spoke.

"Oh," she said, the word more like a sigh.

She didn't speak for a few minutes after that, but Nicholas could tell she was thinking—mostly because she felt relaxed in his arms, and if she hadn't been thinking hard about something, he knew she would be much more self-conscious about lying there, together, on her bed.

"I want to go somewhere where it doesn't matter if I laugh loudly. I want to dance without worrying about how I look, or if I am executing a misstep."

She paused, and he felt his insides coil in anticipation of what she would say next. "But most of all, right now, I would like to kiss you," she said at last.

Which was both the best and the worst answer she could have given him.

It took her an entire week to realize what had been staring her in the face all along.

And then it took her another week to muster up the courage to tell them she was leaving, after having just gotten there.

And yet one more week before she'd finished hearing them say their piece, and try to convince her.

So it was nearly a month before she found herself walking up to the castle door, her heart in her throat, wondering if she was making a huge mistake.

"Princess!" The guard sounded shocked to see her. As well he might.

"Let me in, please," she said. She couldn't wait to find him, to tell him what she felt.

"The prince is gone, my lady. He left a week or so after you did. We don't know when he will be back. He's ordered us to keep the castle closed until he returns. If he returns."

No. No, it couldn't be.

"Where did he go?"

The guard shook his head. "No one knows, my lady."

—THE PRINCESS AND THE SCOUNDREL

Chapter 16

She didn't know where those words had come from. They'd just popped out of her mouth, and now they were out there, floating in the air somewhere, and she couldn't take them back.

Not that she wanted to, exactly; if he rebuffed her, then she would want to take them back. Most definitely.

But right now, he was still holding her, his fingers on her skin, tracing circles. But she knew he'd heard her, since his body had changed after she'd spoken. Gotten more—aware? Alert? If such a thing was possible.

Perhaps he was on the verge of flinging her to the floor and denouncing her as a fast woman.

But she didn't think so.

"It seems you and I have more in common than we might have initially thought, princess," he said. His mouth was still right next to her ear, and his words sent a gentle hum through her whole body.

Her mouth felt suddenly dry. "So you've wanted to

dance badly?" she said in a breathy voice that nearly sounded—yes—*squeaky*.

He chuckled in response, and she had a wild, panicked moment of wanting to leap off the bed in search of water, only it wasn't really water she wished to drink, was it?

It was he. She wanted to taste him, to see how it felt to have that full, gorgeous mouth on hers. He was too kind to refuse her, wasn't he? Even if he wasn't all that intrigued by her. Even though she was his wife.

But he'd said—he'd said they had more in common. That meant what she thought it meant, right?

"I believe the way to do this is for us to face each other," he said, a hint of humor in his voice.

"Of course," she replied, putting her hand on his leg to twist in his arms. He winced, and uttered some sort of groan, and she snatched her hand away, feeling as mortified as it was possible for a virginal wife to feel after a few days of marriage.

So a lot of mortification.

Why hadn't her training gone through this? "How to Deal with Your Husband When It Seems He Might Not Wish to Consummate the Marriage." Or "How Not to Blush and Appear Awkward in Intimate Situations, Not That This Situation Is Intimate at All, Given That They Were Married."

Too long, too much, too—

He placed his fingers on her face, right at her jawline, his blue eyes gazing into hers. And even though two seconds earlier her pulse had been pounding, and all she'd wanted was to run away and never face the embarrassment of having said what she did, she felt—

Well, her pulse was still racing. But she didn't want to run away.

"We will start slowly, princess," he said, his gaze moving to her mouth. She felt his stare on her lips as though it were almost a palpable thing, a caress that lit her up inside.

And then he licked his lips, and Isabella nearly swooned. She'd never swooned in her life, she'd barely exhibited any kind of emotion at all, and yet here she was, being overcome by the simple observation of her husband having a dry mouth.

But what a mouth. It was wide and full, the lower lip larger than the top, the brackets at the side showing he liked to laugh. As though she didn't already know he had a good sense of humor. His mouth was in contrast to the sharp planes and angles of his face, which made it even more enticing.

And then, then when she felt like she might be going cross-eyed from staring so closely at his mouth, he leaned forward and pressed those lips against hers.

His fingers moved to behind her ear, holding her gently in place. His mouth felt warm and delicious, and she imagined she could feel the contact of his lips all over his body, even though they were only touching in—one, two, three places. Their mouths, his fingers behind her ear, his thigh pressed against hers.

How was one supposed to breathe? She didn't want to exhale from her nostrils onto his face, since that seemed like it would be unpleasant, and she couldn't exactly breathe with her mouth, since it was otherwise occupied.

Thankfully, it seemed that he had to breathe as well, since he disengaged and drew back for just a moment, giving her enough time to draw a deep breath, before returning his mouth to hers.

Only now—now it felt as though his lips were parting, and she could feel his breath in her mouth, only it didn't seem odd at all. It felt as though they were joined together in just that one spot, breathing the same air, almost the same person.

Except that he was a very tall, very charming, apparently-very-conversant-with-such-matters duke, while she was a not as tall, very polished, but not-very-aware-of-anything-that-might-happen-between-a-man-and-a-woman duchess.

He drew back again, but only just barely. She felt her insides flutter as his eyes met hers. "You haven't been kissed before."

It wasn't a question, but instead of the sharp, irked feeling she got when her mother said such things, she felt as though he'd spotted something about her no one else ever had. That no one else had ever gotten close enough to know.

That no one had been privileged to know before.

"No," she said, shaking her head a tiny fraction.

An almost arrogant smile came across that mouth, and she felt her own mouth start to curl up in response.

"Is that some sort of thing men like? To be the first one a lady has kissed?" she asked, startled by her own boldness. Not to mention her own ability to form a sentence, given how fluttery she felt.

"Not usually." It sounded as though he was actually pondering her question rather than giving her the expected answer. "But with you—you're different. Somehow it feels different," he said in a wondering tone of voice.

But before she could respond to that, he lowered his mouth to hers and kissed her again, this time using his lips to coax her mouth open as well.

Now where was this going? she thought, before she felt something besides a lip. It was—oh, it was his tongue, and it was moving gently along the seam of her lips, licking them, making sparks fly throughout her entire body, her mouth open beneath his, her heart beating fast in her chest.

She somehow had grabbed hold of his shoulders and was holding on, as though she might spiral off and fall without him as an anchor. Only he wasn't an anchor—he was the one making her dizzy, making her heart race, making every part of her body feel as though it had never been alive like this before.

And then his tongue entered her mouth, of all things, and she gasped as she felt the warmth of his tongue, licking inside, finding her tongue, which seemed to know just what to do without any help from her.

Well, this felt just intoxicating, and for a moment, she was annoyed it had taken them this long—three days?—to get to this place. But then she forgot how to think as he continued to kiss her, long, slow kisses, pausing every so often to take a much-needed breath, the only sound in the room, in fact, that of their breathing and the occasional rustle of fabric.

She couldn't say how long they kissed—a few minutes, a few hours, perhaps a week—but when he finally drew back, his eyes heavy again, his expression that of just pure wanting—it wasn't enough. Would it ever be enough?

"I think we should stop there," he said, in such a low rumble she felt it through her whole body.

She wanted to ask why, but wasn't sure she should. What was the etiquette? Although— Although he was her husband, and she was his wife, and they should be able to dispense somewhat with etiquette when they were alone together.

Not to mention that as far as she knew there was no established etiquette for such a situation anyway. Perhaps she should start compiling one, for future brides and bridegrooms.

So she asked. It would be research for the book, after all. "Why?"

He grimaced, and looked away from her, off into the distance. But she didn't think he was actually looking at anything—he just wasn't looking at her.

A minute, which felt like a lifetime, until he returned his gaze to her face. "I don't think we should continue until we know each other better."

His voice, which before had sounded low and pleasant and incredibly alluring, now held a repressed tone to it that made Isabella straighten instinctively—not easy when one was sitting on a bed.

"Ah," she said, biting her lip.

His eyes tracked the movement, and he looked pained. Which was an odd response, but then again, everything about this was odd—did he really not wish to kiss her? But even though this was her first kiss, she rather thought he'd been as enthusiastic about the activity as she was.

Then why? He still hadn't answered her question. Might not, given how he wasn't speaking.

"Do you have any thoughts as to when you might like us to throw a ball?"

The question was completely unexpected, and made Isabella wonder, still, just what she might have done wrong.

But she really couldn't ask that, because what if he actually answered? And it was something she couldn't change, or was an untenable situation, or something that would be devastating?

Yes, she was cowardly not to want to know, but better to be cowardly than to risk possible misery for the rest of her life.

She'd been trained to respond politely. She could do this. "Two or three weeks? I will need time to review what other affairs might be occurring that evening, and work with your staff. Our staff," she corrected herself, before he could. "All of that will take time." Most ladies needed at least a month or more to plan something so enormous, but thanks to her training, she could do it better in less time. She wished she could do other things better in less time as well.

"Of course, of course," he replied, sounding as though he weren't thinking at all about what she was saying.

"This will be our first public event. We want it to be the highlight of the Season."

"Mmph," he replied.

"I am so glad you agree," she said in a dry tone. "I will hire workers to paint the entire house black, the paint will need time to dry. Plus we will need time to roast the goats."

"Of course," he repeated, still sounding absent.

She tapped him on the arm. "I am tired, Nicholas. If you wouldn't mind—?" she said, gesturing to the door. If he wasn't going to listen to her, he should at least leave her alone.

"Certainly." He slid off the bed quickly, as though eager to leave her company, and she felt the sting of tears in her eyes. Did he not wish to be with her that much? And if so, why was he trying so hard to get to know her, to ensure they had things in common?

Although now it seemed as though they did not have a mutual enjoyment of kissing in common. A fact that made her heart hurt, but she couldn't allow herself to think about any of that now, not until he was safely back in his room and she was on her own. Without even Margaret to talk to.

"Good night," he said, leaning over to kiss her on the forehead, as though she were a child. She nodded, staring off into the distance, willing herself not to cry.

"I hope you sleep well," she said to his back as he walked out of the room. He froze, then turned back to look at her. Something odd was in his expression, something she couldn't figure out. Just like the rest of him—something she couldn't figure out, not at all, but would have to—or else her marriage would be as unfulfilling as her unmarried life had been.

"You too, princess." He opened the door and left, closing it softly behind him.

Leaving her alone with her thoughts, her bruised and tender mouth, and even more unanswered questions.

"Where could he have gone to?"

Jane was pacing the castle's entryway, the only place the guards had allowed her to go. Someone had been sent to her rooms to gather a few things, and the palace cook was packing her something to eat as well.

But now she had no home and no husband.

She could just return home and tell her family it had all been a mistake, her leaving.

But she knew she wouldn't do that.

"I will find him," she muttered to herself, hoping no one was around to hear her talking to herself. "How far could he have gone? Or did he leave because he no longer wanted me? Once he thought I didn't want him?

"What have I done?" she asked, feeling a wave of ~~hopelessness~~ desperation crash over her.

—THE PRINCESS AND THE SCOUNDREL

Chapter 17

If Nicholas were to list the hardest things he'd ever done in his life, telling his wife they had to stop kissing would be first on the list. Even harder than when he'd been ten years old and Griff had challenged him to eat an entire cake, and he'd done it, even though he'd been sick for a week after.

She was far more delicious than cake.

He walked as quickly as he could to his bedroom, counting off the paces—again—so he wouldn't just turn right around and resume kissing her.

Kissing her. He'd gotten the chance to kiss his wife, and it was even more spectacular than he'd imagined, and he'd thought it would be tremendous.

Griff was right when he'd said Nicholas didn't have enough imagination. How could he have imagined the reality of her soft mouth, how her lips felt under his, how she'd grabbed hold of his shoulders and kept him pressed to her?

How much he'd wanted to continue kissing her, moving from her mouth to her neck to her breasts, all the way down to her toes.

But while she'd been responsive—so responsive, in fact, it surprised him—he didn't want to rush things. He truly meant what he'd said when he told her he thought they should get to know each other better. Even though if he were to say that to any other man who had the chance to get under Isabella's skirts, they'd laugh at him and tell him not to be so soft.

Finally he reached his door and entered, Miller springing up as he shut the door.

"Your Grace," Miller said, smoothing his coat. "I trust you had a pleasant evening?"

Nicholas felt himself grimace, but smoothed his expression quickly. "Yes, thank you."

If you could call leaving the most gorgeous woman he'd ever seen alone in her bedroom wishing for more kissing from him a pleasant evening, then yes, he'd had a pleasant evening.

Speaking of which, he needed to douse himself with cold water or something before allowing Miller to help him undress. Likely Miller would be as enthusiastic about seeing Nicholas in a state of excitement as he was about watching him bathe.

"Do you wish to change into your nightclothes now, Your Grace?"

"Uh," Nicholas said nonsensically, trying to gauge

the state of his erection without actually looking down. "Yes, only first could you rustle up a cup of tea?"

That would give him enough time to review some of his dukely accounts or count from one hundred backward or something else to take his mind off her, her softness, and her mouth.

"Yes, Your Grace." Miller left, and Nicholas let out a great sigh of relief.

Now to just keep his mind on anything but her, but that would be difficult, since she was all he seemed to be able to think about.

How about if he pondered what her reaction might be if he'd just gone ahead and fucked her as mercilessly as his body was begging him to do?

That thought made him wince, and yes, made his excitement diminish a little.

When Miller returned about ten minutes later, Nicholas had gotten himself back to relative sanity, and was sitting reading the paper, catching up on the serial he'd neglected while he was telling his own stories to his wife.

The prince couldn't be as much of a scoundrel as the heroine thought, could he?

And what did the prince think about her?

Funny, he'd never thought much about what the characters in these stories actually felt before now. Perhaps Griff was wrong, and he was just developing an imagination late in his life.

Or he was just a married man desperate to know what his wife really thought.

The next morning, Nicholas decided perhaps it would be more prudent not to go to the boxing saloon, since in his current state of frustration he might just ask his opponent to kill him and end his agony.

Plus he knew Griff would likely be arriving soon to start officially being his secretary.

So he lay in bed, rereading the serial he'd caught up on the night before until he felt thoroughly bored and almost willing to take care of his business affairs. He rang the bell and Miller entered, only a few minutes later.

"Your Grace?"

"Yes, I need to get dressed, my new secretary is arriving shortly, and I wish to breakfast with the duchess. Is she up yet, do you know?"

"She is not, as far as I know, Your Grace."

Ah. Had she lain awake as he had, thinking about them? Those kisses? Or was she just naturally inclined to sleep for lengthy periods?

He knew so little about her; he wanted, no, he needed to know more. To know everything about her.

"Good morning, Your Grace." Renning stood at attention just outside the breakfast room. "Her Grace has just arrived."

Nicholas was almost embarrassed at how pleased that made him, then reminded himself she was his wife, the only woman he would be with for the rest of his life, so if he wasn't pleased at the outset of their marriage he was going to have a difficult time of it in the future. "I wish to breakfast with my wife alone, so I can handle things from here, Renning."

His butler looked startled—at least as startled as a butler allowed himself to look—but merely offered a "Of course, Your Grace," and held the door open for Nicholas, then shut it behind them.

"Isabella, you are—" Well, she wasn't looking her best, so he couldn't necessarily say that. Although he'd lied to women before, many times, he did not wish to make it a habit with her. "You are . . . here," he finished lamely.

She smiled that brilliant Society smile and nodded. "I am, as you see, Nicholas." Her tone was brittle.

Had he done something wrong? Besides not ravishing her, that is?

Why hadn't anyone told him marriage would be so hard? Oh, likely because he'd never imagined—given his now self-admittedly poor imagination—that he would be married at all.

He spoke as though he hadn't noticed her tone. Perhaps that was what typical husbands did. "I am glad you are here this morning, I wanted to tell you that my brother will be joining my staff as my secretary. So he can assist with the planning of the ball, should you wish it."

She nodded. "If you wish it, I will utilize him."

Nicholas paused in the act of pouring himself coffee. He turned to look at her, a feeling of annoyance mingling with the distinct feeling that he was making an absolute hash of dealing with her. He apparently wasn't a typical husband. "I don't wish it, if I had wished it, I would have said so. It is that I want you to know that should you need assistance, Griff is at your disposal. That is all," he finished, waving his half-full cup in the air in an aggrieved way.

"Thank you," she replied, still with that distant tone, only not quite as cold as before, thank goodness.

"What are your plans for today?" He sat down at the head of the table, next to her. She was wearing a gown made of the same pink that her bed coverings were made of, and he congratulated himself on figuring out her favorite color.

"Is there something you require of me?"

Nicholas repressed another great sigh and placed his coffee cup firmly down on its saucer, causing both to rattle. He was not the hero of one of his serials, he should not behave like one. "No, I am merely asking. As I mentioned, Griff will be arriving shortly, and I expect our business to take at least a few hours"—God help him—"and so if there was something you wished to do, you would be free at least until teatime."

"Oh." She was looking down at her plate, not at him. Why wouldn't she look at him? It annoyed him, how she didn't seem to focus on him when he was in the room. And now he sounded like a petty child, insistent on having all the attention.

He would have to be content with sharing her attention with the piece of half-eaten toast and the three strawberries currently on her breakfast plate.

"Well, perhaps I will go to my parents' house and see Margaret. I need to start shopping for a gown for our ball—I have many nice gowns, of course, but nothing anybody hasn't seen before, and I want to do you justice."

She met his gaze then, and he took in the lovely, warm brown depths of her eyes, her full, intensely kissable mouth, that porcelain skin, and her figure, which he'd seen enough to know was spectacular. And seen enough to wish he could see all of it, preferably underneath his body.

"You would do me justice wearing a sack, princess," he said, hearing his voice get just a bit husky.

A stain flooded her cheeks and she looked back down at her other object of scrutiny, the toast. "Thank you."

"But if you wish to ensure that every single person there sees how stunning you are, and what an asset you are to me as my wife, then you might want a new gown. Just so that no one will say your new husband is a skinflint."

"I will start working on the guest list this afternoon also. And consult with Renning and Cook as to what to serve."

Nicholas waved his hand. "Whatever you want, I will go along with your wishes. I haven't ever thrown a party"—at least not a respectable one—"and wouldn't have the faintest idea how to go about it."

She pressed her mouth together, as though she were thinking, then spoke in a low, hesitant voice. "I am grateful you are allowing me so much freedom."

Instead of making him feel beneficent, however, her words made him feel as though she was secretly waiting for him to turn into an ogre.

"Well, why wouldn't I? You are my wife, not my possession."

She raised her eyebrow at him then and he felt guilty. Over what, he had no idea.

"But I am. I was bartered to you through neither of our doing, anything I own belongs really to you, and you can do whatever you like to me."

Oh. Put that way, well, no wonder he felt guilty. "But you must know, Isabella, that I do not view you as my possession"—*even though I wish to possess you*—"and that if there is anything on which we disagree, we can discuss it as equals."

That eyebrow was still raised, and he could swear she had a skeptical look in her eye. But she didn't say anything else, just nodded, and returned to her toast.

Nicholas had rarely—well, never—felt awkward around a woman, much less an attractive woman he wished to bed. But it seemed as though there was a first time for everything, whether it was a kiss for her, or a moment where he was feeling as though he had no idea what to do or say, and had no hint of what she felt for him. Except that she did like kissing him, which suited his agenda, since he also liked kissing her.

Could they forge a satisfactory relationship on kissing?

And if the answer was yes, or even maybe, when was the soonest they could return to that?

She set off an hour later, accompanied by the maid the prince had ordered to serve her when she first arrived. She'd tried to go on her own, but the girl had shrieked and folded her arms and said it wasn't seemly, and that wherever the prince had gotten to, the princess couldn't go there without a chaperone.

It seemed preferable to take her along than to spend another few hours arguing with her, so she agreed.

The girl, whose name was Catherine, made sure they both had warm cloaks and provisions for the journey. Then she bullied one of the grooms to saddle up two horses.

Jane knew she could never have accomplished that on her own, so she was grateful for Catherine's presence.

"Which way?" Catherine asked, as they came to a fork in the road.

"Does it matter?" Jane replied. "We don't know

where he's gone, so the sooner we find out where he's not, the sooner we will find out where he is."

Catherine nodded in agreement, and they took the left turn.

Jane just hoped it wasn't the wrong one.

—The Princess and the Scoundrel

Chapter 18

She'd left the house an hour later, with Nicholas ensconced in his study with his brother. Griff, not Gruff. She winced as she considered that Nicholas might find it hysterical to share that gaffe with his brother.

Her parents' house wasn't that far away from her own—goodness, her own house—so it was only about fifteen minutes later that she was alighting from the carriage and ascending the familiar stairs. As a guest now, not a resident.

"Good afternoon, miss. That is, Your Grace." Lowton bowed as he held the door wide for first Isabella, then Robinson, to enter Isabella's parents' house.

Before he could say anything else, however, Margaret was running down the staircase, a delighted grin on her face. "You're here! And I was just planning on coming to see you, only you're here!"

"I am," Isabella said, smiling in return. There were few people as . . . *exuberant* as her sister when she was enthused. And to be the object of that exuberance was wonderful; Isabella had found it the only source of happiness when they were younger. Now she had Nicholas as some sort of source of . . . something, she wasn't sure what yet.

"Lowton, can you bring tea up to my room, please?" Margaret peered over Isabella's shoulder at Robinson. "You can take a cup of tea in the kitchen while we visit."

"Thank you, Robinson," Isabella murmured as Lowton showed Robinson where to go.

"What is even better," Margaret said in a low voice as they began to ascend the staircase, "is that the parents are off doing something, and so we won't be disturbed. And thank goodness, because without you, they have been focusing their attention on me, of all people."

They reached Margaret's room, and walked in, Margaret making sure the door was firmly closed by leaning against it. Margaret's room was substantially smaller than Isabella's had been, and the size was further compromised by the vast amount of books placed on every available surface. Several sheets of paper lay on top of one of the piles, and Margaret flipped them over as they entered the room.

Isabella wanted to ask, since her sister was seldom secretive, but then Margaret might demand information in return.

"I don't know how you could stand it," Margaret

continued, shaking her head as she gestured to Isabella to sit. "They want to know why I am wearing what I am wearing, and who I might be seeing, and why I didn't say this thing when I said that thing. Honestly, I wish they would return to just ignoring me."

Isabella gave a rueful laugh, then drew her bonnet off her head and laid it on one of the shorter stacks of books on Margaret's dressing table. "They are awful," she said at last.

Margaret's eyes widened and she bounced in her chair. "Do you know, that is the first time you have actually said something bad about them that you didn't immediately follow up with some sort of 'Well, but they mean well,' or 'Perhaps they don't know how it feels' comment? Marriage certainly agrees with you," she said, grinning.

Oh, if you only knew, Isabella thought. "It does. I think." She frowned, thinking about how to say things without saying other things.

She'd had a lifetime of saying things without imparting knowledge, as every proper young lady had, so she should be able to talk to her sister without saying the thing that was uppermost in her mind.

"What is marriage like?"

So of course her sister went right to the crucial question, not dancing around the topic like Isabella would. She admired Margaret for that, nearly as much as her parents deplored it.

"It's fine?" She hated how hesitant she sounded. "But it's been such a short time, and we barely know each other." *I can't quite tell, for example, if he likes kissing me, or sees it as his duty because he is a gentleman. And my husband.*

"Still, you must know if you like his company. I like him, not that that matters," Margaret said. "Is he talkative? Or quiet? What does he like to do? What do you have in common?"

The enjoyment of good stories, even if they differed on the best way to tell them. Kissing, hopefully. Possibly rain, but she wasn't certain about the last item.

"He has a good sense of humor, I think," Isabella began. "He is thoughtful." She thought about it some more. "Actually, perhaps you would know. Why would a man, a seemingly reasonable man, want to enter a boxing ring? Voluntarily?"

"Oh, so that is what he was doing!" Margaret looked relieved. "I'd wondered what had happened, but didn't want to ask. Although—now that I know, I have no idea." She twisted her mouth up in thought. "Perhaps he used to get more exercise, and is feeling restless? Could that be it?"

Restless. Maybe that was it. Maybe he was accustomed to being on his own, free to go wherever he liked, and now he had a wife to deal with. Isabella was beginning to feel less like a wife than she did a millstone around his neck. "He has an entire stable full of horses at his disposal. Unless he doesn't like to ride?" She shook her head. "I have no idea, except that the morning you came over, that was not the first time he'd arrived home in that condition."

"All bruised and bleeding?" Margaret did not sound appalled. As a matter of fact, she sounded . . . intrigued.

And as she thought about it, something about the way he'd looked, and definitely about the way he'd smelled, had intrigued Isabella as well. Perhaps there was some sort of unknown mating ritual about which she had no idea that he was enacting? Was she merely being seduced by his bruised knuckles and manly scent?

Or was she just searching for a rational explanation for the way he made her feel, those nights alone in her bedroom?

"But you didn't tell me the important part." And Isabella knew to what Margaret referred, of course, since her sister never shied away from any type of conversation, regardless of how proper it might or might not be.

"I can tell you a few things," Isabella said. She paused, gathering the words. "I can tell you that kissing is one of the most glorious things known to man. And woman," she said with a laugh. "And there are things that happen during it that sound utterly terrible, but when they occur, you wonder that more people don't just spend all of their free time in the pursuit of kissing."

"Oh," Margaret breathed, her eyes wide and sparkling with interest. "I've been kissed before, but I certainly haven't felt that way."

"You've been kissed? By whom?" And how aggrieved did Isabella feel, to know that Margaret had been kissed before her, and she hadn't said anything?

Margaret folded her hands sedately in her lap. "I will not tell, just as you won't tell me what happens after the kissing."

That is because I don't know.

"As I said. It wouldn't be proper," Isabella said in a prim voice. "And I cannot believe you were kissed, and never told me!" She picked up one of the pillows on the chair she was sitting on and hurled it at her sister, who dodged it with a skill that bore testament to how many times the event had occurred before.

Margaret shrugged. "It was nothing. I just needed to do it so I knew what it felt like. But I think the person I kissed must have been doing it wrong, since I really just wanted it to be over."

"You did say my husband had that kind of reputation," even though the thought of him kissing anyone but her made her want to punch someone herself, "so perhaps he is exceptional at it. In which case, I am a very lucky woman," she finished in a smug tone she would only allow herself to use when alone with Margaret. Even if she had to ignore the parts of her brain that were telling her he didn't really want to utilize his vast kissing skill on his wife.

"Hmph."

"Anyway, how are you? What are you doing with yourself now that I am not here to bother?"

Margaret looked up at the ceiling and pursed her lips. "A little bit of this and that," she said vaguely. And irritatingly.

"That, as you well know, tells me nothing." She leaned forward and touched Margaret on the knee. "How is it here? Honestly?"

Margaret's eyes glittered. "Honestly? It's terrible. But don't worry about me, I have a plan."

Isabella narrowed her eyes. "What kind of plan?" Because the last time Margaret had a plan it involved a ferret, a six-foot-long piece of rope, and two cherry pies. It was very messy.

"Never mind that. Take my mind off things here, what have you been doing?"

"Well, starting to think about having a ball. The duke and I—that is, Nicholas and I—decided that we would have it in a few weeks, and he's left everything up to me, so I'll be planning the entire thing."

Margaret beamed. "You are so wonderful at that, if he doesn't love you already he will love you afterward."

Isabella held her hand up. "Wait, the last time we actually spoke about him, and my marriage, you were discussing what I could do to escape, if need be. Now you're talking about love?" That would be entirely unexpected— that he love her. Or, for that matter, that she love him.

It was enough that they tolerate each other, maybe even enjoy each other's company.

Wasn't it?

"But that was before I met him," Margaret said. "Now that I've met him, he seems awfully nice. And good for you."

"What with the bleeding face and the penchant for boxing rings?"

Margaret rolled her eyes. "No, not just that. The way he looked at you, as though he wanted to know what you thought, not just admiring you, like so many of the other gentlemen did. As that duke that was did, too. He just wanted you as a possession, someone to be his duchess and be perfect. This duke seems like he actually wants you—Isabella."

The words, so casually tossed out by her sister, seemed to pierce through to her soul.

Could he actually want her? Want the person inside the beautiful casing?

She'd never imagined that anyone would actually want her, the woman underneath the facade that had been so carefully nurtured.

It terrified her.

"Are you all right?" Apparently her terror must have shown on her face—something the normally perfect Isabella would never let happen.

What if she were to become . . . less perfect? Would she become more truly Isabella?

That thought was almost more terrifying than the first one.

But, she thought, it was most terrifying to remain as she was—pristine, perfect, and polished to such a bright shine she couldn't recognize herself.

"Prince?"

"Catherine, he is not simply going to perk up his ears and come trotting out of the forest just because you call out his name. Which isn't even his name, but his title," Jane said crossly.

They'd been riding for over three hours, and so far they had seen trees, brushes, streams, and grass.

A veritable rainbow of green things.

"Well, how should we call him?" Catherine said reasonably.

"His name, of course." Until Jane realized she didn't know his name. He was just the prince, her husband. "Oh, fine," she muttered. "Prince!" she shouted.

—The Princess and the Scoundrel

Chapter 19

Nicholas left his study and walked into the foyer, relieved that Griff had had another engagement so they couldn't spend all day on the tenant improvements. Just half the day, which felt like an entire lifetime. And now he wanted to find his wife. If only he could spend half a day on wifely improvements, that would feel like the work of a moment.

"Isabella?"

"In here," she called. Nicholas paused, trying to figure out where "here" was.

"The ballroom, Your Grace," Renning said, bowing as he gestured to the door.

"Thank you," Nicholas replied, striding to fling the ballroom doors open.

It had been only a few days since they'd agreed on a date for their ball, but already the house was a whirlwind of activity, none of it involving Nicholas.

He told himself he should be grateful, and yet he

couldn't help but feel as though he were just an adjunct part of the entire thing, an ornament or a dusty lamp to be brought out for view, but not for purpose.

Not, as he well knew, that he had any idea of how to throw a party.

But still. He wished Isabella would just consult with him about any of it, perhaps on whether the champagne should be served as the guests were starting to arrive or wait until it was clear the Queen wasn't coming. Because the Queen never came, but one had to invite her nonetheless.

But Isabella didn't. She just met him at the breakfast table each morning with a furrow already creasing her lovely brow, her hands full of notes and linens and other things he had no idea of, and she would wish him a good morning before heading downstairs to the kitchen to consult with Cook, or to her sitting room to meet with Renning, or basically see anybody but him.

There were no carriage rides, no moments of conversation, nothing that indicated that they were anything more than inhabitants of the same house.

At night—well, that was an entirely different story.

Nicholas had come to count not just the hours until he could arrive in her bedroom, but the minutes. To walk into the room, so peacefully pink, and lie with her on her bed and tell stories to her, and hear her soft reminiscences, and then, oh then, they would kiss for what seemed like hours. But was likely only minutes.

He hadn't had sex in over a month. But it didn't matter anymore; when they did finally consummate their marriage, he felt as though it would be as if they were both virgins—neither of them had been with the other, and for him, it would be the first time he was making love to his wife.

His wife whom he desired with every fiber of his being, but whom he wouldn't touch until she asked him to.

The irony didn't escape him; he could tell her that he wouldn't do anything until she asked him, but then he would basically be telling her to ask him, and that was exactly not the point of it all.

He wanted her to burn for him as he did for her, to forget who she was—or more precisely, who she was supposed to be—and beg him to take her, to make her feel every sweet, sexual moment.

Meanwhile, he was going to the boxing saloon each morning after breakfast and staying there for hours, getting pummeled or doing the pummeling in order to ease some of his frustration.

Most days he returned home more bruised and occasionally more bloody, and he and Griff would go over what seemed to be an endless amount of business questions. He wondered that anybody actually *wanted* to be a duke, given how much paperwork there was.

When she did see him, and his bruises, she seemed to take it in stride, not fussing over him as she had initially.

He missed that also.

And, if he didn't say something, his wife would think he was missing part of his brain.

"You were looking for me?" she said, in a tone that sounded as though she'd already said something, and he hadn't responded.

"Uh . . . yes." He was most definitely unfamiliar, perhaps even a virgin, at having to court a woman. All the women he'd known—both biblically and otherwise—had taken very little coaxing to get them to do what he wished, whether it was to remove all their clothing for him or perhaps just fetch him a cup of tea.

He felt . . . flummoxed at not knowing what to say, or how to talk to her.

"I wanted to know if you would care to go riding with me this afternoon. If your other engagements are not too pressing." He glanced around the ballroom, which was suitably enormous. It was wallpapered in a patterned cream, and there were chandeliers every six feet or so. The floor was so shiny he could almost see his reflection, and it looked, to his unskilled eye, like they could have the ball this evening and have the house be entirely ready. But he knew, from overhearing her morning conversations with the staff, that this was far from the case.

"If you would like."

He closed the distance between them in just a few quick strides. "I did not say I demand it, Isabella." He stood close to her, wishing she would just fall into his arms or something. Anything. "I asked if you wished to go. If you do not, tell me."

They stood there, staring at each other, he quashing the urge to just pick her up and throw her over his shoulder, she thinking—well, he couldn't tell. Her expression was as serene as ever, except he could see a tiny tic at her jaw.

And now he was reviewing minute facial movements just to gauge how his wife was feeling. What kind of mess had he gotten himself into?

After what felt like an hour (but again, was likely only a minute) she opened her mouth to speak. "I would like to go riding, Nicholas, if you can wait for another half an hour."

He wanted to throw his arms up in the air in joy that she actually said what she wanted and asked for an alteration to the plan.

Instead he bowed, nearly knocking his forehead into hers since he'd stood so close to her. "I will return in half an hour," he said.

"Half an hour," she repeated, already turning away to resume her task.

"The green riding habit, Your Grace?" Robinson began to pull the garment from the wardrobe without waiting for Isabella's reply.

"No, actually." Robinson's hand stilled. "I want the black one." She'd gotten it a few years ago, when her father's sister had died. It was severe, matching its color, and it had been the only bright spot, ironically enough, through the entire period of mourning. It fit her like a glove, it made her feel strong, not pretty, and it didn't have any fussiness about it.

In other words, it was not a pink gown designed for a duchess.

"Certainly." Robinson drew the habit out and shook it off the hanger. "Should I dress your hair differently, Your Grace? To better match the habit?"

Isabella glanced in the mirror. Her hair was in its carefully coiffed curls. "No, I don't want to keep the duke waiting." She'd said half an hour, and it was just that now. She had meant to finish earlier, but then Renning had informed her of an issue with the napkins, then Cook had come to consult with a last-minute swap of hors d'oeuvres.

So now she was rushing to get ready, desperate to be with him for just a bit, but worried that he'd find her lacking.

Not that she needed to worry that he didn't like kissing; he'd proven that in the days subsequent to their first kiss. He now rushed through the stories he told her, like a child gobbling dinner to get to dessert, although he was far from a child.

She could definitely tell he was all man. And that

part, the part she wasn't supposed to notice, as a lady, but should be conversant with, as a wife, was definitely enjoying the kissing as well. She could tell that, even though she knew very little about the thing. It. The appendage in question.

"If I could—" Robinson said, gesturing to Isabella's gown.

"Oh, of course." So now she would be late to go riding with him because she was thinking of him. And his—whatever. She was an idiot.

Robinson undid the laces, and Isabella stepped out from the gown and waited as her maid readied the habit for her to put on.

So many times she'd had to stop herself from just blurting out what was on her mind: *Why haven't we done more than this?*, but again, she worried that he'd give her an answer she wasn't strong enough to hear. Not strong enough yet.

But each day she lived here, she felt the long shadows of her upbringing recede just a bit, each decision she made on her own making her feel as though she weren't the helpless duchess flower she'd been bred to be.

Not that she was solving mathematical puzzles or conquering new lands; she was deciding on guest lists and querying her cook about whether they could serve angels on horseback (they could not, it was not oyster season).

"There, Your Grace." She hadn't noticed, but somehow Robinson had managed to get her entirely dressed.

"And your hat, Your Grace."

"Thank you." Isabella glanced in the mirror as she put the hat on. It was encircled by a gauzy black ribbon, the only adornment of the entire ensemble.

She looked severe. Almost mean.

She loved it.

"Nicholas, sorry to have kept you waiting."

Nicholas turned as she descended the stairs. And swallowed, because the woman approaching him was very different from the one he'd gotten accustomed to seeing.

This woman—this tall, elegant, remote woman—was dressed entirely in black, but she didn't look as though she were in mourning. She looked, in fact, as though she were in triumph, as though she were on her way to conquer a country or two or perhaps sentence some hardened criminals to death.

Perhaps even enact the deaths herself, with one fierce glance.

And while it was, to say the least, unusual to see her that way, it wasn't unpleasant.

The opposite, in fact.

But who was he fooling? He would have found her attractive if she were wearing a burlap sack.

"I can wait for as long as you need," Nicholas replied, taking her hand to lead her down the last few steps. And wasn't that an unfortunate truth; he would wait until she was ready, which was definitely going to be longer than it was for him to be ready. Since he'd been ready since the first time he saw her, in her father's drawing room, when it wasn't entirely clear they would have to get married.

Although that had been acquisitive lust; he'd wanted to have her, to make her his, but he hadn't known anything more about her than that she was the most spectacularly beautiful woman he'd ever seen.

Now that he knew her, he knew he'd have to wait.

Agony, but the eventual result would be worth it, he knew. If they ever got there, that is.

He couldn't think about that, or he might end up punching more than an opponent; the side of a ship, perhaps, or maybe he'd go bang his head against the sidewalk for a few hours.

"Are we going to the park?" she asked as she walked to the door. He followed, glancing to where her shape was clearly delineated by the close cut of the riding habit.

He wanted to suggest they do nothing but ride horses forever.

"If that pleases you," he said.

She spun on her heel to face him, coming within six inches of his face. If Renning and the footmen hadn't been there, he would have kissed her then and there.

"I do not wish to do what pleases me," she said, in clear imitation of his earlier words. "Do you wish to do it, or not? I know what I want."

Please say me, a voice howled, deep in that primal want part of his brain. Which was getting to be the majority of his brain lately. He probably had seven percent allocated for drain irrigation, another twelve percent for remembering the names of all his new holdings, and four percent for keeping track of the events in the serial he was reading.

Which left seventy-seven percent for thoughts about what he and his wife could do together.

"I thought we would start in the park, and then see where we wished to go."

That seventy-seven percent was quite good at reading things into the most innocuous of statements. Right now, it was seeing "start in the park" as "begin kissing," and "we wished to go" ending up as "him on top of her, bringing her to climax."

He could definitely not tell Griff about this spurt of his imagination.

"Sounds like a wonderful plan." Oh, maybe she had parts of her brain thinking about that as well.

Or he was just doomed to forever be thinking about his wife that way when she was only thinking about him this way.

It was no surprise Nicholas was an excellent horseman; he was clearly fit, she'd felt the strength and hardness of his muscles whenever he'd put his arm around her. She'd allowed herself to touch his chest, very lightly, of course, when they'd kissed.

Not to mention the constant boxing. That had to do something more to him than just send him home with cuts.

She hadn't expected, however, to get such a visceral, almost carnal, thrill at how he rode; his strong body almost one with the powerful horse, with him clearly in command of the beast.

"Do you want to race?" she asked him after they'd been trotting at a reasonable pace for about fifteen minutes. They were in a more remote section of the park, one not meant to see and be seen in; just ahead she spotted a copse of trees that looked as though one could get lost in there.

She would like that, to get lost with him.

He turned his head to look at her, and she caught the glint of sly humor in his gaze. "It is not a question of if I want to race, it is if you—"

"Fine, then, we're off!" she said, cutting him off as she spurred her horse on. She caught him by surprise, and was ahead of him for about a minute before she heard him at her back, only to pass her with apparent ease.

"And when I win," he called back, but she couldn't

hear the rest of his words because, sadly for her, he was too far ahead.

He kept riding until he reached the trees, and had come to a stop by the time she arrived, his horse even having had enough time to start cropping the grass.

"Glad you could make it," he said, a smug grin on his handsome face.

Isabella tilted her head up in an imperious pose. "One wishes to arrive just late enough to make the other party aware that he is lacking her presence."

His smile changed to something more . . . serious. If a smile could be serious, which she didn't think was possible.

"I would wait forever for you, princess," he said in that low voice that made her insides tremble. "And speaking of waiting," he continued, leaping off his horse with an enviable grace, "I've been thinking of what I will demand as my prize for winning the race."

He strode over to her and leaned against her horse, staring up at her face. "I want you to tell me more of what you want."

Judging by his expression, Isabella now knew absolutely and positively that not only did he like kissing her, he was also nearly as interested as she was in the things that might happen after.

She felt her body start to react, almost before her brain did, her breasts feeling as though they were fuller, her body aware of its every movement, and precisely where he was in relation to her.

"Should I tell you here?" She barely recognized her own voice, it sounded so husky.

A knowing smile crept onto his mouth. She couldn't seem to stop looking at it, even though his beautiful eyes were just above, and as worthy of her attention.

But his mouth. She'd dreamed about that mouth.

And her attention was warranted, since that mouth opened to speak. "Not here. Not until tonight, when we're alone together. Then you can tell me what you want."

She resisted the urge to demand what time it was now, and how much longer they would have to wait, feeling the shivers of anticipation flow throughout her body.

Tonight. If she could just think of the words, she could tell him. Tonight.

Not surprisingly, nobody answered their calls.

Jane and Catherine kept shouting intermittently, just because they'd been in the habit of doing so and couldn't seem to stop. Only there was no answer. Just birds or squirrels or some other woodland creatures scampering off because they were startled.

Jane glanced up at the sky, which was showing signs of darkening. And she hadn't thought the slightest about where they would sleep.

"Over there, my lady," Catherine said, gesturing to where a few plumes of smoke curled up into the clouds.

"Remind me to give you a rise in wages, Catherine," Jane muttered as she urged her horse, who began to trot toward the signs of life.

"Give me a rise, my lady," Catherine replied, a cheeky grin on her face.

—THE PRINCESS AND THE SCOUNDREL

Chapter 20

Nicholas bolted from his room as soon as Miller had helped him with his robe. He would have normally told Miller just to leave him be, but now that he was about to claim his prize—sort of—he wanted to savor the moment.

So he forced himself to patiently wait as Miller helped him remove his clothing, folding everything just so, and then got him into his nightshirt. He even waited as Miller fussed about which robe would be best, given that one was older but that one was warmer.

"Whichever you prefer," Nicholas said, willing himself not to yell at his valet. It wasn't Miller's fault he'd had a cockstand since she'd asked, "Shall I tell you here?" It had been difficult enough not to say yes, and toss her onto the grass.

Not very ducal of him. Not even very gentlemanly, in fact.

"Isabella?" He pushed her door open without waiting for a reply.

And there she sat, as usual, at her dressing table, her lady's maid holding her brush. But there was something different about her face.

Or maybe he was just hoping there was.

But she seemed—*strong*, nearly as strong as she'd appeared while they were riding and she had on that black riding habit.

Only now, now she was wearing some sort of frilly night rail with loads of lace and some random ribbons and what seemed to be an entire window curtain's worth of material.

She should have looked ludicrous, like an overdecorated cake. But instead she looked— He couldn't find the words. His imagination had left him, just when he needed it most.

And he was gaping. "You look lovely," he said at last, not even caring that her lady's maid was still in the room. Not the best words, but at least he'd been able to form some sort of sentence.

She spoke without taking her eyes off him. "You may go, Robinson."

Robinson walked past him, giving a quick bow, but he barely noticed. Except noticing that she was gone. Thank God.

"Come," she said, standing as she held her hand out to him. They walked the now familiar path to her bed, then both sat, assuming their usual positions—with her tucked into his shoulder, his fingers on her upper arm.

"I've been thinking about what we spoke about all day," she said, after a moment. He tried to keep his breaths even, since it felt as though he wanted to hold his breath or breathe hard, and he didn't think either would be useful.

Unless he wanted either to faint from lack of oxygen or to sound like a panting dog. Then, perhaps, he could choose one of those courses.

"And what do you think?"

Damn it, he was holding his breath. Hopefully she wouldn't take too long to speak again.

"I would like to do more than just kiss you. I want to discover what is next. With you," she clarified, as though he might think she was about to go run off with some other man and "do more" with him.

The very thought—theoretical though it was—made Nicholas want to punch something.

"And what would you like to do?" he asked. He needed to find out precisely what she meant, so he didn't scare her. Forever.

"That is the problem," she said in a frustrated tone. "I don't know what is next, so I don't know what to ask for."

"Ah, I see." Nicholas tilted his head back against the headboard. "Well, I think the first thing would be for you to become more familiar with our bodies." He removed his arm from around her and drew his shirt up over his head, tossing it wherever it landed.

After all, he was a duke, and dukes weren't required to fold their clothing. Even though a tiny part of him felt badly for Miller or Robinson or whoever would be tasked with picking up all the strewed clothing he hoped to, well, *strew* tonight.

"Oh!" she said, her eyes wide as her gaze traveled all over him, from his face to his shoulders, down his chest, quickly lower, then just as quickly back up again. "Can I—?" and she reached her fingers out before she could finish her sentence and put them on his chest, so lightly it felt like a whisper.

Even though he felt the impact of her touch all over his body.

"Is this—?" Apparently she was now incapable of finishing her thought, which was fine, because he was having issues with that himself.

She placed her palm flat on his chest, and held it there, her fingers splayed, her expression—well, he wasn't sure what she was feeling, since she looked so shocked. But not necessarily in a bad way. Or in a good way.

Damn it, now he couldn't even process his thoughts in his head. And of the two of them, he was presumed to know what he was doing.

"You feel so different than I do," she said, seemingly able to complete a sentence. Even though he doubted he could say anything at the moment. She smoothed her palm over his skin, and each place she touched felt as though it had been electrified. "It's very hard," she mused, catching her lower lip in her teeth.

Oh, princess, if you only knew, he thought.

It wasn't as though she were precisely in the dark about what a man with no shirt looked like. Although, actually, she really had only seen shirtless laborers working in the fields when she'd been riding in her family's carriage, so she hadn't gotten a close look. So perhaps she was in the dark about it.

Although, thank goodness, her room was lit with candles so she wasn't actually in the dark and could see what she was touching.

His chest was broad and firm, his skin darker than hers, light brown hair, of all things, on the top part of his chest. It felt ticklish under her hand, and she trailed her fingers through it. She dragged her finger across his nipple, so different from hers.

Not that she'd made a study of what hers looked like, but they were not brown and flat, like his. She was certain of that.

He inhaled sharply, and she snatched her hand away. "Did I hurt you?" Were men's nipples so sensitive?

He took her hand and put it back, right where she'd been touching. "No, the opposite." His voice was low and husky and nearly ragged, and she knew—even though she had no way of knowing, but she knew—that he was liking what she was doing, that he was affected by it, and that it was making his voice get all low like that.

And happily enough, she liked that as well.

She rubbed across his nipple again, and he breathed out again, sharp and fast through his nose. His palms were placed flat on the bed beside his body, and it appeared that he was pressing them down. So as not to touch her? Or not to make her stop?

No, but if he'd wanted her to stop he would have said so—"Tell me what you want," after all—and she already knew he liked it.

Was he so afraid of what might happen? Was it possible that the rumors about him weren't true, and he was awkward with women?

If so, they would just have to learn together. And she would encourage him to explore her as much as she was going to explore him.

Which meant she would have to get undressed, at least as much as he was.

She kept one hand on his chest—and just even thinking that she had her hand on a part of him that was normally under clothing made her want to swoon and shout, all at the same time—while she undid the bow at the neck of her dressing gown with the other.

His hooded gaze stayed on her hand, his tongue

reaching out to lick his lip as he watched her shrug, admittedly quite awkwardly, out of the sleeves. She wriggled to let the garment drop to the bed.

She was only in her night rail, an item of clothing that only women, usually her relatives, had seen her in. It hadn't seemed to matter that much before whether the fabric was sheer or opaque, but now she was acutely aware that the shape of her body was likely outlined, with the candlelight behind her, and that he was—well, he was staring.

As though he'd never seen a woman before, poor thing.

"Do you need help with that?" he asked in a strangled voice. His chest was heaving as though he'd just run a race, and she felt a moment of smug triumph that she had rendered him to this with just a few touches to his chest and the removal of her dressing gown.

Although she didn't want to kill him by going too quickly, did she?

But on the other hand, his hands were reaching toward her, as though they really wished to touch her, and she felt bad for him that he hadn't gotten up the nerve yet.

She took one of the hands that was waving about in the air and brought it to her chest. Not precisely on her breast, but just above. She kept her hand on his, then guided his palm down, so that his smallest finger was on the top curve of her breast.

And then it seemed he lost his shyness, because his hand kept going down until he had his palm entirely around her, his thumb resting on her nipple, just as she'd touched his.

No wonder he'd made those sounds and reacted that way when she touched him. It felt wonderful, as though her whole being were centered just there, and she knew she wanted more, wanted to feel both of his hands on her, wanted to have him explore how she felt just as she wanted to continue exploring him.

"You like this." It wasn't a question—honestly, when would someone actually want her opinion about something?—but she didn't care, because she did, she absolutely did like this.

"Yes," she said, surprised to hear how breathy she sounded. As though she, too, had run a race.

He took his hand off her, and she felt her mouth nearly turn into a pout, but then he slid his fingers underneath the fabric of her night rail and repeated the movement from before, moving his hand down, only now it was just his bare skin on her bare skin, and it felt even more incredible.

And then—oh!—his fingers curled around her breast, and he touched her nipple again and she wanted to say something only she didn't think she could form words. Or even really form thoughts.

It must have looked awkward, since his elbow was at a right angle and his hand was down her gown—down her gown!—but she didn't care how silly it must have looked because no one but them was here anyway, and he didn't look as though he wanted to laugh.

In fact, if she had to categorize his look, it would be one of intense scrutiny. His eyes were locked on her chest, watching as his fingers played with her nipple, caressed the round flesh of her breast, and his mouth was slightly open, his tongue licking his lips every so often.

"Dear God, you are lovely," he breathed, then did something even more unexpected than intense scrutinizing and lip licking and fondling of nipples.

He leaned forward and bent his head to her chest, then placed his mouth where his finger had just been.

On her nipple.

It was through the fabric, of course, but it was his mouth. On her.

And then he licked her, through the fabric, dampening it so it clung to her, and her nipple was poking out, like when she was chilled, only she felt the opposite, as though there were a fire burning inside her.

Somehow his hands were on her waist, holding her still, as though she were going to go anywhere. She might never leave this place as long as she kept feeling like this.

She felt something react lower still, where the things were supposed to happen, only she didn't know that ladies could feel this—this heaviness, this yearning ache, that seemed to flow from his mouth throughout her entire body.

"Touch me," he murmured as he lifted his mouth, presumably to take a breath. His hand found hers and placed it on his body, only now her hand was on his side, not his chest, and she ran it down to his waist, feeling the flex of his muscles under her palm.

Meanwhile, his mouth was doing wonderful, wicked things to her, and then he moved to the other nipple while he moved his hand from her waist to cup her breast in his hand.

She couldn't keep track, in fact, of where everything was—his mouth was on her right nipple, his hand on her left, her hand was on his waist, he was leaning forward while her legs were bent to the side, and it should have been much more uncomfortable than it was.

Because it felt blissful. And amazing. And her body and her brain were fully aware of how incredible it felt, and still, both were demanding more. More of what, she had no idea.

Just more.

He lifted his mouth from her and blew on her, causing a shiver to run down her spine. Before she could notice, however, that his mouth wasn't doing wicked, lovely things to her any longer, he was kissing her again, his arms now wrapped entirely around her, holding her tightly against his chest, that gorgeous, hard, muscular chest. The pressure of his body felt right, and she squirmed in his arms to get closer still, until he broke the kiss and put his forehead on her shoulder, gasping.

"You're killing me, princess," he said in a voice so low she thought perhaps only dogs could hear it. Well, dogs and her.

"I am?" Her voice, on the other hand, sounded as though she had just ascended a high altitude carrying a bag of bricks.

In other words, entirely and completely breathless.

"You are," he replied in that same growl, only with a hint of humor in it, as though he knew she'd been mentally comparing his voice to one in a dog's audio range or her to some sort of brave, brick-carrying mountain climber.

But she couldn't think of anything when he leaned back, a quirk of a smile on his mouth, and took her hand, putting it there.

On his whatever.

"Where did you come from?" The farmer strode out from his barn, pieces of hay clinging to his shirt, his boots muddy and who knew what else.

Jane had never actually spoken to a laborer, and she was gratified she could understand him.

"The castle, you dolt," Catherine said. "Where do you think ladies come from?"

The farmer grinned and leaned back, putting his fists on his hips. "Well, if you was to ask me where ladies and gentlemen come from, I'd have no choice but to tell you." He glanced from Catherine to Jane and back to Catherine. "Should I be having that conversation with your lady here?"

Jane's face grew hot. She wasn't naive any longer, she was a married woman, but there were some things that she'd never heard discussed.

"Hush, you," Catherine said in a chiding voice.

"Never mind that, you rascal. We're looking for the prince. Have you seen him?"

The farmer glanced around as though surprised. "Oh, I forgot, he's sitting in my kitchen having a cup of tea." His face creased into a scowl. "Of course I ain't seen your prince. Have you lost him, then?"

"Yes, I have," Jane replied, a thick lump forming in her throat.

—THE PRINCESS AND THE SCOUNDREL

Chapter 21

*H*e hadn't meant to put her hand on his cock.

Although now that it was there, he didn't know why he hadn't done it before; say, perhaps, the first time he met her, in her parents' drawing room.

Never mind, that would have been awkward.

Just as this was, actually. She had frozen, as any young lady might, her hand on him, but not doing anything, not moving, just . . . frozen. Her lips were parted, her eyes were wide, and she was breathing in quick, short bursts.

"Uh," she said, and then, thank God, she did move her palm, placing it more firmly on his erection.

So help him, he was going to spend in about thirty-seven seconds.

He gripped her wrist. "Do you feel what you do to me?" he asked, hoping she wasn't about to run off. Fuck it, he'd ask. He'd demanded to know what she wanted, after all. And that would include what she didn't want, as well. "You're not scared, are you? Or about to run off?"

Her eyes were as huge and round as a full moon, but she shook her head. Thank God. "No, neither." She made some sort of tentative motion that felt incredible, if unskilled (of course), and settled herself more comfortably on the bed. "What do you want me to do?"

He didn't want to tell her what to do, hadn't he decided that? Only his gentlemanly and husbandly resolve was wavering in the face—or rather the hand—of the moment. But he could tell her what to do now without necessarily be telling her what to do entirely, right?

If only he had Griff's ability to argue in circumlocution, he'd have been able to convince himself that fucking her right now, hard and fast, was the most honorable thing he could possibly do.

He had never wanted to be more like Griff in his entire life.

"I want you to do what feels comfortable for you," he said in as firm a tone as he could muster.

She rolled her eyes at him. "What about what is comfortable for you? Because I am here, and we are— and you are—and, and . . ." and she gestured with her other hand, thank goodness, because if she had moved her hand off him he would have sobbed or howled or done some other unmanly-type thing.

"Touch me. Just—touch me." And he waited as she tilted her head and thought about it, her mouth wet and swollen from their kisses, the fabric of her nightgown damp from his tongue, her nipples poking out jauntily, taunting him.

"Like this?" she asked, rubbing her palm over him, frustratingly over the cloth of his breeches, since he hadn't trusted himself to wear just a nightshirt to bed since they'd started kissing.

Still, it felt as good as having your wife, the most beautiful woman you'd ever seen, sitting on a bed with you with her palm on you.

So pretty damn good.

"Yes," he said through gritted teeth. "Yes, only harder, only . . ."

He closed his eyes so he could ask her without begging. Too much. "Would you be comfortable with me removing my breeches?"

And kept his eyes shut because, so help him, if she looked terrified or disgusted or appalled, he might never recover.

"Yes," she said, finally, in a soft whisper. *Whispers are always soft*, a voice yelled at him, probably in Griff's practical tone of voice. Still. It was a very soft whisper.

But, thankfully, he'd heard it.

He opened his eyes and took a deep breath, then scooted back on the bed so he wasn't touching her. He swung his feet over to the floor and stood, his back to her, undoing the falls of his breeches, pushing the garment to the floor so he was only in his smallclothes. One part of him wanted to take those off also—one guess what part it was—only he wasn't willing to push things. He had only one chance at this, and he was going to do it properly.

One thing at a time.

He sat back down on the bed and returned to face her. She didn't look scared, and he congratulated himself on taking it slowly, since he knew that this would have had a much different outcome if they had begun it all that first night, when he'd been drowning in passion for her, when he'd only longed to see her naked and underneath him.

Well, so exactly like now, only now he had gotten to know the woman underneath, and that just made him more determined to ensure she was as comfortable with this as he was. Or uncomfortable, given how his erection was throbbing, thrusting out from his body demanding—no, requiring—attention.

"Oh my," she said, looking down at last.

He didn't want to preen at how she was looking at him. But his cock certainly did.

He leaned forward and took her hand in his, pulling her so she had to move. He returned to their usual positions against the headboard, pulling her into his arms.

"Are you all right?" he asked, allowing himself to rest his hand on her hip. Her night rail was rucked up, and he could see her legs from the knees down. Even her feet were beautiful, long and slender and elegant, currently wiggling around at the end of the bed as though dancing.

Horizontal dancing. If that wasn't a euphemism, he didn't know what was. And Griff said he wasn't good with words or imagination. Ha! He just had to have the right material to inspire him. Like her.

"I am fine," she said, reaching her hand across his body, mirroring his action by placing her hand on his hip. "Can I touch you again?" she asked.

Oh my God. He might just die from joy now, only then that would mean he'd never get to touch her more thoroughly. "Yes," he said, his voice a rasp as he drew himself out from his smallclothes, "please do."

And she moved her hand over and gripped him. Both of them were looking at her fingers encircling his cock, neither one of them moving.

He should probably tell her what he wanted. Because if he didn't, he might die from frustration.

"What should I do?"

He exhaled and put his hand on top of hers. "Move your hand up and down, like this," he said, running her hand up and down his shaft. He kept his motions at a steady pace, then let go when he thought she had probably gotten the rhythm down.

And she had. She kept right on touching him, rubbing him, up and down, her fingers barely meeting each other around his cock. He couldn't stop looking at how delicate and fine her hand looked against him, her skin pale against the flush of his erection.

"It's so hard and soft at the same time," she said, not sounding as though she were horrified, thank goodness, but merely observing.

"Mmph," Nicholas replied, not able to maintain a conversation.

"And then what—oh!" she said as he climaxed, spilling all over his hand, his smallclothes, her hand, his stomach, and likely on the bed as well.

Not quite thirty-seven seconds, but not nearly as long as he usually could go for. To be fair, however, it had been quite a long time. And it was she. So he couldn't feel bad about how quickly it had all occurred.

She let go right away and scooted away, and if he'd been able to, he would have tried to reassure her that what she'd done had been marvelous, and that this was the desired effect.

But all he could do was feel the pleasure coursing through his body, along with a substantial amount of regret that he hadn't explained things better.

"Isabella," he began, when he could finally speak. She hadn't left, but her posture wasn't exactly what a man wished to see after a woman had just brought him release; she was leaning away from him, her eyes darting from the mess on his stomach to the mess on the bed, all the while she was wiping her hand on her nightgown.

He'd made an actual mess of things.

"That was . . ." she began, her brow creased in thought.

He barely dared to breathe waiting for what she might say—horrible? Disgusting? Never to happen again?

Please don't let it be the last one, he thought. The first two he might be able to get through, but not the last one.

"—unexpected," she said at last, nodding in satisfaction, it seemed, for having found the right word.

Nicholas couldn't help but laugh. "Not quite, since that is what generally happens when—well, when," and now he was unexpectedly surprised to find he was embarrassed to discuss the subject with his wife.

He'd never shied away from frank talk with his partners, but on the other hand, his partners hadn't been delicate virgins who didn't know how a man's penis functioned.

"When what?" she said, as though she were interested.

"When a man has an orgasm."

"Oh," she replied, as though she understood. Which she did not, since then she asked, "What is an orgasm?"

Oh, princess, he thought, *that is such an excellent question.*

Even though he'd made intriguing noises, low in his throat, and he'd seemed unable to speak at certain points, and even though she'd touched him there, right on that part that she was only supposed to encounter as a married woman—which she was, thankfully—she still didn't see signs of his being an animalistic beast, intent only on his own desires.

Because, for example, instead of just leaving after he'd had his own pleasure, he'd tucked her up in his arms again, after making sure she was comfortable, and was now stroking her side, just under her breast.

His mouth was positioned just above her ear, and she straightened up so his lips were actually right at her ear, hoping he would say something. Or kiss her. Or something.

"Do you trust me?" he asked, at last, after a few moments of touching and silence and her feeling an urgency in that area that she'd been told was just for his pleasure, not hers.

She was beginning to wonder if her mother had been seriously mistaken about all of this. And then chided herself—of course her mother was mistaken.

"I do," she murmured, then put her palm on top of his hand where it lay on her, and moved it to her breast. She couldn't think about how bold she was being, because if she did she'd stop, and that was the last thing she wanted, what with all the tingling sensations down there, and how his soft, warm breath sent shivers down her spine.

"Good. Then allow me to demonstrate what an orgasm is," he said, thumbing her nipple so it rose into a stiff peak. God, she wanted his mouth on her again, wanted his whole weight on her, in fact, and wanted to find out just what would happen next.

She thought it likely wouldn't happen quickly enough. But instead of being impatient—well, she was impatient, but in a deliciously anticipatory way—she was savoring the moments even as her mind was wondering what was next.

And it seemed she might not have long to wait. He undid himself from behind her, then slid alongside her, running his fingers along her jaw and turning her face to his. "Kiss me," he said in that low, luscious voice, and she sighed, raising her mouth to his.

He didn't put his tongue into her mouth, as he had before, he just held himself still as she pressed her lips to his. Frustrated, she let out a little growl in her throat, a sound she barely recognized as coming from her, and licked his lips, then slid her tongue between them. His hand was on her breast again, and he was caressing it, rubbing his palm over the nipple, holding the weight of her in his hand.

She reached around to his back and pressed herself closer to him, the part that was aching and needy now pushed up against his hip. She wanted more.

Her tongue danced and licked inside his mouth, and he responded, but didn't take the lead. She understood, without his saying it, which would have been difficult, given that they were kissing anyway, that everything was up to her pace. She knew, somehow, he didn't want to frighten her, and, oh God, he wasn't. If anything, she was frightened of all the passion that seemed to be lurking inside her, hidden from her for all this time, until right now.

He broke the kiss first, gasping as he pressed his forehead to hers. His hand moved from her breast to her waist to her hip. "You might be the death of me," he said in a low rasp, and she felt oddly proud that she'd brought him to this place, this pleasurable place where they weren't the duke or duchess, or even really Nicholas and Isabella, but instead were just man and woman.

"There has to be something more," she murmured, realizing she was pushing that spot into his returned erection. It made for an exquisite ache, but it wasn't enough. It might never be enough.

"As long as you trust me," he said, gripping her hip tighter.

"Yes," she said, wondering if now was the time he would enter her. "Unpleasant and awkward," her mother had said, but she felt the opposite. Maybe that would all change when they were joined?

But it didn't seem as though that was in his plan, because he moved lower down her body, sliding his palm from her hip to her leg, then putting his fingers between her thighs and moving her leg so it was over his shoulder.

Which put his mouth right—"Ah," she yelped as his mouth closed on her. Now he was kissing her *there*, causing tremors of sensation throughout her entire body, that delicious ache now intensified so it was almost painful, but she would die if he stopped. His fingers were holding her legs apart, her instinct to close herself up against him, even as she exulted in what he was doing.

"Mm, so sweet," he said as he licked, one long, slow lick she felt all the way to her toes. "Do you like this?" he asked before he did something that made her unable to answer except in a moan that he seemed to understand.

He chuckled against her, and she found her hands were in his hair, holding him to her, even though he showed no signs of wishing to leave.

"Oh, oh," she said, flinging her head back against the pillow, her body feeling as though it were on fire, as though something was lighting her from within. And she knew the source of the burn—his mouth, his tongue, doing amazing things to her as she felt herself spiral up toward some heretofore unknown destination.

She fell into the feeling, losing herself entirely, not thinking, not conscious of anything but how it felt, how good it felt, how she had never felt so entirely good in her life. And she knew there was still more.

"Nicholas," she breathed, and looked down at him, at his head which was between her legs, his strong hands holding her thighs, his back which was just as muscular and intriguing as his front, of course.

He increased his rhythm, and she was lost, feeling herself crest on a wave of pleasure that made her shake with its intensity.

"Oh," she said, finally, when she had fallen down enough from the feeling to speak again.

He was watching her, a knowing, satisfied look in his eyes. His mouth moist from her, from where he'd been—"Oh!" she repeated, turning her head to bury it in her arm.

She felt his fingers nudging her chin up. "Don't be embarrassed, princess," he said, his voice husky. "It was amazing watching you have your first orgasm— that was your first, was it not?" She nodded, keeping her eyes focused anywhere but his face. "And I look forward to giving you many more."

She finally felt brave enough to meet his gaze again, and she felt like melting all over again when she saw his expression—so proudly male and smug she nearly laughed.

"Thank you," she said, finally releasing the death grip on his hair.

He grinned at her and raised himself up on his arms over her body, as though he were going to—

But he didn't. Instead he kissed her on the forehead.

"Let's go to sleep, shall we? We have our ball the day after next, and we both need to get some rest."

Isabella barely suppressed an irritated hmph, but allowed him to curl up behind her, his hardness pressing into her backside. "Doesn't that hurt?" she mumbled, suddenly feeling very sleepy.

"I'm fine," he said into her neck. "Sleep, princess."

"We have misplaced him," Jane replied.

The farmer looked askance, as he might. The prince was not an item of clothing to be mislaid, after all.

"Or he has misplaced himself," Catherine added, not helpfully at all.

The farmer put his hands on his hips and leaned his head back. "He hasn't been here. But you might be able to find out where he might have gotten to. We've got our own witch, she can answer questions. For a price."

Jane nodded firmly. "Where will we find this witch, then?"

—THE PRINCESS AND THE SCOUNDREL

Chapter 22

Nicholas felt the punch throughout his entire body. He'd thought, mistakenly, that perhaps he wouldn't need to go to the boxing saloon this morning, because of what they'd done the night before, but if anything, his need for her had increased.

Eventually, he was able to wear his opponent down, but not without taking quite a few hits himself. Which Griff noticed.

"What in God's name were you thinking?" Griff snarled, unwrapping Nicholas's hand. "Because you sure as hell didn't have your mind on the boxing."

The way she shuddered under his mouth, how her hand felt as she grasped him, not to mention how smooth and beautiful her skin was, even though he had yet to see her entirely naked.

"This and that," Nicholas replied, shrugging. He knew he'd feel the effect of the punches later, but right now all he felt was euphoria. That he'd gotten her to trust him enough, that he'd finally tasted her, that there was even more to come—so to speak—between the two of them.

That marriage was, thus far, more than he'd dreamed of.

"You're an idiot," Griff replied through gritted teeth. He reached into a tub of some sort of unguent, then began to smooth it over the places Nicholas had gotten hit.

"Ouch, that smarts," Nicholas said, flinching at the contact. His brother just shook his head and kept rubbing it in, ignoring Nicholas's increasingly virulent cursing.

"Heard you're throwing a ball." The voice was instantly recognizable, even though he'd only heard it the once. The duke, or former duke, that is, standing in front of him, fists planted on his hips, a disdainful look on his face.

"It seems your invitation was lost in the post," Griff said. Nicholas was startled to hear his brother speak so disdainfully—maybe being a duke's secretary had made him more assured? Or perhaps Griff was feeling more confident in general.

Not that he could think about anybody but himself now.

The man shrugged. Nicholas would have to get his name in one of these encounters. Especially if they were to be meeting in the House of Lords. He couldn't very well address him as "the former duke" or "the duke that was."

"It doesn't matter," the man sneered. "Soon enough I'll be back where I belong, and you'll have nothing but your memories of being important for a few weeks. I wonder if your duchess will stay by your side when you lose your title?"

Nicholas's chest squeezed at the mention of Isabella. "Leave my wife out of this," he said, feeling his fists clench. Griff stepped to the side, as though making room should Nicholas wish to stand up and punch the bastard. That was what he should just refer to him as— the bastard.

And he did want to punch the bastard, of course, but there were at least ten other gentlemen in the room, all of them watching the conversation. If any of them happened to be sympathetic to the former duke's cause, Nicholas might find himself not a duke, with Isabella not a duchess. He didn't care much himself, except as it affected her, his holdings, his entire staff, and—

Well, it seemed he did care. Damn it.

"Your wife only married you because of the title. That's why her parents made the bargain with me, after all. What will happen when the title, the land, and the money are all gone? Because I will see to it, Mr. Smithfield, rest assured." He bent down to get right in Nicholas's face, his words coming fast and sharp. "And you won't be able to do a thing. Maybe I'll let her stay as my whore."

Nicholas snapped then, leaping up, fists cocked.

Only to find that Griff was holding his arms in back of him, kneeing him in the leg to make him buckle at the same time.

"Don't do it, Nick," Griff said. "That's what he wants."

"No, that's not what I want," the former duke replied. "I want my title back. I want what is mine. And I will get it," he said, punctuating his words with a poke to one of the sore spots on Nicholas's chest.

"What is your name, anyway?" Nicholas asked, causing both the bastard and Griff to start.

"My name? The Duke of Gage, of course," he replied.

"No, not that name. You have to have another name, don't you?" Nicholas strove to keep his tone as polite as possible. As polite, that is, as he could be, given that Griff was still holding him back from punching the bastard who, as yet, had no name that Nicholas knew.

"Lord Collingwood." The man sounded as though he wished he were in a position to punch Nicholas as well. At least they had their mutual desire to pummel each other in common.

"Not pleased to make your acquaintance, Lord Collingwood. I will be glad to meet you in the ring at any time of your choosing."

"I will prefer, Mr. Smithfield, to see you in a more formal setting. Parliament will do."

He punctuated his words with one final poke to

Nicholas's chest, then spun on his heel and walked out of the saloon.

"I don't believe holding one's employer back from making an ass of himself is within a secretary's purview," Griff said, releasing Nicholas.

"No, but it is damn well within a brother's right," Nicholas said. "Thank you."

Griff put his hand up to his ear. "What was that? Did my brother actually thank me for something?"

Nicholas scowled and punched Griff none too gently on the arm. "Don't get used to it, from either employer or sibling."

"Unless it happens again," Griff said in a sly tone of voice.

"Watch yourself, or I won't teach you all I know about a certain subject." Although he now was only going to teach the subject himself, not practice it. At least not on any woman but Isabella, and he wasn't going to share any of his experiences with his wife with his brother. That would be—well, it would be wrong. And distasteful. He'd never felt as though his allegiance lay with anyone but his brother before, but now, now that he'd felt her tremble under his touch, and heard her soft moans, and shared what he liked with her in a way he hadn't with anybody, ever before, it felt entirely different. As though his heart had been doubled in size, with one part remaining tied to his brother, and the other part sworn to her.

It made him feel oddly vulnerable. He'd never felt vulnerable, not in terms of a woman before. Or ever, actually. Griff was his younger brother, Nicholas had always been the one to lead.

Now, he realized, he wanted her to lead. He wanted her to tell him what she wanted, and he wanted to do it. For her. For them, eventually, but mostly for her. Since it seemed as though no one had ever wanted her to choose what she wanted. They wanted her to choose what they wanted so it would be more convenient for them.

He wouldn't ever do that to her, even if it meant it was less convenient for him. He just hoped he would never have to face that eventuality.

"The duke is out again, isn't he?" Did the man ever get a full night's sleep? Was getting himself hit, and presumably hitting another person as well, worth losing sleep over?

"He is, Your Grace." Renning held Isabella's chair out as she settled herself into it, sniffing at the pleasant smells of breakfast. She hadn't expected to be so hungry today—perhaps her hunger today was due to what had happened the night before. In which case, no wonder so many men were able to eat so much more than she was. From what she'd heard, men were always having such occurrences. That they were able to function normally and not wander about in search of their next orgasm was a marv— Oh, she thought, nearly giggling. Many men did seem to do that, she just hadn't known what they were about before.

"Sausage, Your Grace?" Renning held out a salver piled high with sausages, which resembled— *Stop it, Isabella*, she chided herself. Really, how did people function with part of one's brain constantly thinking about those types of things?

"No, thank you." She couldn't actually bear to eat one of the sausages. Even though she absolutely was not going to think such salacious thoughts. "Just tea and toast, please."

She'd be surprised if she could actually taste any food today. Maybe she wouldn't taste ever again. She felt as though she'd fractured last night, and had been put back together even stronger. As though all that— she still couldn't name it even in her own mind—had opened a door that she just had to step through.

And she would. Or at least she would try. He wanted her to say what she wanted, didn't he? She just had to open her mind to the possibilities of whatever those things might be. And not just those things, but all sorts of things.

It was exciting, and terrifying, and absolutely what she wanted.

She heard the door open as Renning was putting a plate in front of her, and within a few moments Nicholas himself had arrived, looking—as usual—as though he'd been planting his face into the side of somebody's fist.

She would not share that thought with him, however. He kissed her brow, grabbed a sausage and bit it in half, making Isabella wince.

"Sorry, awful table manners," he replied, noticing her expression, then took the napkin Renning was holding out and wiped his mouth. He sat in the chair adjacent to hers, nodding as Renning approached with coffee and a plate.

Isabella waited until Renning had finished, then spoke to him. "If you'll excuse us?"

"Of course, Your Grace, Your Grace." Renning bowed his way out of the room, leaving Isabella, Nicholas, and a half-eaten sausage.

"How are you this morning, Isabella?" Nicholas's face had a smug expression as though he knew precisely how she was.

And he was right, damn him.

"I am fine, Nicholas. And you?" She gestured to his face. "How was your daily thrashing?"

"I beg your pardon," he replied, sitting up straight. "I was not thrashed. I was *boxing*."

She waved her hand dismissively, her tone almost flirtatiously light. "Whatever you call it." And then paused as the thought occurred to her. Like a door opening, showing her something she'd never imagined before. It made her catch her breath, but in a good way. And what was to prevent her from asking? "I was wondering—would you be able to teach me some of the sport?"

He gaped at her, the expression on his face so comical she nearly burst out laughing. Although that would not be at all duchesslike, would it? Or even ladylike. It definitely would not be Isabella-like, that was for certain.

In which case, perhaps she should burst out laughing once in a while. Just to see how it felt.

But the moment had passed.

"Teach you how to box?" His voice held an incredulous note she'd never heard. And she felt herself stiffen, as though he'd criticized her. Had found her less than perfect.

I am not perfect, she wanted to yell. To him, as well as to herself.

"Yes. Precisely." She deliberately looked away and put another lump of sugar in her tea, even though it already had enough. Just so she could feel what it was like to do something unexpected.

Pathetic, really, that putting an extra lump of sugar in one's tea was unexpected, but she had to take tiny steps. Or tiny punches. The question was, did he really mean what he'd said? What he'd seemed to promise, last night, and the other nights when he'd encouraged her to say what she wanted?

"You haven't said if you would. Will you teach me how to box, Nicholas?"

Of all the things she could have asked, he would never have thought of this question. Perhaps he was, indeed, lacking in imagination, as Griff said. But the thought of her—his lovely, fragile, beautiful wife—getting into a ring, allowing anyone near her perfect features, was enough to make him want to punch somebody himself. Even if that somebody was she.

"Uh . . ." he stammered, watching as her expression changed from one of mere curiosity to something darker.

"You don't want me to say what I want, then," she said, glancing away from him as she poured more tea into her cup.

"I'll teach you, you just—you just surprised me." He sounded lame. He sounded as though he were lying. He sounded as though he didn't want her to say what she wanted, even though he'd been encouraging her to do so almost from the first moment they were wed.

"You needn't." She had that icily polite tone to her voice, the one she used with everyone but her sister. The one he hated.

"I will."

She shrugged, as though she didn't believe him, but was too polite to call him on his subterfuge. "After the ball, we will see."

"After the ball," he repeated, knowing full well she was doubting his promise.

"Speaking of which," she said, still in that falsely bright tone, which he continued to loathe, "I will be collecting Margaret so she can help me decide which gown to choose." A pause, then she turned her gaze to him. "Unless you wish to decide?"

It was a challenge, he knew that, but he'd be damned if he could figure out what precisely she wanted. Did she want his advice, or did she want him to allow her to choose on her own? If he did offer an opinion, how could he trust that she wouldn't just go with that because that was what he wanted, not what she really wanted?

Women—especially wives, especially this wife— were very complicated, he was discovering.

"Uh," he said again, feeling as uncertain as before, only now with an entirely new topic, "perhaps you and Margaret should go on your own. I trust you will choose what is best."

Her expression froze. "You trust I will choose what is best?" she repeated. He winced at how it sounded when she said it.

But damn it, he had no clue what to say now. He should probably just stop talking.

"Uh, yes." He speared the other half of the sausage from his plate and stuffed it into his mouth.

Now, oddly enough, she looked as though she were going to laugh. But at least it was better than an icy glare.

"I will see you later then?" he said, after he'd swallowed.

She inclined her head, apparently not even wasting the breath to speak.

And Nicholas felt as he never had before around a woman. And didn't like it at all.

"Are you the witch?" Jane winced as she realized just how blunt she'd sounded. Thankfully the woman—the witch, as it happened—didn't seem to mind.

"I am, as long as you're the one with the money," she replied, cackling after she spoke.

"Yes. Yes, I am," Jane said, gesturing to Catherine. Her maid reached into her gown and drew out the purse Jane had made sure to bring, appropriately stuffed with coins. Catherine handed it to her mistress, who dug her fingers in and extracted a handful of coins.

"Is this enough?" she said, holding her hand out to the witch.

The woman nodded, picking only half of the money from Jane's palm, then folded Jane's fingers over the remainder. "More than enough. What can I do for you, my lady?"

"I need to find my husband," Jane replied. "Before he is lost entirely."

—THE PRINCESS AND THE SCOUNDREL

Chapter 23

The dressmaker's felt like a refuge, if only a refuge from her increasingly muddled thoughts. Half of her had wanted to find him and confront him about—well, about all sorts of things, none of which she could put her finger on now—while the other half wanted to go fling herself onto her bed and cry.

And the other half, which she knew perfectly well was a mathematical impossibility, wanted to find him and finish what they'd started.

But she had a gown to choose. All part of being a duchess about to give a ball.

"Are you decided then?" Margaret stroked the fabric of one of the gowns—the less pink one—and turned to Isabella.

"I think so. This one, please," she said, pointing to the more pink gown. The dressmaker beamed, as though Isabella had chosen what she herself had been hoping for.

Join the queue, Isabella thought sourly. First there

was Nicholas trying to pretend he really wanted her opinion and her choices, when all he wanted was for her to choose him, and now the modiste was smiling as though Isabella was brilliant in her gown selection when all she was doing was what was expected.

Hmph.

"It is quite pink," Margaret said in a skeptical voice. At least one person wasn't urging her to make a choice that was their choice. "Don't you like this one?"

Then again, Margaret was like the rest of them. Not that she could blame any of them; of course one wanted one's opinions and choices to matter, but not at the expense of another person's choice and opinions. Not that Margaret was doing that, so perhaps her sister could escape Isabella's ire.

"It is very pink," Isabella agreed, schooling her features to keep from revealing her true opinion. She would just see what he had to say about this.

It was entirely irrational to be grumpy that he would likely approve of this gown—after all, she did look lovely in it. It was a suitable color for a recently married young woman, and she had told him she wanted to make her own choice.

But a part of her—an irrational, emotional, heretofore unknown part of her—wanted him to see through her disguise to what she really felt and thought.

How could a man bring her such ecstasy, as he had the previous night, and yet still not really know her?

Maybe this was the animalistic beast part of marriage her mother had warned her about. That a husband could seem to be all that was lovely and correct and frankly delightful, only to discover that he didn't really care after all. Except for the things that affected him.

"If that is what you want," Margaret said, but not as though she were secretly judging her sister. Just as though she'd accepted that was what Isabella wanted. "We need to find some ribbons for your hair, don't we?"

"Never mind that. What are you wearing?"

Margaret's eyes widened. "Do you know, I don't believe anyone has ever asked me that before."

Isabella felt a sharp pang of guilt. "Really? I never did?"

Margaret shook her head, but not as though it was a problem. Her sister was too accepting. Isabella was too accepting as well. Something she planned to change. Was changing.

But meanwhile, she would not stop listening, especially if it was to her sister.

"Whenever there is—was—an event, the only concern would be what you were wearing. I generally just got to choose what I wanted out of the things the countess would allow. Which was generally white, off-white, and occasionally cream," she said with a smirk. "I wish I could just dress in black all the time," she added with a grin.

"So if someone—say, your now lofty older sister—were to ask you what you wanted to wear, what would you answer?"

It felt good—and entirely new—not to first think about what anybody else would say about it. Well, except for Margaret, whose opinion was the only one that mattered.

Although Isabella would have to object if Margaret wished to wear olive or yellow. Both of those colors would look horrible with Margaret's coloring.

"What would I wish to wear?" Margaret's expression was wondrous, as though entertaining all sorts of intriguing possibilities, and Isabella felt an old, familiar stab of anxiety. Anxiety that Margaret would want something unsuitable, or untoward, or inappropriate. Or black.

But that was just the old Isabella worrying. The new Isabella—the one that had come into being just that morning—wasn't worried about anything.

Except, possibly, that she was wrong about her husband when she'd thought she might be able to trust him.

"I would love a gown in this," Margaret said, putting her fingers on a bolt of blue satin. It was the blue of a summer twilight, and would look marvelous with Margaret's coloring, even if it wasn't precisely appropriate for her age and station.

"Excellent," Isabella said quickly, nodding to the dressmaker. "My sister will need her gown tomorrow as well. I presume that will not be a problem?" She raised one eyebrow, feeling terribly guilty at employing her duchess-ish station, but also knowing that otherwise

Margaret wouldn't get her gown in time. "I will pay double the amount for your trouble," she added. Money went a long way to soothing people's ruffled feathers.

"Of course, Your Grace," the woman replied, the smile on her face a reassuring sign that Isabella's money was indeed overcoming the imposition.

"Thank you." For once, Margaret didn't sound like her own exuberant self. She spoke in a subdued tone, but then her lips curled into an extravagant smile, and she launched herself at her sister, hugging her so tightly Isabella's corset cut into her side. "That is the nicest thing anyone has ever done for me."

Isabella immediately felt horrible that one gown was enough to provoke this response, but knew that Margaret was speaking the truth. She'd never been in a position to do anything for her sister before, and there was simply nobody else who cared enough about Margaret to do anything. Their parents certainly didn't. "You're welcome, Margie," she said, using the nickname she'd called her sister for the first few years of her life.

All the paperwork was laid out, neatly, on his desk, with Griff discussing each piece in turn, making Nicholas's head ache. Or ache more, that is.

"Where are you, Nick?" Griff asked, waving one of the many papers they were reviewing in front of his brother's face.

Not in bed with her, he thought, shaking his head to try to dislodge any thought that wasn't of ducal documents and legal papers proving he was the rightful duke.

He hated paperwork at the best of times, and this was definitely not the best of times. What had been the issue this morning? What had made her go from soft, willing, orgasmic woman to the nearly frowning, distant female he'd seen at breakfast?

"Sorry, Griff. Tell me again, where is that parish record?" Nicholas made a helpless gesture over the papers.

"Here, you idiot." Griff thrust a different paper, this one clearly well-aged, under Nicholas's nose. He sneezed, but Griff snatched it away before he could ruin it.

"Nice, Nick," his brother said dryly. "We're sorry, my lords, but we cannot prove that the Duke of Gage is actually the duke because someone saw fit to blow his nose on the document."

"I did not!" Nicholas replied. Was everyone grouchy at him today? Perhaps by tomorrow things would return to usual. Griff would—well, Griff would speak to him this way, as he always did, but she would be pleasant. Amenable. Preferably while naked in bed.

With that happy thought in his brain, Nicholas returned to his work with renewed energy, agreeing to purchase new farm equipment for one of his holdings, signing some bills promising payment, and at last understanding the legal basis for the claim that the former Duke of Gage was not, actually, the Duke of Gage.

It was a productive day, even if it was less naked and not as full of fucking as Nicholas would have wished.

But there was always the nighttime.

He entered immediately after knocking, but tonight she wasn't at her dressing table. Nor was her maid in attendance.

Nor, unfortunately, was she disrobed and in bed.

"Good evening, Isabella." He strode over to where she sat, on one of the cozy pink sofas, and sat down next to her. She placed a bookmark in the pages of her book, closed it, laid it down on the table beside where she sat, and then looked at him. Without speaking.

"Good evening, Nicholas," she said, at last. "I trust you had a pleasant day? I could ring for tea, and you could tell me all about it." Her expression—damn it, she wore that frozen societal expression he'd seen when they were entertaining callers. As if he were only a caller, and not the man who'd brought her to climax for the very first time not twenty-four hours ago in this room.

He felt something tighten inside, and he gritted his teeth. And immediately felt like the worst kind of man, since her eyes widened at the sight and she flinched.

Flinched! As though he were going to hit her or yell at her or something.

But weren't you? a small voice asked inside his head, *Weren't you just thinking about upbraiding her for not being grateful for your attentions the prior evening? Weren't you going to demand the respect due a husband?*

But that was what he should expect, damn it. He was her husband. She was his wife. And as such, she should welcome him in her bedroom, in her life, whenever he chose to come into it. Them. Whatever.

After all, he hadn't mistreated her. He'd done the opposite, in fact; he'd wooed her, he'd listened to her, he'd told her stories, he'd shared parts of himself he hadn't shared with anyone before, not even Griff.

"Tea?" she repeated, her hand poised above the bell. It almost looked as though she were daring him to call her bluff—if ringing for tea was a bluff—and he stared at her for a long moment, wondering what the hell had possibly gone wrong. What was going wrong now, of all times, when they should be continuing their sexual and marital explorations, hopefully bringing everything to its natural conclusion. Instead she was fully clothed sitting on a sofa, giving him a look she would bestow on a mere acquaintance.

"No thank you. I find I am not hungry. I will leave you to your rest, Isabella, since the ball is tomorrow. Perhaps there we will find a moment to have a beverage together then."

That last part didn't come out as scathing as he'd wished, but it seemed to have its proper impact, since her face paled and she put the bell down quickly on the table.

"Good night, Nicholas," she said, her eyes never leaving his face.

There were so many things that rushed through his mind—*What did I do? Are you all right? Don't you want to feel as good as you did last night?*—but he didn't say any of them.

Instead, he bowed. "Good night." And walked out the door to make the twenty-three-step walk to his own bedroom.

"Do you have an item of his? A piece of clothing,
or something that meant something to him?" the witch
asked, as though Jane would be gallivanting all over
the country with a bundle of the prince's possessions.

"No."

The witch frowned. That was not the answer she
wanted, clearly.

"She means something to him," Catherine
interjected. And then pointed at Jane, just in case it
wasn't clear who "she" was. "The princess. She means
everything to him."

The witch glanced from Catherine to Jane and
then smiled. "Of course. You will just have to do one
thing for me then, my lady."

—THE PRINCESS AND THE SCOUNDREL

Chapter 24

*O*f course she felt terrible as the door shut behind him. She even rose halfway off the sofa to go to him, to beg him to come back, to say that she didn't mean to be so cold, so—so rude.

But when she thought about it, she had meant all of it. She had said, and done, what she wanted, as he'd asked. As he'd insisted, several times.

So he could not be angry with her because she had spoken her mind.

Except he very clearly was. Which, she presumed when she thought about it some more, was his right, just as it was her right to want something herself and be disappointed that she wouldn't get it.

Being imperfect was far more honest than being perfect all the time, even if it was also far more difficult.

"Hmph," she muttered, getting up to yank on the bellpull for Robinson. She was still dressed, after all; she'd deliberately stayed in her clothing rather than change so she wouldn't be tempted by the thought of resuming the kissing and—and the other things, she couldn't even say the words in her mind, that they'd been doing. Not that she wasn't tempted, she truly was. He'd strode in, a warm, knowing smile on his face when he saw her, and she'd nearly succumbed then and there. He could have undressed her himself, if what Margaret had heard about him was true.

But then she'd reminded herself about how he'd faltered at doing what she wanted, even though it was a minor thing. Because what if the next time she expressed her wants it was something truly important? And he denied her?

She needed to know now what kind of marriage she was in, what he would—and would not—do for her.

"I am being entirely selfish," she said, going to sit at her dressing table. Saying it aloud, even if it was just to herself, made it feel as though it wasn't something to be ashamed of. Yes, she was being imperfect in her selfishness, but that was preferable to being perfect and unselfish, to always do what someone else wanted, to wear what they thought was best, to act and behave in a way that wasn't her.

It felt so odd, as though some mischievous and cantankerous woman had taken over Isabella's brain. But perhaps this was really she, she just didn't recognize herself yet.

And if she didn't know herself, how could she possibly expect her husband to? So until then, she would strive to be as selfish and imperfect as possible.

It was a goal, even if it wasn't one she was particularly proud of. But it was far truer to herself than striving to be the best hostess, or the ideal debutante, or the complacent and welcoming wife.

It would have to do.

She woke early the next morning, her mind already running through all the things she'd need to get done that day—it was true she could plan a ball in less time than most could, but there were still so many things to be done.

At least it would take her mind off her own marriage. This ball would be their actual coming-out party; him as the legitimate duke, and her as his rightful duchess. It was crucial that this first event go perfectly. Even though she was coming to realize—happily—that she was not perfect herself.

The gown had arrived the afternoon before, and it hung in her closet, all the pink perfection of it, waiting for Isabella to put it on and don her social persona. It was pretty, she had to admit, even if she did not care for the intensity of the color. It had a wide skirt and a low neckline that would have been too daring for an unmarried lady, but was perfectly respectable for a married one. There were a few ruffles toward the bottom of the skirt, and its sleeves were overlaid with lace, but it was just as simple as most of her other nonpink gowns, which she appreciated. She didn't want to be decorated with fussiness, just as she didn't want to be more than what she actually was.

She leaned over to her bedside table and rang the bell for Robinson. The day and the night needed to be conquered, and she could not waste time thinking about herself.

Now all that was left was for the ball to actually begin. The day had passed by in a blur, filled with decisions and last-minute changes, and she'd barely had time to breathe, let alone eat. Robinson had cornered her at four o'clock and insisted she take tea and a biscuit, and then at dinner she'd been too anxious to eat much. He, she'd noticed grumpily, had no such problem.

And now she was ready. She frowned as she stared at herself in the glass. She looked perfect. Not imperfect, not even a little. And because of the glass, she was able to see when he entered her room, able to school her features into the look of a perfect duchess.

His perfect duchess.

He nodded in approval as he approached her, and she turned to regard him. "You look lovely, Isabella." Thank goodness he hadn't said perfect.

Nicholas himself was remarkably, ridiculously handsome in his evening wear, his face freshly shaved, his hair even managing not to swing into his face.

"Thank you, Nicholas." She spoke in a reserved tone of voice. "You look handsome as well." She saw his jaw tighten and first got confused at what she could have said to set him off and then got angry—if he'd just ask her what was wrong, perhaps then she could find the words to tell him. But if he didn't ask, she couldn't, and wouldn't, just tell him what was bothering her. In which case perhaps they were doomed to be forever asking each other the wrong questions.

"Thank you." He glanced at the clock behind her. "Our ball begins at ten o'clock? So we have a few minutes."

Was he going to ask her what was wrong now, fifteen minutes or so before the biggest social event of her life? When all she'd had to eat was tea and a biscuit? When she was wearing the pinkest gown ever?

She wanted him to, of course, just not *now*. Not now when more than half of her mind was on whether the musicians would gauge the room to ensure the guests were kept entertained, and whether Renning had his staff prepared adequately, and whether Cook had figured out how to rescue the dinner rolls that had gotten burned in the frenzy of cooking.

"I wanted to give you these," Nicholas said. "I was hoping you would wear them this evening." He drew a box from behind his back and flipped the lid open, revealing the most ostentatious and gaudy display of diamonds she'd ever seen.

A necklace with rows upon rows of diamonds, so large that it would cover nearly all of her exposed chest, with a matching set of earrings that looked remarkably like the chandeliers she'd just been overseeing the dusting of.

And the bracelet, which more resembled an armband, with the same loops and rows of diamonds.

"My goodness," she breathed, taking in the splendor. Because, ostentatious and gaudy though the set most definitely was, she also had to admit, in her heart of hearts, that she loved it. She'd never been allowed to wear anything close to this outrageous before. Her beauty, she and her mother both recognized, was best set off by simple gowns and demure decoration, one of the reasons she'd insisted on few decorations on her very pink gown. But this—this was entirely different.

"This belongs to the Duchess of Gage. Griff got it from the bank this afternoon; thankfully the former duke hadn't gotten his hands on it yet." He drew the necklace out. "May I put it on you?"

"Please," Isabella said, turning her back to him and bowing her head. His fingers were warm on her skin as he placed the necklace on her, and after he fastened the clasp he kissed her on the back of her neck, making her shiver.

"Thank you, Nicholas," she said in a soft voice, placing her hand on his where it rested on her shoulder.

"You look perfect," he replied, kissing her again, this time on her neck just under her ear.

She froze at his words. Damn it. Of course she looked perfect. But that didn't mean she was perfect. She wished they weren't having this ball, that it wasn't so important that they show themselves to Society, that they could just continue to get to know each other. Perhaps then she would be able to share some of her doubts and concerns instead of freezing up into her own perfect persona.

But that was impossible. The invites to all the best members of Society had been delivered, the ballroom floors had been polished and waxed, and right now Cook was preparing approximately six hundred tiny perfect sandwiches.

"We should go downstairs to prepare for our guests," Isabella said, instead of saying all the things she wished she could say. All of that would have to wait until after the ball.

Isabella looked as beautiful as he'd ever seen her—well, in clothing at least. She stood beside him at the entry to the ballroom, greeting their guests perfectly, putting each one at ease with a few words, ensuring that everyone had enough to eat and drink. She'd even managed to secure dance partners for two fiercely blushing debutantes in between all that, and Nicholas saw the two ladies whirling on the floor, their faces alight with happiness.

"The Earl and Countess of Grosston. Lady Margaret Sawford," Renning said. Nicholas turned from his viewing of the dance floor to see his in-laws at the door, Isabella's parents' faces both with the same frozen, icily polite expression currently on his wife's face.

Margaret was just grinning as she looked at her sister.

"Isabella," her father said, walking forward to kiss her on the cheek. Nicholas noticed how she stiffened up even more. He would have to find a way to talk to her about her parents at some point. Of course, he would have to find a way to talk to her in general, since it seemed as though he'd done something wrong, although he'd be damned if he knew what it was.

He'd thought about asking her when he'd given her the jewelry, but didn't think it would be fair to either one of them to embark on that kind of conversation when their party was about to begin. He wanted to point that out to her, but that would have defeated the whole purpose of not asking in the first place.

Marriage was very difficult. It was becoming one of his most frequent thoughts.

"Father, Mother," she murmured. "Nicholas and I are so glad you were able to attend."

He heard his sister-in-law utter some kind of snort, which she quickly smothered into her hand.

"Margaret, you look lovely this evening." And she

did—he hadn't really noticed before, since next to Isabella any woman paled, but Margaret was lovely in her own way, her chestnut-brown hair pulled up off her neck with a few errant curls spilling down. Her eyes sparkled, as though she were in on a joke nobody else was, and her gown was a deep, rich blue, very different from the whites he vaguely recalled most single young ladies wearing to such events.

"Thank you, Nicholas. And thank you, Isabella," she added with a meaningful glance at his wife.

"You are very welcome, Margie," Isabella replied.

"We do not use diminutives of names, Isabella," her mother said in a sharp tone.

Isabella looked as though she were going to apologize, then she straightened her shoulders and regarded her mother with a cool gaze—for once, Nicholas didn't begrudge her hauteur.

"If Margaret objects, of course I won't." She tilted her head to look at her sister. "Do you mind, Margie?" she asked, a hint of a smile on her lips.

Margaret shook her head vehemently, dislodging a fat curl that rested on her shoulder. "Not at all, Izzy," she said, that mischievous grin back on her face.

Nicholas bowed. "Margaret, would you do me the honor of a dance?" He glanced at Isabella. "Unless you wish me to stay?"

Isabella shook her head. "No, it appears most of our guests have arrived."

Margaret turned that grin to him. "Since Izzy says it's all right, Your Grace, I would be delighted to dance with you."

"Excellent. My lady?" Nicholas held his arm out for Margaret.

"Thank you for asking me to dance, Your Grace," Margaret said as they walked onto the dance floor. "Because otherwise I would have to stand there with the earl and the countess, and that is never pleasant." Her tone left him in no doubt as to how she felt about her parents.

"You're welcome," he replied with a laugh. He wished that Margaret's sister was able to be as blunt as Margaret. Although perhaps not, because then she might have told him just how she felt about being forced into marriage with him, and then shared her genuine fear about what would happen between them in the marriage.

When Margaret smiled, it was as though her whole face was alight. "This event is marvelous, there are so many people here, and some of them are actually pleasant."

Pleasant. That word again. Perhaps that was the word that was drilled into the young Sawfords in the schoolroom? Dear Lord, he hoped Isabella wouldn't say their sexual relations were pleasant. If they even got to have them, that is.

"You're supposed to say something, Your Grace." His sister-in-law's voice was mocking, and Nicholas found himself grinning in response.

"Do you think your sister is happy?" And where had that come from?

She snapped her head up to look him straight in the eye. As straight as a woman who was more than a foot shorter could, that is.

"If she wasn't, you would have me to answer to." Her tone was fierce, not at all the humorous voice she'd had a few moments ago.

"I promise to do everything in my power to make her so," Nicholas replied, surprised to find that it was true. He wanted her to be happy, just as happy as he thought he might, eventually, be himself.

If he ever got to sleep with his wife, that is.

He was beginning to bore himself with how much he was thinking about it, but the alternative to that was to actually do it, and he couldn't—or rather, wouldn't—do that until she wanted it, too.

She squeezed his hand as they danced. "I do believe you will, Your Grace."

Isabella watched her husband and her sister walk off, pleased that the two people she lov—that is, the two people for whom she cared the most were getting along.

Of course that meant she was now alone with her parents.

"You have done well, my girl," her father said with a falsely hearty tone in his voice. "Not that we didn't expect it of you, but this party could not have been easy to plan within only a few weeks."

"It is what she has been trained for," Isabella's mother replied in a reproving tone. "I would expect nothing less than perfection."

And that, Isabella thought, was the problem.

But it wouldn't do any good to discuss it with her parents.

She gestured to a passing footman. "Father, would you care for a glass of champagne?"

Her father plucked the glass from the tray, handed it to her mother, then took another for himself.

Her mother noticed Isabella's look of surprise. "No, I normally do not indulge, but we have something to tell you."

A feeling of dread passed over her, like a shadow. "What is it?" She took her own glass of champagne from the tray. She hadn't yet figured out if she liked wine, much less champagne, but tonight seemed as good an evening to find out as any. She drew the glass to her mouth.

"Your sister is to be married," her mother said, a smug expression on her face.

And then put it down again on another nearby servant's tray. Tonight was not the night for wine deciding after all. "Married?" Isabella couldn't disguise her astonishment. Margaret hadn't said a word to her about it, so that meant— "Does Margaret know?"

Her mother's expression grew even more conde-
scending, if such a thing was possible. "No, of course
not." She raised her own glass and took a sip as Isabella waited, wishing she could shake the information
from her mother. "We just finalized the details this
afternoon. And this match will benefit you and your
husband also."

"How?" Isabella took a look over her shoulder at the
dance floor. Nicholas and Margaret were still out there,
apparently engaged in some sort of animated discussion. At least they looked happy. Unlike the expression
that must be on her— No, of course not, she probably
looked the same as she always did. Perfect.

Her mother nodded to Margaret and Nicholas. "We
have affianced Margaret to the man who held your husband's title formerly. In exchange, he will stop pressing
forward with his case in Parliament, leaving you and
the duke free from any kind of concern."

Nicholas hadn't told her that there was any kind of
case in Parliament. Was this something he didn't want
to bother her with, or thought she couldn't help with?
Even to listen? It wasn't the most important thing to
concentrate on at the moment, but for a few seconds,
Isabella had the urge to stride out on the dance floor
and demand to know just what he was thinking, not to
share something so significant with her.

Although if she had known, she would have known
how much more important this ball was, and this—

despite her own desires for imperfection—had to be perfect, to settle them in the eyes of Society.

"Why would the man who was—" She gave up, knowing they'd know who she was talking about. "Why would he do such a thing?"

Her mother smiled. And not in a nice way. Never in a nice way, actually. "Because Margaret is a poor exchange for the chance of being a duke? Precisely, but he knows the case could drag on for years, and he doesn't have the funds to pursue it, and the case is not all that strong in the first place."

"So why would you do such a thing?" Bartering their daughter for the chance of a ducal title, certainly, but this was far less of a prize.

Her mother shrugged. "It is not as though men are clamoring for your sister's hand, and this way, we solve two problems—she is married off, and we ensure the duke's title is safe. The former duke balked, at first, but he is a businessman at heart." She nodded. "He knows a good bargain when he sees it."

Her mother's words made Isabella's body freeze. He didn't even *want* to marry Margaret? What kind of hellish bargain had her parents made? How could they have done it?

Although if there was something to be gained it didn't matter that they were losing their daughter. Their less appealing daughter, according to them.

"The dukedom was in rough shape before we lent

him the money," her father added. "Now it is solvent, and even if he's not the true duke, he knows his way around money matters. That can only serve us in the long run."

Isabella really, really wished Nicholas had begun to teach her how to box at this moment. Not just for the reasons she'd gotten upset about before, but because now she would like to hit both of her parents. Starting with her mother, who was undoubtedly the instigator.

Instead, she focused on not screaming. "When do you plan on telling Margaret?"

"Later on this evening. I wouldn't expect you to keep a secret from her, but I wanted you to know precisely why we were doing this, and convey the news to your husband. He can thank us later." Her mother spoke as though this was something the duke would be thrilled by. Isabella knew her husband well enough to know he would be appalled, and wished he were here to hear the news.

Although he did know how to box, and it would not put them into Society's good graces if he punched his in-laws. Especially at his own ball.

Meanwhile, she had to pretend as though this wasn't the worst news she'd received—worse than being told she'd have to marry Nicholas. Because the former duke had always made her uncomfortable, and the thought of her sister having to endure his attentions for the rest of her life made her ill. But there would be no remonstrating with her parents, she knew that, so her only option was to behave as though she was fine with it as she discussed what to do with Margaret.

And Nicholas, the thought popped into her head. He might have some ideas, especially since it pertained to his title. Although he hadn't seen fit to tell her any of what was happening, so perhaps she shouldn't be looking for his advice, given how it seemed he might view hers.

She would speak first to Margaret, and then consider telling Nicholas, if she and her sister couldn't resolve it between themselves.

"Excuse me, Mother, Father." She pretended to gesture to someone over their shoulders. "I am required elsewhere."

She left without waiting for a reply, her whole body shaking, her mind racing with the injustice of it all.

A few people tried to engage her in conversation, but she just nodded, continuing to walk. Renning, however, she could not ignore.

"Your Grace, we are running out of champagne."

"Already?" Maybe all of the guests were just as upset by her parents and were drowning their sorrows.

Or they were all overjoyed at being entertained by the newly minted Duke of Gage and his perfect duchess.

"Yes, Your Grace." Renning tilted his head. "If I might make a suggestion?"

Run over her parents with a carriage? "Of course, what is it?"

"If we could begin to offer white wine on the trays it is unlikely"—he coughed, to show his discretion—"that any of the guests will notice."

"Excellent idea," Isabella replied. *Although I'm still holding out for the carriage.*

"Your Grace!" She turned to see Lord and Lady Truscott, both with huge grins on their faces. They, at least, she knew, weren't going to do anything to vastly disappoint her. She forced a smile onto her own face and walked toward them, her hands outstretched.

"You look perfect, my dear," Lord Truscott remarked, a twinkle in his eye. At least coming from him she didn't feel as though it was a stricture, as though she would have to be perfect forever.

"Thank you, my lord. Are you enjoying yourselves?"

All three of them looked around them. There were people Isabella didn't think she had ever met before dancing and smiling and eating. And drinking white wine now, of course. Everywhere there was a hubbub of conversation, and the musicians seemed to be playing just the right type of music, and she could tell— given how many of these affairs she'd attended as a debutante—that the evening was a rousing success.

If only her whole self wasn't in a tumult about Margaret, and her parents' plans for her, she might actually enjoy the moment.

"It is spectacular," Lady Truscott said, nodding her approval. "I so appreciate that you have enough chairs for us older folk, and that the food is so delicious, and not at all too fancy. I swear, sometimes I don't know how I am supposed to eat half the food served at these functions!" She shared a conspiratorial look with her husband, sending a pang through Isabella.

Would she and Nicholas be like that, in twenty or so years? Or would they have settled into some sort of banal routine where they each lived their lives, parallel but not together?

Would he allow her to have what she wanted? Whenever she discovered precisely what that was, of course.

"Thank you, I am so delighted you came, and are having an enjoyable time." Isabella nodded to both of them, then went off in search of her sister, knowing she had likely reached the limits of her ability to make polite conversation.

At last Isabella spotted her, in conversation with Nicholas's brother, Griff. He graciously bowed as Isabella made some nonsensical excuse about needing her sister for some reason. She tried not to feel resentful that likely Nicholas had shared the information about the former duke's activities with his brother.

"Over here." Isabella took Margaret's hand and led her through the ballroom, nodding at people who seemed as though they wished to speak to her, steadily threading her way through the crowd until she reached the door to Nicholas's study.

"Where are we going? Don't you have to be a duchess or something?" Margaret replied, her tone light and mocking.

"This is more important." Isabella thrust Margaret in front of her into the room, then closed the door and locked it.

Margaret turned to face her. "What is it? What is so important that you have to take yourself away from your sparkling social occasion?"

"It's not about me, it's you. It's . . ." She stepped forward and took both of Margaret's hands in hers. "The parents are planning on marrying you off."

For once, Margaret was speechless.

Until she was not.

She snatched her hands back and began to pace. "Are you in earnest? They are planning on wedding me without my permission and even told you first?" She rubbed her eyes with the back of her hand. "I knew they didn't care about me, but the extent to which that is true is remarkable." She spun back around. "Who is my bridegroom?"

"Lord Collingwood." Judging by Margaret's blank face, she didn't remember who that was. "The former Duke of Gage. The man I was supposed to marry."

"Oh! But why?" As always, Margaret knew precisely

what question to ask. Unlike some people in Isabella's acquaintance, but this wasn't the time to be thinking about Nicholas.

She said it as bluntly as she knew Margaret would want to hear it. "It seems that he is good with money, and he's promised to stop contesting Nicholas's ascension to duke if he marries you."

Isabella clasped her hands in front of her in a supplicating position. "You cannot agree to do this, even for me."

Margaret gaped at her, then she flung her head back and laughed.

Perhaps her sister had already been driven mad by the thought of her future bridegroom. Because laughter was absolutely the last response Isabella expected.

Margaret shook her head. "Of course I wouldn't agree to it, silly. Why would it even make sense for me to do something like that? No offense to either you or your lovely husband, but I see no need to sacrifice myself just to maintain a title. The idea!"

"Well, you don't have to be so mocking about it," Isabella said, feeling like an idiot for assuming her sister would even entertain such a notion. Margaret was her own person, able to express her own opinions—which she did, often—and she valued herself enough, even if her parents did not, not to give up on any future chance of happiness for another.

That was Isabella's job, and she had done wonderfully at it. Except despite it all, and unexpectedly, she was happy. She liked Nicholas, when he wasn't being an obtuse ass. She also had to admit that it was a lovely bonus that he was as attractive as he was, and that she liked kissing him so much.

"So what will you do?"

Margaret smiled, as though she knew something Isabella did not. Probably something to do with self-confidence and refusing to back down from any situation. "I will take care of it, don't worry about it."

"But what will you do?"

"The less you know, the better," her sister replied, patting Isabella's hand. Apparently keeping things from Isabella was a common occurrence. And Isabella did not like it at all.

"What do I have to do?" Jane braced herself for what the witch might say—pluck out a hair, or an eye, or a tooth.

The witch smiled. "You just have to keep looking, and never lose hope."

Jane felt relief that she wouldn't have to go through any pain, but then annoyed that the witch was telling her to do precisely as she was doing.

Although perhaps the witch was telling her to trust herself and her instinct, such as the instinct that had brought her back to the castle in the first place.

"Thank you," Jane replied. "You have been very helpful."

She took Catherine's arm and walked to where their horses stood.

"She didn't tell you anything! If it were me, I'd ask for my money back," Catherine said in a whisper.

"She told me everything I need to know," Jane said, a feeling of hope blossoming in her chest.

—THE PRINCESS AND THE SCOUNDREL

Chapter 25

The evening was as dull and full of platitudes as Nicholas had feared. Plus he had only gotten to dance with his wife once, and even then, she kept looking around the room as though searching for problems to solve. She certainly hadn't met his gaze more than a few times, and that definitely irked him.

But now the ball was over, it was a rousing success, according to all the guests who bid him goodbye, and it seemed to have reassured Society that he and his wife were entirely respectable people who could maintain the proper dignity required of a duke and duchess. How that was proven through spending vast amounts of money to give people food, drink, entertainment, and a place to congregate he couldn't quite figure out, but it seemed to be the case.

He strode the twenty-three steps from his bedroom to hers as quickly as he could, eager to see if her mood had changed. Perhaps she had been anxious about the ball, worried that her efforts wouldn't reflect well on him and his new bride. She shouldn't worry, he would tell her, she was perfect.

He knocked, then entered, relieved to see that not only was Isabella's maid not there, but Isabella was also in her nightclothes. Things were looking up.

She was seated at her dressing table, brushing her hair, the diamonds he'd given her lying in a heap on the table.

She met his gaze in her glass, and he knew, immediately, that things were not back to normal. The woman looking at him was angry. Very, very angry.

"When were you going to tell me? That is, if you were going to tell me at all?"

Thoughts of what he could have possibly forgotten to tell her flashed through his mind—that he really could tell a better story if he put his mind to it, that he was nearly desperate to bed her, that he'd chosen her room decorations himself, you're welcome—but it didn't seem as though any of that would cause as much ire as she was currently expressing.

"Tell you what?"

She narrowed her eyes at him, put her hairbrush on the table, and stood, spinning to face him. "That the former duke was causing problems for you in terms of the title. That he is—was—threatening to bring the case to Parliament. Didn't you think to tell me something that important? I'm your *wife*, Nicholas."

His insides tightened as he processed what she'd said.

She was right.

He hadn't told her, not because he didn't trust her, but because he wasn't accustomed to sharing anything with anybody, especially not a woman. True, he'd told her he liked reading serials in the newspapers, but that wouldn't affect his—their—future.

"I'm sorry." He held his hands out. "I didn't think—well, I just didn't think."

Her expression softened, and he felt an overwhelming relief that perhaps, at last, he'd managed to say the right thing.

She nodded and bit her lip. "If we are going to make this marriage work, Nicholas, you need to tell me things. Not just things like if you've had a pleasant day, or not, but important things like that your title is possibly in jeopardy."

Nicholas glanced away from her penetrating gaze. No wonder she had found the carpet so irresistible—it was much easier to have a difficult conversation when one was looking at it, and not the other conversationalist. "You're right. I made you promise to tell me things, didn't I? So of course you have the right to demand the same thing of me."

Nicholas walked to the bed and flopped onto it, holding his arms out. "And now I would like to tell you that I want you in my arms right now, my lovely, perfect wife." It was a tactic, but it was also the truth. If he didn't feel her near him, and soon, he didn't know what he would do.

She began to walk to him, but the look in her eye made him wary. As though she were going to pounce, not lie against him. Although pouncing could be pleasurable in its own way, so perhaps he should not be concerned.

"Thinking about you not sharing things made me realize that I haven't been entirely truthful with you, either." She sat at the foot of the bed cross-legged, not in her usual position against him. Her dark hair flowed down her back, and her night rail wasn't fastened all the way up, so Nicholas was distracted. But trying desperately hard to pay attention to her words rather than how much he wanted her.

"Not truthful about what?" God, she wasn't about to tell him she had been in love with someone, was she? Or that she had secret aspirations of becoming just like her mother?

"I don't like the color pink." She spoke as though she were confessing some terrible crime, not a dislike of—

"Oh," he said slowly, glancing around the room that he'd decorated for her. Entirely in pink, ranging from shades found in the deepest rose to the lightest wisps of sun-kissed clouds. He really did not know her at all, did he? "So why did you choose the gown you wore this evening?" Did she harbor a secret self-loathing? Or maybe was practicing some sort of self-sacrifice, only instead of a hair shirt she was donning a pink gown?

"I did it to punish you," she replied, as though that made any sense at all.

He felt his eyes widen in surprise. "What? How would that punish me?"

She must've thought about what she'd said, since she laughed as she shook her head. "I can understand why you'd be confused. It doesn't make a lot of sense." She looked off into the room. The exceedingly pink room. "I asked you yesterday for something I wanted, and you didn't seem to want to accommodate me."

"What did you ask for?" Had he not passed her the milk for her tea or something?

She met his gaze. "I wanted you to teach me how to box."

"I told you I would after the ball." He winced at how defensive he sounded. For all his years spending time with women, he didn't know if he'd ever truly understand them. Or this one, at least, the only one he wanted to truly understand.

"But you didn't sound pleased about it."

"Isabella," he said in an exaggeratedly patient tone, "there are going to be times when I say something in a different way than you might expect. That does not mean you go off on some sort of mad punishment by wearing a gown whose color you hate— not that that makes any sense," he said in a mutter, "but what you should do, what I am asking you to do, is to talk to me."

She arched a brow. "Just as you talked to me about the former duke's case?"

He winced again. She was right again, damn it. "I promise as well. I will speak to you about important things, even if I don't wish to bother you with them, and furthermore, I promise not to go dressing in colors I loathe to spite you."

She laughed, then began to move toward him. Thank goodness. "And now I would like to tell you what I want. I want to"—but before he could hear what it was, there was a sharp knock at the door.

There had better be a good reason for this interruption, he thought as he looked at his wife.

"Who could that be?" she asked aloud, not that Nicholas would have any more idea than she would. She reversed her movements, getting off the bed and walking to the door. She grabbed her dressing gown and put it on quickly, wrapping the edges together to ensure she was as proper as a woman in her bedroom with her husband could possibly be.

"What?" she said, flinging the door open.

Her mother stood there, still wearing the gown she'd worn to the ball. Her father stood just behind, two hot patches of red on his cheeks. Renning followed, his face flushed, his expression outraged. Isabella wished she could tell him it was no use to try to stop her mother when she had a purpose. As she well knew.

"Where is she?" her mother said, her eyes blazing.

"Where is who?" Isabella replied, even though she knew perfectly well to whom her mother was referring.

"You know who." Apparently her mother knew Isabella knew perfectly well also.

"I have no idea." What had Margaret done? More importantly, where had she gone?

"What is it? Where is who?" Nicholas said, coming up to stand behind her at the door. "Is Margaret missing?" Because it seemed everyone knew who wasn't there.

Her mother gave a short nod. "She left your house with us, and then I went to remind her to return my necklace, and she was missing. Gone," her mother added, as though it was unclear.

Isabella felt a low panic begin to unfurl in her belly; Margaret had said not to worry, that she would handle it. Was this Margaret's way of handling it, by running away, or had something else happened? Where was her sister?

"You two are close, surely she must have mentioned something." Her mother punctuated her words with a sniff, as though it was beneath her to even imagine that the two sisters were close. Or that Margaret would have confided anything to Isabella.

But since she hadn't, her mother wasn't far off.

"She must have said something after you told her about the marriage, at least."

Isabella was grateful that Nicholas didn't interrupt with any questions—such as what marriage, and why Isabella was telling her things about it.

Isabella shook her head. "No, she didn't. When is the last time anyone saw her?" They were all still standing at the door, as though this was going to be a short discussion. She gestured to her state of undress. "Nicholas and I will be downstairs in five minutes, perhaps you could ask Renning to show you to the drawing room."

"Five minutes," her mother replied, giving one assessing look to Nicholas. At least it wasn't disapproving, although if anyone could find something to disapprove of in someone as handsome as Nicholas, it would be her mother.

Once the door was shut, Isabella stared at Nicholas, who was already drawing her into his arms. It felt so right there, even though things weren't precisely right. She'd deal with all of that later, right now the most important thing was finding her sister. Her marriage, her imperfections, her life now had to take second place to her sister's safety.

"I'll call for my horse, she can't have gotten far. You and your parents can stay here while I am out."

"Pardon me?" Isabella drew back and looked up at his face. "Are you thinking for a moment that I wouldn't come with you to look for my sister, who I love more than anything in the world?"

His face was a duplicate of the confusion he'd had in his expression when she'd asked him about boxing. And caused her to feel even more upset.

"But it's not . . . It wouldn't be . . ." he said, as though that were something she could understand.

"You mean it's not appropriate, and it wouldn't be suitable, is that what I am to understand?" Well, never mind, she did understand. She continued, not waiting for his reply. "We just talked about this, didn't we? I want to go look for my sister, with or without you, and that is just what I plan on doing. You don't even know why she ran off, do you? You're just dashing off into the night to go look for someone you barely know." She held her hand up as she saw him open his mouth. "You can join me, or you can stay here with my parents and wring your hands. It is your choice," she said, moving away from him to the bellpull.

She would have to get dressed quickly and then figure out the most efficient method of transportation—she couldn't see Margaret jumping on a horse and taking off by herself, so she must have left by coach, somehow.

Coaches would be slower, by necessity, than a single horse, so at least they had a benefit there. Although she and Nicholas would also be in a coach, but a private one wouldn't have to stop as often.

Though the thought of her sister being alone on a public coach made her ill. So she wouldn't think about it. She took her dressing gown off and flung it to the floor, striding past Nicholas on the way to her wardrobe.

"I can't talk you—"

"No," Isabella interrupted, yanking open the door to her wardrobe. "Ring the bell for Robinson, please."

"Fine." He rang the bell as she glanced inside the wardrobe. "Then I'm coming with you. I care about your sister," he said. "And if anything were to happen to you—" His words trailed off, but Isabella knew he did care, that he wouldn't say it if he didn't feel it. She knew that about him, at least. So there was that, even if she wasn't certain he cared enough. But not fighting her on going out in the middle of the night to look for her sister was a step in the right direction.

It was better than how most any other man in this situation would behave, she knew that, too.

Was it part of her selfish imperfection that she was no longer content to settle? That she wanted to live for herself as much as it seemed Margaret was?

She had no idea what the answers to those questions were, but she did know her sister was out there on her own, and needed rescuing. Everything else would wait.

An hour later Nicholas was fully clothed and sitting with his wife in a carriage. Not the scenario he'd been hoping for that evening. They'd talked it through, and decided that taking the coach was the more prudent action; when they found Margaret (neither of them was entertaining the thought that they might not find her), they would need to do something to rescue her reputation, so likely that would mean taking her to one of Nicholas's estates, none of which he'd even visited.

Of course he'd also had to listen as his mother-in-law demanded that Isabella stay in town, that they summon a policeman or someone else in authority to go hunt for her sister. As though something so important should be left to the next morning and to a stranger.

And when he'd found out why Margaret left—that her parents were bartering her to a loathsome man who had already fixated on her sister—it made Nicholas determined to find her and do whatever he could to help her, if only to keep her from being under her parents' control.

Small wonder that Isabella valued herself so little, if this was who had raised her.

Plus if the authorities were told of Margaret's disappearance, her reputation would be ruined permanently. That was the only thing that had persuaded the earl and countess eventually—not Isabella's clear worry for her sister, or the fact that their daughter had run off into the night in the first place—and so they agreed to return home to wait for word as Isabella and Nicholas went out to search themselves.

They'd taken only the coachman and the groom Michael. There would be no need to dress formally, or even bring that many items of clothing, so they left Robinson and Miller behind.

That was definitely Nicholas's doing; he wanted to be the one to undress Isabella. Having to head off in the middle of the night to hunt for a missing relative could have its benefits, after all.

It was another hour later, and they were in the coach. Isabella's expression hadn't altered from the one of concern that was now making her frown. Even frowning, she was still lovely. "What did the footman say?"

Nicholas leaned forward and took her hand. "You've asked that at least four times already." He smiled as he spoke to let her know he wasn't complaining. Just aware. And that he could count.

He spoke slowly, not to insult her, but to ensure she could absorb it all. "I'll repeat precisely what he told me. Your sister returned home with your parents, told them good night, went upstairs for approximately half an hour, then came back downstairs and told the footman she and her maid were going onto the balcony to watch the meteor shower. The poor man had no idea if there was a meteor shower or anything, and there wasn't much he could do or say anyway, so that was the last time anyone saw them. That was at about three o'clock in the morning, and your parents came to our door at just about half past four, I believe."

She nodded, biting her lip. "At least she had her maid with her. At least she's not alone. I wish she had said more in her note. But at least we know she wasn't kidnapped."

Dear Earl, Countess, and Isabella:

I am off to the country. Don't worry about me, I will be fine. I have money, I have future employment, and I have my maid.

What I don't have, and what I will not have, is Lord Collingwood for a husband.

Not Yours,
Margaret

"Of course she had to be witty in her note," Isabella said, a mingling of tears and laughter in her voice. "And thank goodness she left one, at least it gives us a clue about where she went, even though it took my parents forever to find it—she's very clever."

"She is." Nicholas got up to sit beside her. He put his arm around her, and drew her close. "She is very clever, and she will keep herself safe, you can trust her enough for that."

Isabella uttered a little snort at the word "trust." "It seems as though I don't trust anybody now—I trusted that Margaret wouldn't do anything foolish, and yet she's run away, and I trusted that you would share things with me, which you've promised to do, I know that, but I'm still not sure." Her words trailed off, and Nicholas felt a tightening in his chest, a squeezing of his heart, for disappointing her.

"Tell you what," he said, after a moment. "As soon as we stop for the night we will start your boxing lessons." Because it would be callous for him to want her to continue their intimacies, even though he was secretly wishing he were that callous.

She glanced up at him, one eyebrow raised. "Are you certain you want me to have an opportunity to punch you?" She nudged him with her shoulder. "After all, I said some things that were not entirely pleasant."

"But what you said is what you felt. You were right, I asked you to tell me what you wanted, and that includes how you are feeling." Who knew that telling the truth could be so complicated? "Besides which, if you can strike me, I deserve to be punched."

She grinned then, as though the prospect pleased her. "So you won't be angry? To be bested by me?"

He smiled down at her. Even in the dark coach, he could see her eyes sparkling with delight. "As I said, princess, if you can hit me, I deserve to be hit. We'll start this afternoon, we'll have to change out the horses by then anyway."

"I look forward to hitting you, then, Nicholas." She

leaned up and kissed him on the jaw. "In the nicest possible way, of course."

The thought crossed his mind that she'd already planted him a facer, in the emotional sense, at least. She was definitely more than how she appeared on the outside, and that was already spectacular.

If only he could ensure he didn't mess it up somehow, he might have a long and happy future. And hopefully he'd consummate his marriage before he was too old to do so.

"Why are we returning home?" Catherine asked.

Jane urged her horse to go just a bit faster. "He trusted me enough to let me go. I have to do the same. If I am right, he will be at the castle when we return."

"And if you are wrong?"

Jane took a deep breath. "Then my heart will be broken."

—THE PRINCESS AND THE SCOUNDREL

Chapter 26

"*P*rotect your body." Nicholas stood opposite her in the small bedroom of the inn. They'd traveled for most of the day, but had stopped at three o'clock to swap out the horses and find a place to spend the night. They'd eaten, and walked around the village, asking a few people if they'd seen a coach passing through. No one had, but a few of them knew the route of the closest coach, and Nicholas and Isabella had plans to chase that coach down the next day.

Since it was a mail coach, it would by necessity move much slower than a private coach, and Nicholas had every expectation they would find Margaret soon. There were only a few places in the country Margaret was familiar with, Isabella had explained, and since she hadn't taken a private conveyance, she would be limited in her direction.

The footman and coachman were downstairs in the public room. She and Nicholas had taken a glass of wine together there as well, which reminded Isabella that she still had so much to learn about herself, about her likes and dislikes. She liked the wine well enough, but much preferred how it made her feel after finishing the glass.

Later, when everything was fine again, she would experiment some more.

And now they were back upstairs, with Nicholas doing what he'd promised, beginning to show her the rudiments of boxing.

She'd heard of ladies boxing before, but usually the reports had been told by scandalized members of society, who couldn't believe that a lady would so demean herself to indulge in something so physical.

Which made Isabella want to point to childbirth, since from what she knew about it, that was likely one of the most physical things a person—specifically a lady—could do.

But meanwhile, her husband had stripped to the waist, which was its own distraction, and she'd removed all of her clothing except for her chemise, for more ease of movement, Nicholas had said, but judging by the look in his eye it wasn't just for that.

"Like this?" Isabella asked, trying to position her fists as Nicholas had them. He looked for a moment, then got a sly smile on his face and moved to stand in back of her. He wrapped his arms around her and took ahold of her wrists, one in each hand.

"Like this," he said, positioning her arms in front of her body. His chest was pressed up against her back, and she could feel the damp heat of his body. It wasn't unpleasant. The opposite, in fact.

And of course since he had been moving about, and was sweating, he smelled like he had before, one of the first times he'd arrived home from boxing. She inhaled, trying not to make an audible sniff, feeling both appalled and intrigued by her reaction to his scent.

"Did you just smell me?"

Apparently her inaudible sniff was, in fact, audible.

"Um—yes?" she said. She turned in his embrace and wrapped her arms around his neck. "It's just so different from how I smell. I like it," she admitted, twining her fingers in his hair. Of course some of it had fallen forward into his face, which just made him look more rakish.

He laughed. "The more I know you, Isabella, the more you surprise me."

"I promise always to surprise you, Nicholas," Isabella replied, a wicked thought crossing her mind as she spoke. She removed one of her hands, wound it up into a fist, and punched him, right in the stomach.

"Ouch!" He held his hand to where she'd hit him and glared up at her through the strands of fallen hair. "Nice work," he added, a grin on his face.

She giggled, then put her fists up into boxing position. "And now you can see if you can get any hits in.

It might not be possible, given your expertise in comparison to mine."

He snorted and raised his own hands. "You mean your element of surprise. That's gone, Your Grace, you are going to have to rely on your pugilistic skill." His fist moved so fast it was a blur, ending up on her arm. He only tapped her, but it stung nonetheless. Her pride, that is. He had barely touched her.

"Hmph," she said.

"That's it, keep your hands up. Protect your body." He lowered his fists and regarded her over them, a look of desire in his eyes. "Because it is well worth protecting." And then his gaze traveled from her face, all the way down to her feet, and back up again. She felt a tingle everywhere he looked, which meant that by the time he was done, she felt as though she had been jolted by a bolt of lightning. Or Nicholas, whichever was more electric.

"You are not playing fair," she complained, trying to hit him before he returned to his fighting stance. Not fast enough—her fist went right past his body into the air.

"I could say the same of you, princess, since here you are in barely anything, your hair tumbling down your back, your feet bare, alone with your husband in a bedroom at night, taunting me with your . . ." and he paused as she started to blush, wondering how he would finish his sentence, ". . . quickness."

"Thank you, Your Grace." She planted her feet again and assumed the stance he'd shown her. She felt so different, and yet still so her; was this a product of selfish imperfection? How did she ever think being perfect was . . . perfection?

She far preferred this messy, sweaty, sensual, irrational way of being. Perhaps especially because of him, but not only because of him. That, too, felt important—that she did something because of her own thoughts and feelings, not because she wished to please him or be who she thought he might want.

Even though she knew, judging by the look in his eye, that he wanted her very much. And, she thought, she might want him just as much.

But the new selfish, imperfect Isabella was first going to see if she could possibly land another punch.

"That's it. Keep your hands up. Don't let me predict where you'll be." And wasn't that prophetic, Nicholas thought. She stood in front of him, clad only in her chemise, a thin glisten of sweat on her brow, her cheeks flushed from the exercise, her eyes bright as she tried to find a way to penetrate his defenses.

Little did she know—or perhaps she did know, judging by how she'd verbally sparred with him—that she already had. He had admired her before, had desired her from the moment he met her, but he hadn't appreciated her various parts. The part that was hesitant and confident, sometimes within moments of each other, the part that could throw a party for the whole of Society and have it be perfect, the part that asked for what she wanted, and demanded to know why he hadn't confided in her.

All of her parts, in fact. He loved her.

Why hadn't he realized that before? Oh right. He'd never been in love before. Not even when he'd first discovered women, figured out that their soft curves brought him pleasure, and he knew precisely the way to bring them pleasure as well.

He had known all that going into this marriage, with her, but he hadn't known what it would be like to join with a woman when he also loved her.

Not that he knew that precisely now, but he was hoping he would know that very soon. He didn't know how he could tell, but there was something in the way she was looking at him, the way she was speaking to him, that let him know that not only was she not afraid of him any longer, or what they might do together, but that she wanted it.

She'd just need to say it. To say what she wanted, and hopefully what she might want would be him.

Meanwhile, he would have to hold back his own desires so she would come to him because that's what she wanted—not what she thought he might want. Or need, given how overwhelming the need to possess her had grown.

"What I'm not precisely clear on," he said as he dodged another one of her strikes, "is why your parents felt they had to betroth your sister to Lord Collingwood in the first place. He's not the duke, unless someone has forgotten to tell me something"—at which point he winked to let her know he was teasing—"and from what I know about him, he is thoroughly unpleasant."

Isabella dropped her hands. "You don't know? You can't even guess?"

Well, now he felt stupid. But—"No," he replied. He had promised to be truthful, open, and honest, hadn't he? Even if he ended up looking like an idiot? "I have no idea."

She furrowed her brow and looked at him for one long moment. At least, it felt like a long moment. "They made a deal with him," she said, spreading her hands wide in front of her body. "If he would stop pursuing the matter in court, the matter of his wanting the title back, they would marry her to him and probably give him money. It seems that while he held the title he managed to make some money, and my parents want him to share his acumen. At the price of Margaret."

His mouth dropped open. "I had no idea." And then froze as another thought struck him. "I didn't ask them for that, you know that, don't you?"

Her expression tightened. "Of course I knew that, if I had even thought it, would I be here with you now?"

"Oh. Right." He reached out and cupped her jaw,

leaning in close. "If you did think it, though, I could see why you were so eager to hit me."

She laughed, as he'd meant her to, and now their mouths were close together and he could lean in and kiss her—he knew she wouldn't rebuff him, her eyes were on his mouth, and he knew that look well—but he wouldn't.

He wouldn't.

Would he?

Damn it. He closed the space between them and let his mouth hover over hers, not kissing her, not yet, but right there so there was no mistaking what he intended to do. What he wanted to do. More to the point, what he wanted her to do.

Oh, thank God. She tilted her face to his and pressed her lips to his, placing her hands on his arms as though to hold him in place. As though he would want to be anywhere else but here.

What about the bed? a traitorous voice whispered.

Fine, he wouldn't want to be anywhere else but here, if here meant kissing her.

Her lips were so soft, and she opened her mouth and her tongue darted inside his mouth, sending a shock of feeling straight to his—well, not just his penis, but his entire body, in fact. Had he ever felt like this with any other woman? He didn't even want to ponder the question, since thinking about other women—even as they related to her—was not thinking about her.

And she was all he wanted to think about. How she was sucking on his tongue so gently, her fingers reaching up to his shoulders, her body moving up against his, her breasts pressed into him. He had hold of her elbows, but that wasn't enough, he didn't think anything would ever be enough, and he slid his hands onto her waist, then reached around to the small of her back, pulling her entirely into him.

Her body was soft and warm and curved in all the right places, and he heard himself groan as his erection pressed against her. If she hadn't known what she did to him before, she certainly did now.

She broke the kiss, gasping, her mouth so moist and red, her eyes heavy-lidded, a spark of desire within the chocolate-brown depths. "We should stop."

He barely restrained himself from telling her that was the worst idea she had ever had. Not that he knew all of her ideas, but he already knew that this was the worst one. Ever.

But he'd promised himself he wouldn't push her, or rush her, or seduce her with his tongue and his hands until she was ablaze with sensual passion—damn. He'd promised, he had to remind himself of that.

But he could talk to her, because they'd said that they would. "Why?"

She bit her lip, and that action made Nicholas almost forget he'd asked a question in the first place. He wanted to be the one biting her lip, damn it.

"When this happens"—thank God she said "when," not "if"—"I want to be fully engaged in it. Right now there's a part of my mind that is worrying about Margaret, and that isn't fair to you."

He admired his own restraint in not telling her that he was absolutely fine with her not being fair to him if it got them supine and naked sooner.

"Ah," he said, putting his hands back on her arms. She had somehow gotten her hands onto his waist, and was sliding her hands up and down his side, the sensations of pleasure posing a serious threat to his peace of mind.

"You have to stop as well, princess," he said in a ragged voice, putting his hands on hers. He moved her hands so they were now in front of her, not anywhere near him, then stepped back so he wouldn't just resume everything.

She had said they should stop, she was his wife, and he was going to respect her wishes.

And thank goodness she had said "when," because if she had said "if," he might have just sat down in the middle of the inn bedroom and howled in frustration.

"So," he said, moving back one more step, "we should think about getting some sleep. We have to find your sister," he added through gritted teeth. The sooner they found her, the sooner the marriage would be consummated.

He'd never wanted to see someone as much in his entire life as he did Margaret.

It was another hour before he returned to the room. He'd muttered something and had left, barely allowing himself to look at her. And even though it had been an hour, it felt like there wouldn't be time enough to ever stop wanting her.

"You're back," she said, looking up at him from the bed. In the bed. Tousled, delicious, and still wearing her chemise.

"Yes, I am," Nicholas replied. At this point, he was just glad he could put words together, even though he sounded ridiculous.

"Did you have a pleasant time?" she asked, shooting him a grin that indicated she knew just what she was saying.

He sat down on the chair by the door and began to remove his boots. For once, he wished Miller were here. They were damn hard to get off.

Thump went one, then the other, after he'd yanked and stomped for a few minutes. It didn't help he heard her giggling.

"Oh, I was about to help you," she said after the second boot dropped to the floor.

He raised his head and looked at her. She had a mischievous look on her face, as though they were sharing a joke. Well, in fact, they were, weren't they?

He'd certainly laughed with women before, but had never felt this kind of warm camaraderie. Was this what love and marriage was, as well as all the stuff he knew about?

The thought made his throat thicken. If they—if he and she—could find a place to be with each other where this was how they interacted, how they behaved with one another, that would be a rarity, he knew enough about marriage to know that was true. And yet it seemed like they might make it happen.

"Why did you go out, anyway?" she asked in a curious voice. Not accusingly, as another woman might have done.

"I told you. I wanted to check on the horses."

"The truth, Nicholas," she said in a soft voice.

Ah, the truth. He stood up and began to unknot his cravat, nearly tossing it to the floor before recalling that no, Miller was not here. He folded it and placed it on the chair. His shirt followed, then he sat on the edge of the bed and began to remove his trousers, his back to her.

"The truth. The truth is that I went out and exhausted myself so I wouldn't think too much about how you and I are about to sleep in a bed together and yet not—" He gestured vaguely in the air, hoping she would comprehend his meaning without his having to say it.

"Ah, I see!" She had a musing tone in her voice. "So your leaving my bed every night and then going to the boxing saloon every day was somewhat of a preventive measure?"

"Precisely." He looked over his shoulder at her. "Not that it worked all that well, mind you. I still want you, princess, I want you so much it hurts." He uttered a snort. "Hurts more than the punching, that is for certain." He leaned back on the bed, his head near her waist. She put her hand on his head and smoothed his hair back. "But that first night, remember? You were terrified. Shaking." He shook his head, her fingers still on him. "I couldn't force you to do anything."

"You could have. Most men would have." She spoke in a soft voice.

He twisted so he was on his side, his head on his hand, looking at her. "I hope most men wouldn't have. I know that man would have, the one your parents are trying to have your sister marry. But I'm not him, even though I have his title. Or he had mine."

She bit her lip and nodded. He could tell she was thinking about Margaret, and wishing they were rescuing her already rather than here talking. He needed to distract her. "Why do you want to learn to box, anyway?" He pulled himself up on the bed so he was lying face-to-face with her. It was remarkable that she remained as beautiful as she was so close—most people, when you looked at them so minutely, had something wrong with them. An oddly shaped eye, less than perfect teeth, a bit of hair that did something odd when it wasn't controlled. Not her. Up close, she was still gorgeous.

She glanced past him, clearly thinking about his question. She drew her lip into her mouth and chewed in what Nicholas was beginning to realize was her thinking mode. "I suppose it was first just to see what I would feel when I did it. But the more I thought about it, and thought about why you might be doing it, the more I realized it was about control, and power." She met his gaze. "I've never had either. I wanted to see what it was like."

The simple statement—"I've never had either"— made his chest hurt. He'd never thought about it before. How young ladies of her class were bound first to their parents and their family, and then to their husbands. Later on, perhaps, to their children. Always to their duty. They never got to choose for themselves. And he'd done her the disservice of making the choice of her decorations for her, even, when that would be one area where she could have her freedom of choice.

"And how did it feel?"

She frowned in thought. Then her expression cleared, and she smiled, a delighted, joyful smile that made his chest open back up again.

"It felt wonderful. It feels wonderful. I want to do it more. I might even want to try boxing someone who isn't you at some point."

His eyebrows rose. "Punch someone who isn't me? If I were a less confident man, I'd be jealous."

She laughed, and hit him—appropriately—on the

shoulder. "I won't hit anyone the same way I hit you, Nicholas."

And then she smiled again, only this smile was far more seductive. As though she was thinking about the same things he had been trying not to think of since they stopped kissing.

And he felt as though he might stop breathing. His chest must look like an accordion by now.

"Uh, well, thank you." He didn't care that he sounded like an idiot; he was her idiot. Not that that should make it him feel better, but it did.

"You're welcome," she said, leaning forward to kiss him.

He'd expected a gentle kiss, which he got, but then she lingered, and her hand went onto his arm and her mouth was open, her tongue licking his mouth, and he drew back, clamping his fingers on her wrist. "You can't do this, princess, I can only be so strong."

She looked at him from under her lashes. And his breath caught, his throat suddenly thick.

"I have changed my mind. That is a lady's prerogative, isn't it? I mean," and then she smiled wryly, as though at a private joke, "I'm not perfect. I'm allowed to change my mind."

"Yes, of course you are," he began, only to realize what she'd said. She'd changed her mind. She wanted to—they were going to—and he forgot what else he was going to say, forgot his name, definitely forgot to breathe.

Until she leaned forward and kissed him again, murmuring as she did so. "But if you're not ready, we can wait."

At which point he pushed her arm onto the bed and lay his body on top of hers, planting his elbows on either side of her so he wouldn't crush her. "I'm ready, princess."

"Good," she said, reaching up to pull him down to her, lifting her mouth to his and kissing him, open-mouthed, sensuous, and as unafraid as she should be.

Dear Lord, he hoped he'd survive. Because if he didn't, that would mean he wouldn't get to do it again, and he already knew he wanted to do it many times this evening. And the rest of his life.

From the unedited version of A Lady of Mystery's serial:

Jane felt anxious as they neared the castle. What if he wasn't there? What if she was wrong?

"It will be fine," Catherine said, as though she knew what Jane was thinking.

Would it? What would happen if he wasn't there? What would she do? Would she be all right?

Who would she become?

—The Princess and the Scoundrel

Chapter 27

*F*inally. She was finally going to find out what that was all about, in an obscure inn in the country without even an enormous bed to flounder around in together.

And she'd never been more pleased.

He kissed her with far more ferocity than he had before, even though before she'd thought their kisses had been spectacular. This, now—his mouth was devouring hers, and she responded in kind, thrusting her tongue into his mouth, pulling him as close as she could, even though he was already as close as he could possibly be, since he was lying on top of her.

He was being careful of her still, though, resting his weight on his arms so he wouldn't be entirely on her. His body was pushed up against her there, and it felt wonderful, and she wanted more. She wriggled underneath him, delighted to hear him utter a groan low and deep in his throat and feel his hardness against her.

Why had she waited so long, anyway? Oh right, well,

she hadn't precisely waited. That is, he had brought her pleasure with his mouth, and she had done something with her hand to him, and there apparently was more to be done.

For once, she was excited about learning things and getting new skills. This wasn't pouring tea, or curtseying to the Queen, or even dancing, which she did enjoy. This was something far more important, the learning of another person's wants and desires as you explored their own.

And now she was about to find out just what it was all about, although she thought, perhaps, that this was only a small part of it—that what they'd been doing for the past few weeks was part of all of it, from playing card games to talking to riding in the park.

He lifted his head, breaking the kiss, and gazed into her eyes. His eyes had darkened to an evening sky blue, and she felt as though she could see through to him, to his very essence, and there was nothing at all to fear there. Because it was he, and she trusted him. She wanted him. She desired him.

She loved him.

That thought made her eyes widen as she realized the truth of it, and he paused. "Is everything all right, princess?" He spoke in a low, rasping tone, as though it pained him to ask, but he had to.

Which just made her love him more, if such a thing were possible in the space of just a few seconds.

"Everything is wonderful," she replied, sliding her hands from his shoulders, down his back, to his backside. Once there, she grasped the firm flesh and caressed it, which had the added benefit of pushing his body more into that place that needed it the most. There.

"Good," he said, lowering his mouth to her neck and kissing it, soft, openmouthed kisses that felt as though he were savoring her. He bit her gently, right on the neck, and she felt a shiver course through her.

Meanwhile, his hands were stroking her arms, and then he raised his body up slightly so he could lower his mouth to her breast, kissing her less gently, moving his way to her nipple, which he found and drew into his mouth.

"Ahh," she sighed as he licked and sucked her nipple through the thin fabric of her chemise. It wasn't enough. "I need to take this off," she said, taking her hands away from his delicious backside to tug at her clothing. "Now," she added, since if she didn't take it off now she was going to explode from the sheer wanting of it. "And I want all this off, too," she said, putting her hands back to tug on his smallclothes.

He smiled, a knowing smile that sent a shiver of an anticipatory promise through her, and got off her to stand by the side of the bed, his eyes never leaving her face.

His hands—God, those strong, wonderful, capable, knowing hands—went to the waistband of his clothing. His—his penis, she knew what it was called, she just hadn't had an opportunity to mention it before—jutted out from the fabric, bold and proud and so intensely and thoroughly male it made her mouth water.

Could she do the same thing to him that he'd done to her? Put her mouth on him there? Just thinking about it was enough to make her move closer to him, wondering what he would do if she did just that.

He hooked his thumbs underneath the fabric and began to draw the smallclothes down his body, revealing the divots and cuts in his hipbones that she knew she didn't have, the trail of hair leading down his belly to his—ahh! And there it was, his penis, large and erect, and even just seeing it did something to her insides.

He dropped the smallclothes onto the ground and straightened, his hand going to touch himself as he gazed at her. "Your turn, princess," he said, stroking his shaft as his eyes traveled down her body. "Slowly," he added, a sensuous expression on his face.

She nodded, her eyes on him, on what his hand was doing, stroking, pulling, his penis defying gravity as it thrust out from his body. And that, that thing would be inside her, and they would be joined, and she would finally get to know what it was like. And that it would be with her husband, Nicholas, the man she loved, was perfect. Even though—and she smiled as she thought about it—she was imperfect.

But this wasn't getting her own clothing off, and them closer to consummating their marriage, at last.

She sat up on the bed and tugged at the bottom of her chemise, but frowned as she thought about the logistics. She got up on her knees, making sure the fabric wasn't caught underneath her, and began to raise the hem. Up, past her knees, past her thighs, pausing as she came closer to revealing her sex, his eyes focused on her, on her hands, his own hand stroking himself, his other hand cupping underneath, holding the things that weren't his penis.

She raised the garment up past there, to her belly, then slowly, slowly, eased it up over her breasts, the press of the fabric against her erect nipples an exquisite torture. Until, finally, she was able to pull it over her head and threw it to the floor.

He was back on the bed within just a few seconds, on his hands and knees, prowling toward her with a predatory look in his eye. And she knew, if she were to look at herself, that same look—that same wanting, hungry look—would be on her own face.

She lay back down on the bed and he lay down as well, on his side, his fingers on her breast, on her nipple, sliding his palm on her flesh, rubbing the hard nub of her until she didn't think she could stand it any longer.

She leaned forward and kissed him, putting her hand on his hip, touching the indent that defined his hipbones, moving her hand across his belly, down lower, feeling the prickly hair tickle her skin.

Until she reached down and touched him there. He

groaned when her hand made contact with him, and thrust his hips more into her hand. He was so hard, so throbbing, and she felt as though she were in control of this strong, proud man, felt as though she were the one leading them, even though he was the one who had all the knowledge of what they were doing.

But none of that mattered, not now, not with him at her mercy, with him gasping and groaning, clearly wanting her touch on him.

"Does that feel good?" she asked, even though of course she knew the answer. She wanted to hear him say it, to hear how his voice sounded now, now when he was so vulnerable and yet so powerful—because, after all, he was just as commanding in this as she was, and she knew, because she knew him, that he would bring her to that same gasping, breathless, wonderful place he'd done before. She couldn't wait.

"You know it does," he said, his words coming out in a short burst, as though it was hard for him to speak at all.

Something in her thrilled to have him so out of control when he'd been the one to guide what they'd done thus far. She stroked him, imitating the action she'd seen him do on himself, her other hand at his chest, playing with his nipples, rubbing her palm against the light sprinkling of hair there.

Suddenly it seemed as though he couldn't stand it any longer, since he pushed her onto her back and got back between her legs, only now, without fabric between them, it was so much more than before. His penis was just there, and she wanted it inside, wanted him to be joined with her, wanted to know what it felt like because she couldn't stand not to know anymore.

"I want you, Nicholas," she said, arching her back so she could press more of her body into his. "I want you," she repeated, knowing he knew what she'd said, but not able to control her words.

"Yes," he replied, then took hold of himself and guided his penis to there, where she ached and wanted and throbbed herself. It was odd, feeling him there, and she bit her lip as he went just a bit further.

"Does it hurt?" he asked, his expression concerned.

"Not yet," she said, returning her hands to his backside, feeling the thrust and clench of his muscles as he moved. It felt amazing to have him, to have his body, so different from hers, on top of her. Going into her.

He kept pushing forward, and then it did hurt as he encountered the barrier of her virginity, but she was beyond caring about that, not now when it was all so close. She pulled on his body to draw him the rest of the way in, and he groaned as he thrust home, her sex feeling stretched and full and absolutely right.

"Are you all right?" he asked, his words punctuated with harsh breathing.

"Yes. Please, Nicholas, please."

"Please what?" he said in a more teasing tone, still ragged, but with a note of humor threading through.

"Please do whatever it is we should do," she said in an irritated voice. She hadn't known that having sexual relations with him at last would make her grumpy. Only perhaps she was grumpy because the sexual relations were delayed, and right now she couldn't imagine anything she wanted more than him inside her, for her to feel that pleasure again as his body—that gorgeous, hard, muscular, delicious body—brought her to climax.

He didn't reply, but began to move, easing his penis out of her body and then back in again, his harsh breathing punctuating each thrust.

It hurt, but in a pleasant way, which was odd to think about. She ran her fingers to the lowest curve of his backside and gripped him, pulling when he went in and releasing as he released.

It seemed as though she was doing the right thing because he closed his eyes and groaned, his thrusts getting faster, his skin warming on hers, his chest hair brushing against her sensitive breasts.

It was all too much, and yet not enough. She found his rhythm and moved her body under his, his motion getting faster and faster until, finally, he froze and shouted, flinging his head back as she felt him throbbing inside her.

Then he collapsed on top of her, this time not seeming to worry about his weight, but it felt right and wonderful to have him there, a warm wetness inside her, his body damp with sweat as he lay on top of her.

"Mmph," he mumbled at last somewhere in the vicinity of her neck.

"Mmph yourself," she replied, her hands rubbing the skin on his back.

She didn't ever want to move, she wanted to stay here like this forever, so she uttered a sound of disappointment as he moved off her to lie next to her, putting his arm under her head, his other hand on her belly.

"That was everything I thought it would be," he said, his voice a low rumble. Then he lifted his head and looked at her. "And now it's your turn."

*FROM THE UNEDITED VERSION OF A
LADY OF MYSTERY'S SERIAL:*

"Thank you, Princess Jane." Jane smiled at the
young girl, no more than twelve, who was curtseying
in front of her.

"You are very welcome. Now, tell me again, what
are you going to do with what I've given you?"

The girl's expression grew fierce and determined. "I
am going to put half of it away, and I am going to pay
the schoolteacher to give me extra lessons and then I am
going to buy a new, serviceable gown and I am going
to walk to the castle, where I will ask for a position."

She looked so proud and spoke so strongly Jane
knew it would be all right. For the girl. For herself.

"Perfect."

She would never stop looking for him, but even
if she never found him, she would be all right. She
would be all right.

—THE PRINCESS AND THE SCOUNDREL

Chapter 28

The last thing Nicholas wanted to do now was—well, anything. He wanted to lie here next to her, perhaps drowse a little, feel her soft warmth next to him as his mind wandered.

But on the other hand, he didn't want to stop doing any of this, and she hadn't climaxed yet, and he didn't want to leave her poised on that precipice when he was so thoroughly sated. Or not so thoroughly, since he was already anticipating doing it again.

He sat up and leaned over, finding his smallclothes from the floor where he'd dropped them. He pushed her legs apart and cleaned her, gently, one hand on her belly caressing her skin. "That's it, let me take care of you," he said in a low voice as he felt her relax. Her hand was on his arm, and she was sliding her fingers on his biceps. He had to admit it felt glorious to have her so clearly reveling in his body. All the boxing he'd done was worth it if it resulted in her admiring his form so much.

When she was clean, he tossed the fabric back on the floor and nuzzled his face into her belly, chuckling as she giggled when his hair tickled her skin. He put his hand on her breast, her lovely, full, round breast, and stroked her, teasing the nipple until it was hard.

Her hands were in his hair, holding him to her, as though he would want to be anywhere else. He kissed the skin under her belly button, then moved down lower still, sliding one finger into her folds as his mouth found her clitoris. She made a low, soft sound deep in her throat and he had to chuckle again. She was so ready for it, ready to be brought to the edge of climax again, and he was determined to make it as good as he possibly could.

Not that climaxes could ever really be bad, but given that this was her first time having intercourse he wanted to ensure the experience was the best it could possibly be.

He licked that little button and moved his finger inside her, stroking her wetness. He could feel his cock already perking up with interest at what was happening, and he smiled to himself as he thought about doing it again. And again, and again, until morning.

There was something to be said for anticipation. Not that he wouldn't have enjoyed every moment of this if it had happened on their wedding night, but this—this, when he knew he'd gotten to know her, had gotten to share some of himself with her. When he loved her. That made it so much more important and real and made it feel, too, as though he was just as virginal as she.

Fanciful thought, but it also felt true.

He kept up his licking, keeping to a steady pace as he felt her begin to writhe under him. He lifted his head and licked his lips. Her eyes were closed, but when he stopped, they flew open and she gazed at him, her pupils dilated, her cheeks flushed, her mouth soft and open.

"Do you like this?" he asked, in clear imitation of what she'd said earlier.

She gripped his shoulder, trying to push his head back down. "You know I do," she replied in a grouchy tone. He laughed, and resumed his work, teasing her with his tongue, caressing her with his fingers.

The grip she had on his hair was tight, and he was guessing she was actually pulling some of his hair out, but he didn't care. Not if it meant he was bringing her pleasure, and he knew, for certain, that he was.

Now just to bring her over the cliff. He could feel her body trembling as the sensation built, and he kept up his steady rhythm, his tongue and fingers working her, bringing her to the edge, until—

"Oh, Nicholas," she cried out, her body tightening with the climax, her hands now holding him to her so tight he doubted he could get free. Not that he wanted to.

She put her head to the side, her eyes shut, her expression relaxed, and he raised his head, feeling a slow, satisfied smile on his face.

Eventually she opened her eyes and met his gaze. Thank goodness she didn't look embarrassed. Instead, she looked—pleasured. Happy. Content.

She smiled back at him and he drew himself up to lie next to her again, drawing her into his arms, pulling the covers over their bodies and curling into her.

"That was lovely," she said, her voice the barest whisper.

"Perfect," he agreed, and her smile was the last thing he saw as they drifted off to sleep.

"Good morning."

"Mmph," Nicholas mumbled, his face buried in her hair. He seemed to have completely enfolded her in his arms while they slept, so his arm was across her chest while his leg was flung over hers. His cock was nestled right in her hip, and it, at least, was awake even if he was not. His cock had been remarkably alert, in fact, and they'd engaged in more sexual relations after that first time.

"We have to get up, Nicholas," she said, sounding irked. "My sister? Rescuing her? You remember?"

He opened his eyes and lifted his head, meeting her gaze. "Of course I remember." So much for some early morning sex. Was she grouchy every morning, or was this a special occasion because of her worry?

He wouldn't know, would he, since he'd never spent an entire night with her. He'd always slipped out before the morning. But it didn't matter anyway, she was concerned about her sister, and he shared that concern.

He leaped out of bed, naked, and went searching for his clothing. His smallclothes were soiled, so he just grabbed his trousers and put them on, then drew his shirt over his head. They'd packed a change of clothing, but he'd forgotten to retrieve it from the coach the night before.

She got out of bed also, and he froze for a moment as he saw her. The early morning light streamed in through the one window, highlighting parts of her body. She had a glorious figure, he knew that, but the light and dark contrast made it look even more stunning, and he wished they could just spend the day in bed, his exploring each and every aspect of her.

But they had her sister to rescue, and he cared too much about both of the sisters to regret—at least, not too much—not being able to indulge his own desires at the cost of someone else's.

"You're going to have to do up my buttons," she said, having gotten her chemise on. She picked up her gown and dropped it over her head, then turned her back so he could begin to work on them.

"How do you feel?" And was there a nonawkward way to ask your previously virgin wife how she felt after consummation?

She turned her head to look at him, her earlier grouchiness apparently gone, for the moment, at least. "I am fine." She raised her eyebrow and smirked. "How are you?"

Well, when you look at me like that I am undone. "Fine, thank you." He concentrated on finishing up his buttoning task, trying to ignore all the instincts that insisted he try to return them to the bed as soon as possible. "Tired," he couldn't resist adding, a knowing tone in his voice.

She turned when he finished and stepped close into him, putting her arms up to wrap around his neck. "I am fine. Thank you for coming with me."

"As though I could stop you," he interrupted, at which she smiled in acknowledgment.

"And thank you for last night. It was lovely."

Her words, even though she didn't mean them that way, made it sound as though she was leaving him, and he felt a cold fear flow through his body. He lowered his mouth to kiss her cheek, whispering in her ear. "Thank you for changing your mind."

"Just keep that in mind, that I'm not perfect," she replied, giving him a final squeeze before stepping away. "And now let's go find my sister," she added, making him remember that they were there for a different purpose than "find out how many times he could have sexual relations with the wife he loved."

Eventually he hoped he could resolve himself to that purpose as well.

She walked downstairs into the common room, a welcome soreness between her legs. Hopefully not a beaming smile on her face. Could everyone tell? She hoped not. She felt her face flush at the thought.

"Good morning, Your Grace, Your Grace." Michael the groom—funny how she remembered his name now, even though she'd never thought to remember a servant's name before—and the coachman (whose name she didn't know, she would have to remedy that) were waiting for them in the public area of the inn, the signs of their breakfast on the table in front of them.

"Coffee and tea, please," Nicholas said to the innkeeper, who was behind the bar. "Quickly," he added, with an understanding nod to Isabella.

She didn't think that she could eat anything anyway, even if they had the time to spare. Margaret's running away, what they'd done last night, how twisted up and odd she felt today, all combined to make her stomach a jumble that would probably tolerate only tea, and that just barely.

She'd been too exhausted the night before—from all her activities, she thought, hopefully without blushing too much—to do any thinking before she went to sleep, but this morning, it was as though there were two Isabellas inhabiting her brain; one, the responsible sister in pursuit of her sibling, while the other was a wanton hoyden who just wanted to do more of all the pleasurable things she and her husband had done last night.

It was difficult to reconcile, but the responsible sister had to take precedence. At least until Margaret was safe.

The innkeeper brought the beverages and laid them on the table, then cleaned up the breakfast things. Isabella sat and drank her tea, barely registering how it tasted.

"Your Grace," Michael said, "we heard that the mail coach stops for a change of horses at about noon in a town not five miles from here. We should be able to catch it today."

If Margaret was on it. But she had to be. Because if she wasn't, then there was no telling where her sister was, and that thought couldn't be borne.

"Thank you," Nicholas said, putting his hand on Isabella's shoulder. "Go get the coach ready, the duchess and I will be out in just a few minutes."

The two nodded and left, while Nicholas beckoned the innkeeper over to settle up the bill. Isabella could hear they were talking about something—the weather, the accommodations, whatever—but didn't hear anything, her mind was already too full of words, the two Isabellas chattering inside her brain.

Margaret, Nicholas, bed, pleasure, worry, lost, found, find, skin, touch, marriage. All of it a maelstrom in her mind.

"We'll find her today," Nicholas said in a confident tone.

"We will," Isabella replied, hoping he was right.

FROM THE UNEDITED VERSION OF A
LADY OF MYSTERY'S SERIAL:

"Have you seen the prince?" Jane felt ridiculous
talking to each person she and Catherine encountered
on the road, but each time when she spotted someone,
she thought, What if this is the one who's seen
him? What if?

None of them seemed to mind her asking, but then
again, none of them had seen him, either.

The shadows of the day grew dark. "We should
stop soon," Catherine said, and Jane nodded,
glancing up at the sky.

"What if his name is Algernon?" Jane blurted out.

Catherine looked confused for a moment, then
laughed. "Or Ichabod."

"Or what if it is just absolutely plain, like Robert
or Michael or William. It wouldn't suit him."

"Well," Catherine reasoned, "that might be why
he's just called Prince. Maybe he doesn't like his

name. I know I hate it when people call me Cathy."
She looked at Jane. "Nobody can shorten your name,
can they? That's lucky."

"I am lucky," Jane agreed. And she was—yes,
she couldn't find her husband, but she knew what
she wanted. And she would be fine if his name was
Algernon. Or even Moloch or Nebuchadnezzar.

—*THE PRINCESS AND THE SCOUNDREL*

Chapter 29

They were on the road again within half an hour. "It won't be long." Nicholas leaned forward to touch her hand, but decided he'd be far happier sitting next to her, so he did so.

And, just as she'd done when they'd been in bed, she tucked herself under his arm and put her cheek on him, curling in like a cat wanting to nap.

What a happy coincidence that he wanted to pet her. But now was neither the time nor the place.

He felt her heave a sigh next to him. And then she spoke in a soft, but clear, voice. "She was right about them," and Nicholas knew she meant their parents. "I always hoped that somehow what they planned, what they did, it was for our good. To keep us safe for the future." She shook her head. "It was only to secure their own."

Nicholas squeezed her arm. "Now you have other people to keep you safe." Did he sound maudlin? Perhaps. But he absolutely meant it, and he wanted her to know it, to know that he was there when or better yet if she needed him.

She leaned up to kiss his jaw. "I know." Then she drew back, a questioning look on her face. "You asked me about boxing. Why I wanted to do it. How did you start? Besides the distraction"—and she blushed, as though recalling that there would no longer be a need for distraction—"there has to be something that compels you to—to get punched."

"And do plenty of punching myself, thank you. I don't usually lose," he said, knowing he was bragging, but it was the truth. She wanted the truth, didn't she? That was the only reason he'd said that, of course. For truth's sake.

"Well?" Oh, right, she was waiting for his answer. Not the answer where he told her how wonderful he was, either.

He leaned his head back against the cushions, the movement of the carriage making him sleepy. Well, that plus he hadn't gotten very much rest the night before, he'd spent most of the night making love to his wife.

Making love. The phrase caught him short, but that was it, wasn't it? He'd made love to her. Not had sexual relations, or even consummated their marriage, even though they'd also done that, but they'd made love.

God, he really was maudlin.

"Anyway, where was I?" he asked, glad she couldn't read his thoughts.

"Nowhere. You hadn't started," she said in a dry voice.

"Oh. Well." When had he started? It had been so long ago. "Well, I think the first time I actually hit anybody was when someone was mocking Griff. He didn't used to be the confident gentleman you know now."

"You don't say," she interrupted in that dry tone, and he chuckled.

"And when we were younger, there were some boys who thought that because Griff was quiet, and liked to read, that he was different. That is, he was different, but they seemed to think it was unfortunate that he was different." He shrugged, as though it weren't important. "I made them see it was unfortunate that they found him so."

She turned more into him and put her arm across his chest to his side. "You're a protector. First Griff, then me." Her voice held a warm tone that indicated her admiration, not to mention her surprise.

"What did I protect you from?"

She hesitated. "You."

"Oh." The thought that she needed protection, even from him, made him want to roar and claim ownership of her, even if it was against himself. Which made no sense at all, but then again, being in love didn't make sense, either. And he was that as well.

"And then it just felt right." It was hard to explain. Like that other activity he liked doing so much—he hoped she wouldn't ask him why he so enjoyed that, or he would know he had done something wrong the night before and would also, likely, be unable to come up with an answer anyway.

"I think Margaret protected me," she said after a few moments. "I never realized it before, but with her always taking the brunt of our parents' disapproval, it meant I was the perfect one." It didn't sound as though that was something to be admired. "And then when I was gone, when they had gotten me married off to a *duke*"—at which point she poked him in the side—"they didn't need her around any longer. Don't need her around, that is." She sounded so sad and disappointed and as far away from the perfect ice princess voice she used in public that it made him happy, even though she was so sad. Which was a horrible contradiction, but there it was.

He was not always a wonderful person, he'd known that about himself for a long time.

"We have about half an hour yet," he said, even though he had no idea if that was true. Anything to distract her from her pain. "How about I tell you a story?"

She ran her hand over his stomach and then back to his side again. As though he were now the cat that needed petting. "I would like that, thank you."

Nicholas cleared his throat, feeling silly, but also feeling as though this was what she needed. And therefore what he would provide.

If only she'd asked for—well, he couldn't let his thoughts go there. "Once upon a time," he began.

He couldn't stop laughing at her outraged expression as he finished the story. "You expect me to believe that the evil witch was actually the hero in disguise?" She whacked his arm. "How did he fool the entire court?"

He grinned at her mock indignation. "By wearing a dress, of course. You, of all people, should know that what you wear is ninety percent of what people perceive about you." He kissed her head. "Such as when you put on that ferociously pink dress to wear to our ball, knowing it looked lovely on you, but also knowing that it was what people were expecting you to wear. Whereas when you wore that black habit to go riding . . ."

He paused. "What?" she asked.

"Well, you did not look at all as I'd been led to believe."

"And that was . . . all right?"

He made a tsking noise. "I cannot believe you still have to ask that. It was glorious to see, you descending the stairs like a fearsome dark goddess rather than the princess I'd married. I knew then, even though I couldn't actually say it to myself properly, that there was more to you than what you present."

"Yes, there is, isn't there?" she asked, sounding surprised.

He should tell her now, and if it was under normal circumstances, he would. *I love you.* Three little words to say, three enormous words to reveal. But these were extraordinary circumstances, and he wanted to wait until he had her full attention.

You're nervous, a voice whispered inside himself. Well, of course he was. He'd never told a woman he loved her before. He hadn't even *thought* it before. He hadn't even thought he would be thinking it before. So naturally he was nervous.

And besides, it appeared that they were nearing the inn where the coach might be. So he couldn't tell her, not now. Later, he would definitely tell her.

Isabella spotted Margaret descending from the mail coach just as their coach pulled into the yard of the public house. She had opened the door even before the coach came to a complete stop, and was out of the carriage within seconds, running to her sister. "Margaret!" she called, and her sister turned, an enormous smile lighting up her face.

"Isabella, you found me!" she said in a delighted voice. "I was hoping it would be you, and not the earl and countess." She peered past Isabella to where Nicholas was getting out of the coach. "And you brought your handsome husband along, too. Even better!" she said.

"You sound as though you just went shopping and needed retrieving," Isabella said in a stern tone. Wonderful, she sounded like their mother. Not who she wanted to model herself after. Ever.

But at least Margaret looked the same as she had a few days ago, definitely not as though she'd been through some horrific experience. Isabella felt a pang of resentment that her sister had so gleefully run off and looked just fine, still. And then felt immediately guilty for having wished Margaret had gone through some suffering.

Goodness, she was a bundle of contradictions. Not perfect now, was she?

Which just made her smile, adding yet another contradiction.

"What were you thinking, running off like that? Your sister was beside herself with worry," Nicholas said as he walked up to them.

Margaret glanced between the two of them, not looking at all contrite. "Well, I knew I would be fine. I brought Annie with me and I have plenty of money and I knew you would find me eventually." She frowned. "Look, can we discuss this all not in public? I feel as though we might be attracting a crowd." And sure enough, some of the mail coach passengers were lingering close by, no doubt intrigued by the private coach and its occupants.

"Come along," Isabella said, tugging Margaret by the arm into the inn. "A private room, please," she said to the innkeeper in her most imperious duchess-like manner.

It worked; the man bowed and led them to a small room. The three of them went in and Nicholas shut the door.

"Are you going to answer my question?" Nicholas asked.

Isabella held her hand up to him. "I would like to speak to her first, please," she said. Nicholas made a motion as though to leave, but she shook her head. "You can stay." She looked at Margaret. "Why didn't you just come to me? We could have solved this without you running off and causing so much worry."

Margaret sat down, emitting a huff of frustration. "I knew you would want to sacrifice yourself for me, and I couldn't—*can't* have that. I know your first instinct would be to want to take me into your home, or worse, have just the two of us go off together somewhere until we could solve the problem, and that wouldn't be fair to you. You've just gotten married," she said, as though Isabella didn't know that herself already, "you didn't even take a honeymoon, for goodness' sake, so if you are to have any kind of chance of happiness, you need to be on your own, not have your sister hanging around."

As she spoke, Isabella felt—was it anger? Yes, it was, and even as she thought about it, the anger grew from a tiny seed to a full-blown flower. If there was a flower of anger, that is.

"How dare you presume so much?" she replied. Margaret's eyes widened in surprise. She'd never seen Isabella's flower of anger before; hardly surprising since Isabella had never grown one before. "That I would sacrifice myself for you. How can you be so selfish to think I would do that for you?" She tapped her chest. "I am important, Margaret, just as important as you, and I have to say that I love you, but I am not a martyr."

Margaret put her chin up. "Just as you weren't a martyr to marry the duke in the first place?" She stepped forward so she was within a foot of Isabella. "Tell me that you didn't just sacrifice yourself because of our parents, who informed you that you would be marrying a duke, it didn't matter which one. And you did, didn't you?" She glanced toward Nicholas. "Thank goodness it was this duke, not that one, but you still would have done it—wouldn't you?"

Out of the corner of her eye Isabella saw Nicholas stiffen, but she couldn't—no, she *wouldn't*—take time to reassure him now.

"It wouldn't be a sacrifice to have you in my home, Margaret," she said in a soft voice. "But I know what you're saying." She paused and took a deep breath. "And you're not wrong. I did marry Nicholas because of our parents." She darted a quick look at him. "And he married me for the same reason, because someone told him he had to. Does that make him weak?" She shook her head before Margaret—or Nicholas, for that matter—could respond. "No, that makes both of us responsible. If we hadn't done what we did, people's livelihoods would be in jeopardy. Neither of us has ever seen our parents when they're thwarted—and that's probably for a good reason. Can you imagine what they would have done if I hadn't agreed?"

She folded her arms over her chest. "We could have found a way out of this that didn't rest on you just running off with only your maid. That was irresponsible and reckless, Margaret."

Margaret pondered that for a moment, then nodded her head slowly. "It was. You're right. I apologize, Isabella, Nicholas," she said, looking at them each in turn. "If I had been in your position—that is, I *was* in your position, faced with a marriage I didn't want, and I didn't think I had any choice."

"You always have a choice." Nicholas spoke, his voice rough and raw. It hurt to have had to admit she hadn't wanted to marry him. Not that he didn't know that already, but to be reminded of it now, on the day after, of all things. That must have been hard to hear. But she'd promised him the truth, always, hadn't she?

But she couldn't spend time on that now, not with her sister here, and found. And not yet safe. "We'll take you to one of Nicholas's estates, I'm sure there is one around here somewhere, and then we'll—"

"No," Margaret interrupted. "I don't want my reputation to be salvaged. I want to be ruined. That's the only way I can be free, don't you see that? You couldn't have done it, I know that, but I can." Her expression turned rueful. "And I should tell you, I haven't been entirely truthful with you." She paused, and Isabella felt her chest constrict. What had Margaret been lying about?

"I am the Lady of Mystery," she said at last.

"The what?" Isabella replied, confused.

She heard Nicholas begin to chuckle. "Of course you are! A Lady of Mystery! Your sister here is the author of those serials that I read to you. *The Princess and the Scoundrel*? You also wrote that other one, *The Dangers of Dancing with a Dragon*. That was a good one," he said in a reminiscent tone.

"Never mind that now," Isabella said in an impatient tone. "What does it matter that you are a writer?"

Margaret rolled her eyes. "It matters because my writing provides income, which means I won't be dependent on anyone. It means I can do what I want, and it means that I will threaten to reveal my identity if the earl and countess try to force me to come back."

"Oh." Of course. Unlike Isabella, who was merely a decorative object, Margaret seemed to have actual skills. "So now what?"

Margaret shrugged. "I suppose we return and I tell the earl and countess there is no way I will ever marry that awful man, or anybody they want me to. When I marry—if I marry—I want the man to be of my choosing, not theirs."

Margaret's words hung in the air as though floating

above Isabella's head, reminding her that she hadn't had the same choice.

"Could you excuse us, Margaret?" She had to talk to him alone. Now, while the words were there, and what she wanted to say was burning so bright on her tongue she thought she might burst.

"Don't go further than the main room, though," Isabella warned as Margaret made to depart.

"I won't," Margaret replied, casting a curious glance between Isabella and Nicholas.

She left, closing the door behind her.

There was a moment of silence as Isabella gathered her thoughts. "You said, just now, that you always have a choice," she began. She turned to look at him, meeting his gaze. He looked . . . hesitant, not at all the way she was used to seeing him. "And I didn't think I did when they told me I had to marry you." She raised her chin. "But now I think it is only truthful to tell you. If I had to choose now, I would choose you."

He moved as though to go to her, and she held her hand up. "No, wait, just a moment. I want to give you that choice as well." She felt the prickle of tears in her eyes. "You didn't ask to be married to me, either, only here we are. I have to tell you, I have to be truthful with you. I love you, Nicholas," she said, and she saw him draw a sharp breath, "and I love you enough that I don't want you to be with me out of obligation. Obviously we can't undo our—our union, but if you choose to live your life separately without me, I would respect that." Not that she could bear to see him with another woman, but she wouldn't have to—she would be off living in the country somewhere, perhaps escaping to wherever Margaret was, ironically enough.

"Are you actually asking me to make a choice, Isabella?" he replied. "Because there isn't one. No, we didn't come into this marriage willingly, but I am unwilling to give up on it. I love you, too, Isabella, which I should have told you last night. Or this afternoon." His lips curled into a wry grin. "That is not the first mistake I have ever made, princess, nor will it be the last."

"You're not perfect either, then," Isabella replied, and then she moved to him, stepping into his arms, feeling his warmth, his love, surround her.

"We can be imperfect together, my love," he said, lifting her chin with his fingers and kissing her.

"Prince?" It was idiotic of her to call for him as soon as she entered the castle's courtyard, but she couldn't help herself.

"Yes?" Oh, it was he. He stood just past the huge gates, his hair disheveled, his clothes messed, his face dirty.

She'd never seen anything so beautiful in her entire life.

She leapt off her horse and ran to him, his arms stretching out to enfold her. She buried her face in his shoulder as he held her tight. He smelled like sweat and horse and dust, if dust smelled.

"What is your name?" she mumbled.

He drew away, looking down at her with a puzzled expression. "What?"

"Your name. What is it?"

He laughed, his hand going to push her hair away from her face. "I thought you'd never ask," he said, pulling her back into his arms.

—The Princess and the Scoundrel

Epilogue

"Lord Collingwood?" Isabella called out his name as she entered the coffeehouse. It was not normally a place for a lady, much less a duchess, but she had business here, like all the men who were currently sitting at the tables, earnestly discussing whatever it was they were discussing.

She saw him turn his head in recognition, and then he rose, planting his hands on his hips. His lips curled up into an unpleasant smile. Likely as not he did not have a pleasant smile in the first place, but still. It chilled her heart.

Nicholas had wanted to do this himself, but she had insisted she be the one, and so he stood just behind her. Letting her do this, knowing how important it was to her. As though she didn't love him enough already.

Michael the groom and John Coachman (his name was John, she'd asked) were waiting outside with the carriage.

"What can I help you with, Your Grace?" He spoke the honorific in a disdainful and yet leering way. Very adroit of him, she had to admit.

"I understand that you have put it about that my sister was not suitable to be your wife." She shook with her anger. Margaret didn't care, or at least she said she didn't care, that she was just happy she wasn't marrying the "loathsome toad," but it was still gossip being spread about her sister. Thankfully it seemed the Queen hadn't heard about it. "When the reality is that my sister refused to marry you. And further . . ." And here she glanced back at Nicholas, as though to assure herself he was there. He was, of course he was. ". . . that my husband's brother discovered some interesting accounting you'd done while you'd been the duke."

He raised his chin. "Your point?"

He was not making this easy, was he? Well, of course he wouldn't. He'd had his title taken, his marriage put off, and Griff had discovered enough financial misdoings to force him to stop the legal proceedings, so Lord Collingwood was in a tough spot.

If she were in his position, she'd be upset as well. But she wasn't, and he had said some things about Margaret that weren't to be borne.

Hence what she had convinced Nicholas to let her do.

Thwack! She drew her fist back, kept her aim true, and hit him, right on the jaw, right where she'd planned.

His head snapped back, and his mouth and eyes were wide with surprise.

Of course she wouldn't knock him unconscious or anything close, she wasn't strong enough for that. But she was good enough to leave him with a bruise, not to mention leaving her with the satisfaction of having done something herself.

"That is for Margaret," she said, brushing her hands together.

The coffeehouse was completely silent, all the men just staring at her, for once not because she was beautiful, but because she was dangerous. Unpredictable.

Imperfect.

She nodded to the room in general, then turned on her heel, taking the arm Nicholas held out for her.

"Nicely done, princess," he said in a whisper. "Only next time, try to keep your fist tight through the whole punch. Makes for a better impact." He drew her through the pub to the outside.

"I love you, do you know that?" she replied, leaning into him.

"I do."

Don't miss the other delightful and sexy
stories in the Dukes Behaving Badly series
by Megan Frampton!

The Duke's Guide to Correct Behavior
Available now from Avon Books!

When Good Earls Go Bad
Available now from Avon Impulse!

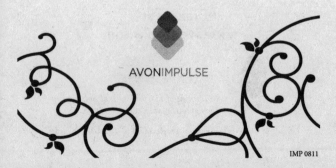